PRAISE FOR BOOK OF KNIVES

"Lise Haines, in *Book of Knives* as in all her work, is an astute psychologist, a cool, unsentimental investigator of humans, who often locates the hard truths. In a time of circumspection, her bracing recognition of a more complex human consciousness hits the spot. I admire her work and her sensibility."

—Rick Moody, author of
The Ice Storm and *Hotels of North America*

"*Book of Knives* is a beautifully written, richly compelling, Jamesian novel of creeping claustrophobia and menace. Haines spins a web so intricate, and so well constructed, that you're unaware of its strands until you are completely enmeshed in it."

—Craig Russell, author of *Hyde* and *The Devil Aspect*

"In *Book of Knives*, Lise Haines has created a believable world of terror where nothing is what it seems. Seen through the perceptive eyes of complex characters, a series of vivid scenes unfolds. One finds all one's worst fears echoed here in an increasingly suspenseful and surprising crescendo of events. Wonderfully done."

—Sheila Kohler, author of the literary thriller *Open Secrets*,
one of *Vogue*'s best books of 2020

"Lise Haines's *Book of Knives* is an utterly absorbing, extremely suspenseful, and elegantly written literary ghost story. I was intrigued, and scared, and ultimately deeply moved by this compelling novel about family and the love that transcends death."

—Jessica Treadway, author of *Infinite Dimensions*

"In Lise Haines's subtly menacing and spooky mystery, Nora, a young widow, and her new husband, Paul, join his family at their decaying lakeside summer camp. As a collection of knives disappear from the camp one by one, other unsettling things start to happen, and Nora begins to suspect a ghostly presence is haunting the lake and cabins. Beautifully written and endlessly absorbing, this is a novel to read with the covers up around your chin and a candle burning."

—Sarah Taylor Stewart, author of the Maggie D'arcy mysteries

PRAISE FOR *WHEN WE DISAPPEAR*

"*When We Disappear* tells the story of a family and a country fallen on hard times and burdened by the weight of the past. Lise Haines is a novelist of great empathy and penetrating insight."

—Tom Perrotta, *New York Times* bestselling author

"*When We Disappear* is a singularly gorgeous meditation on the wild complexities of family life. Lise Haines is a wonder, and this is her most thrilling book to date."

—Laura van den Berg, author of *I Hold a Wolf by the Ears*

PRAISE FOR *GIRL IN THE ARENA*

"Vividly rendered...an immersing read..."

—*Booklist*

"What Lise Haines has wrought is a kind of comic book without pictures, a wild pop novel that—rocking with violent energy and bopping with social satire—can generate suspense, horror, laughter, and even twinges of tenderness."

—Tom Robbins, *New York Times* bestselling author

"The showdown is cleverly designed, and the novel's girl-power heart is in the right place, but what makes *Girl in the Arena* tick is Lynn's engaging, often sardonic voice... She makes it easy to root for her."

—*L.A. Times*

PRAISE FOR *SMALL ACTS OF SEX AND ELECTRICITY*

"Whether Lise Haines's characters are doing needlepoint, or playing miniature golf, or exchanging lives, they are fiercely intelligent, provocatively funny, and profoundly aware of the complexities of love and friendship. Here is an author who writes like no one else. Our world is richer for her glittering work."

—Margot Livesey, *New York Times* bestselling author

"Lise Haines's wonderful new novel, *Small Acts of Sex and Electricity*, holds the reader enthralled from beginning to end as it explores the boundaries of sex, love, and friendship. Very few writers could have pulled off the twists and turns within these relationships with such grace and strength."

—Jill McCorkle, *New York Times* bestselling author

"Haines skillfully creates a tenuous idyll that's reminiscent of sections of Ann Patchett's *Bel Canto* or even Rebecca West's *The Return of the Soldier*—here we have the same blissful ménage based on impossible circumstances that carry the seeds of their own destruction."

—*San Francisco Chronicle*

PRAISE FOR *IN MY SISTER'S COUNTRY*

"Beautifully compressed, sensually charged… A wonderful novel."

—Steve Almond, NPR

"An authoritative fictional debut."

—*Boston Globe*

"A darkly comic novel of sibling rivalry and family dysfunction… There's a sinister, dreamlike quality in the way Haines handles this material… Not for the psychologically squeamish, this inventive twist on family malaise makes the unbelievable believable and lingers creepily after the last page."

—*Publishers Weekly*

ALSO BY LISE HAINES

When We Disappear
Girl in the Arena
Small Acts of Sex and Electricity
In My Sister's Country

Book
of
Knives

Book of Knives

a novel

Lise Haines

Poisoned Pen

PRESS

Published by Poisoned Pen Press, an imprint of Sourcebooks
P.O. Box 4410, Naperville, Illinois 60567-4410
(630) 961-3900
sourcebooks.com

Library of Congress Cataloging-in-Publication Data

Names: Haines, Lise, author.
Title: Book of knives : a novel / Lise Haines.
Description: Naperville, Illinois : Poisoned Pen Press, [2022]
Identifiers: LCCN 2021056033 (print) | LCCN 2021056034 (ebook) |
(trade paperback) | (epub)
Classification: LCC PS3608.A545 B66 2022 (print) | LCC PS3608.A545
(ebook) | DDC 813/.6—dc23
LC record available at https://lccn.loc.gov/2021056033
LC ebook record available at https://lccn.loc.gov/2021056034

Printed and bound in Canada.
MBP 10 9 8 7 6 5 4 3 2 1

for Suzanne and Barry

A world in which there are monsters, and ghosts, and things that want to steal your heart is a world in which there are angels, and dreams and a world in which there is hope.

—Neil Gaiman

It occurred to me that if I were a ghost, this ambiance was what I'd miss most: the ordinary, day-to-day bustle of the living. Ghosts long, I'm sure, for the stupidest, most unremarkable things.

—Banana Yoshimoto, *The Lake*

Materializations are often best produced in rooms where there are books. I cannot think of any time when materialization was in any way hampered by the presence of books.

—Shirley Jackson, *The Haunting of Hill House*

Main Characters

Nora, narrator, documentary filmmaker and editor
Nora's parents, mother is a psychiatrist, father is a film
  professor
Takeo, Nora's husband, ceramist
Satchiko, Takeo's mother

Paul, Takeo's best friend, contractor
  Paul's son, Leon, musician, eighteen years old

Gabe, Paul's brother, ornithologist
Salish, Gabe's wife, cook
  Gabe and Salish's Children:
  Jones, sixteen years old
  Timothy, eight years old
  Mason, five years old
  Lily, three and a half years old

Elizabeth and Emmett, Paul and Gabe's parents

CHAPTER ONE

A Secret or Two

I often stand by the sink when I'm trying to figure things out. As if answers to loss will drop like small bundles in the backyard. I will have only to run out and collect them to feel safe again, the way I did when my husband, Takeo, cut the agapanthus he grew and placed the blooms in my arms.

I seem to be at this exact spot in the kitchen whenever Paul comes and goes. Though he's lived here three months, he never looks over as he walks down the drive, past the house, the hardy bougainvillea, and up the stairs to the loft. The loft is the studio apartment with a Pullman kitchen, above my husband's pottery studio. Tonight, Paul's clothes show signs of sawdust, and he takes the stairs two at a time. Even from the house, I hear the rush of water from the shower, and how quickly it shuts off.

I set dinner out, take a seat, and unfold my napkin just as a text lets me know Paul's purchased raw honey and plans to stop by with a jar. Hurrying into my bedroom closet, I drop the new dress over my head. I fasten the difficult buttons at the back and get a trace of lip balm in place before a breeze rushes through the house, scooting me forward.

The way he comes up to the back door, he looks like a census taker who can't imagine I'll cooperate. "Nora," he calls out.

Then he sees me standing there by the sink, tracking him.

Pushing the screen door open, I say, "Welcome, stranger."

The lintel is high enough, but he's a tall man who routinely ducks through most doorways. I'm not sure how he fit in shaving. There's a nick on his chin with a bit of blood and tissue stuck there. Dressed in a fresh shirt and jeans, he holds a pint of bright yellow honey with both hands. Maybe he's worried it will slip and hit the floor. "Fireweed honey."

Taking the jar, I hold it up to the light. It's thick as paste. I've read about the way fireweed seeds remain dormant in the ground. Then a wildfire sweeps through, and they come to life.

"Good for the immune system," he says. "Got it down in Cayucos."

"What were you doing in Cayucos?"

"Driving around."

I can tell by his smile he's feeling shy about something. "Have you eaten yet?" I ask.

He hunches a little, as if he's going through another door. "I don't want to trouble you."

"Actually, I could use a taster." I nod toward the salmon. My only way of knowing if it's done is to cut into it as it cooks. Same with chicken. Even with a meat thermometer, a chicken breast can turn into a series of holes like a newly aerated lawn. Takeo cooked most of our dinners and never made a single cut.

"Just have to make a quick call first. I'll be right back." Paul steps out to the yard and strides to its limits, dialing his phone. He begins to pace, cutting a swath in the lawn around the oriental cherry and the copper beech. His voice elevates before he hangs up and he takes a few steps toward the house. His phone rings again. Once more he returns to his spot at the back of the yard and his shoes dig into the lawn near the neighbor's fence.

Waiting to see if I should set another place, I pour myself a glass of chardonnay. This one from the Russian River.

There's an exchange of five calls altogether. When he enters the kitchen once more, the blood has congealed, and the dot of tissue is gone from his chin. A little winded, he says, "I'll just run over to the store and get a bottle of wine."

"There's more than enough."

"Let me open the bottle," he says and tucks his shirt in a little. But then he sees I'm holding a full glass. We both reach to get the other plate down and bump into each other. I back off and let him do this, along with getting his silverware, a cloth napkin, and another glass. He knows where everything is kept. But without Takeo, we're like a chair with two legs. I wonder if we're going to find a way to balance again.

"Can I fix one of your buttons?" he says.

I feel around my back and realize the top two buttons are confused. I'd do it myself, but I've known him too long for that kind of awkwardness. "Thanks," I say and stand very still. Those steady hands capable of doing fine wood inlays shake just a little as he unthreads and rethreads the buttons. Maybe I didn't want to recall how intimate this gesture can be.

Once we're seated, I ask, "How long have you been seeing her?"

He gulps some of his wine and says, "Not exactly *seeing* her."

"That's like a four-hour drive." I poke at a slice of tomato.

"What is?"

"Cayucos."

"No, that's where I got the honey. She lives in Petaluma."

"Ah. Tell me about her."

His phone rings again, and he shuts it off. "She's…persistent. And she's an EMT. Has a ten-year-old son. But really, I've been too busy to make it work, or she has."

"My mom would say you have to get less busy if you're going to find someone."

"The salmon is wonderful," he says.

The pink center does look right, even if the fish is cold now. Yet he's eaten this same basic salmon with salt, pepper, and dill many times before at our house. I wonder if he's hiding the way he feels about this woman. I've never seen him so hungry. "More salad?"

He takes the bowl from my hands, gestures to see if I want more, and when I shake my head, he mounds the rest onto his plate.

"You know, my immune system is just fine," I say.

"I didn't mean—"

"Of course." I look out to the flower beds that seem as confused as I am now that Takeo's not here to tend to them. "There's something I've been meaning to ask."

"Anything."

"Okay, how to put this? Did Takeo say something to you… about me? Toward the end?"

Letting his fork rest on the edge of his dish, Paul looks puzzled. I follow those pale gray eyes as they search for clues. "He *always* talked about you. Of course he asked me to be there for you, if that's what you mean. But that goes without saying, I—"

"I'm going to just say this so neither of us will be squirrelly about it. A few days before he died, Takeo said you and I…if I ever get ready to see someone…we should… I wondered if he said something like that to you."

His face gets vibrant with color. He pushes against one of the new potatoes with his fork tines, and it rolls halfway around his plate. "Kill me if I'm wrong, but are you saying he gave us permission…to date?"

"More or less."

"No. No, he never did. I—"

"The thing is…I barely see you. I mean… And I've been worried there's something uncomfortable between us."

"Well, you'll probably be seeing more of me, now that I won't be driving to Petaluma anymore."

"I guess if you have enough honey to last."

"Cayucos for honey."

"I'm teasing you."

He spears the center of the potato, and keeping his eyes on his plate, he says, "I'd be happy to barbecue some night. And if there's anything at all that needs fixing…"

"Only a cabinet door that's a little unhinged. It can wait."

We finish the bottle of wine as we talk about his son's band. I tell Paul about the film I'm working on and almost mention the idea of finding a sperm donor but resist. He was very kind when I lost the baby a couple of years ago, but that might be another awkward conversation.

I set a cup of espresso in front of him.

Gradually, he stirs in some sugar. "Okay, now it's my turn. Something happened the other day."

The way he says this, the salmon turns in my stomach as if it might head upstream. "Go on."

"I went out to the house we're working on. Framing done, subfloors in. I told you about it, right? The one that looks out to the bay?"

"You did."

"What I wouldn't give… Anyway, I drove over after the crew had taken off for the day. I made some notes, and sat down on the edge of the deck, feeling the breeze, looking at the currents. I was mesmerized until the crickets started up, and I heard the distinct sound of someone walking across the floorboards. No one was there, and it wasn't just loud, I could feel the vibration. Maybe an echo from another house in the canyon, the movement of a car passing by. Shortly after that I felt Takeo's presence. As if he were right there next to me, studying the water. I could almost hear him talking to me. Crazy, huh?"

My breath gets a little short. "No, not crazy." I'm not ready to tell him this, but the same thing happens to me. I have even seen Takeo. As if his death was a mistake he's trying to correct.

Paul runs a hand along the edge of the table. I know his deliberating face, the way his lower lip pushes out. "When a strong breeze came through, that feeling left me, that Takeo was somehow there in that stillness. I gathered my things, walked back to the truck, and found a card stuck under the wiper on the driver's side. On the front was a drawing of a home. Below this, *In my Father's house are many rooms. If it were not so, would I have told you I go to prepare a place for you? John 14.* That drawing is identical to my childhood home. You know, at my parents' campground?"

"Now *that's* peculiar."

He reaches into his back pocket and hands me the card, warm and creased by his body.

I put it on the table and smooth it down. "It makes me think of a lodge." What I don't say is *a lodge that might be in a horror film*. Maybe it reminds me of a ghost movie I once saw. It's the second floor with its small windows and the lack of a large front door that feels off. *Forbidding* is the word I'd use.

"At the camp, we lived upstairs, so we called it our house even though it has a dining hall that can seat a hundred. But the campers slept in the cabins. The windows, the U-shaped structure—I could have drawn this from memory."

I hand the card back, and he tucks it away.

"It had to be someone out walking. I just don't know why they picked my truck. I didn't see any cards on the cars I passed on the street when I left."

"I'm glad you felt Takeo's presence at least."

"Me too."

I can see he's unsettled. I don't push in about the campground or his family. He's been estranged from them for some time. And I've found he lets things come to the surface in his own time.

Jumping up, he insists on doing the dishes. Then he fixes the cabinet door, a minor leak from the bathroom faucet I hadn't thought about, and a drawer in the kitchen that tends to jam. I actually made it jam so he'd have something to do when he came over, but I've probably revealed enough secrets for one night, so I don't bring this up.

We say good night with an odd hug, and I wonder if I've

been stupid in too many ways. If I had enough steam, I would think again about who I could set him up with—who might be especially good for him. But all I can do is go off to bed and pull Takeo's pillow close.

———

A week later, I wake up at 1:48 in the morning. This is the exact time my husband left this world. My brain is flooded with light though the room is dark. Sounds are amplified—the settling of the house, the HVAC system kicking in, an animal noise outside. The raccoons are having a busy year.

I go online, looking at sperm banks again, and discover that in Seattle, there's a Japanese one. And another where I can select donors by the famous people they resemble. A couple of my friends have gone through this culling. I could reach out to one of them for a reliable place, but I'm still at the just-looking stage. After an hour, the whole idea pushes down on me. Takeo didn't look like a movie star. I don't. Our child shouldn't. We talked about freezing some of his sperm, but we kept thinking he'd get well. That everything would turn out. And then he was awfully sick.

I go outside and sit in the dark thinking of what I might do with the flower beds I can barely see.

I've tried everything for insomnia. Melatonin, caffeine regulation, chamomile, CBD oil. The list is long and unsuccessful. This is the worst stage of the night, when I can't read or watch movies anymore. It's too easy for dark thoughts to dig in about the purpose of life, the purpose of losing Takeo, the purpose of me. The loneliness begins in my chest and radiates outward through my neck and jaw, and down my arms like a heart attack. The therapist I saw for a while said, *Be conscious of where the feelings are held in your body. Try to breathe through them.* When I sat in her patient chair, I looked at the framed photo in which she appeared to be happily married and had two darling kids—the four of them on a sailboat moving through the water, fresh with life. I stopped going to see her and understood how envious my mother's patients would get if she carelessly placed a photo of one of our happiest moments on a table across from them.

In my mother's practice, she does a fair amount of grief counseling. She lectures on this subject and has written two books on loss that I've not been able to bring myself to read. She always helps when I want to understand psychological things, but I noticed she stopped offering unsolicited advice around the time I got married.

When I tell her I'm unsure if I'll ever stop mourning, she says people who love deeply tend to grieve the way some people build collections. The only answer is to build the other parts of my life until I have more than one collection that needs my care. She admitted this is far from easy.

My whole body aches at the thought. I go back into the kitchen as if there's something waiting for me. Something to eat or drink that will change my outlook. But there's nothing I want. It's too dark to go for a run, my brain too weary to take photos or movies.

Takeo wanted love for me. Maybe I just need to be held.

I step into a pair of flip-flops and start across the back lawn and the gravel drive. The stairs to the loft are on the outside. I climb slowly, gripping the railing in the dark, and when I get to the top, I find Paul doesn't bother to lock his door. Before we built the loft, sometimes he stayed over in our guest room when it was late and we had had too much wine. I know him to be a very sound sleeper.

The temperature is cooler up here, the doors to the balcony wide open. I find him in a pair of boxers, sleeping on one side of the mattress, bedding kicked to the floor. I get in and cover us up to our shoulders, curling around his back. He moans just a little but doesn't stir. His hair smells like lemon, his skin radiating the day's heat.

Maybe it's his snoring that wakes me at first light. Whatever it is, I have a chance to head back to my place before he's up.

The second time I slip into his bed is more intentional, more planned. I don't fall asleep, and I leave the minute he rolls over and his breathing shifts.

The third time feels like the start of a habit.

The fourth, fifth, and sixth, more like early addiction. I don't have the excuse of hypnagogia—a half-sleep state. And there is no specific term I can find for those who slip into another person's bed when they're sound asleep and disappear before dawn. Each night I give him an hour after his lights go out, and sneak over to the loft. The odd thing is I fall into my own deep rest and wake eager to get to work in the morning without setting an alarm.

On the thirteenth and fourteenth evenings, I have to restrain the impulse to touch his hair, to touch his mouth when he turns toward me. I know I would not be the first widow on earth to want intimacy in the middle of her grief.

On the eighteenth visit, I wake up in the morning to find him sitting in bed, drinking a cup of coffee. He hands me a cup of black tea with fireweed honey.

"I could always come to your house," he says, "if you'd rather."

"How long have you known?"

"A while."

"Do you want me to explain?"

"No." He takes a sip of coffee. "I'm just happy you're here."

That night, he pretends to be asleep, and I pretend he isn't pretending, and when I slip into bed, we make love with tender confusion.

———

After Paul moves into the home he's newly remodeled, he comes over several nights a week, rarely planned in advance, as if this would have us admitting to something. We continue to sleep in the loft. I notice one day, as I search his bedside table for a pen, that he kept the religious card.

When we begin to spend time together on Sundays, we visit museums, take hikes, go on picnics. It's hard to believe he's never been up Mount Tam. We drive into wine country and add an overnight there. His son, Leon, used to stay over at his house on weekends, but Leon's a senior in high school now and has a band and a girlfriend. I've met him briefly over the years when Paul pulled up to the house for something, but Leon tended to stay in the truck and wait for his dad. Both are quiet men.

A shift occurs after Paul takes me to a French restaurant one

Saturday night. On the drive home, I ask, "What happened back there?"

"Meaning?" He's practically racing through the streets.

"In the restaurant you became…somber."

"Sorry."

"I'm not asking you to be sorry. I'm asking you to help me understand."

"I got a call this morning. From my brother. From Gabe."

"Wow. Is he okay?"

"He got a call from old family friends who live near the camp. Emmett and Elizabeth—our parents—are in bad shape. Gabe is planning to drive up to Hidden Lake to see what they need, once he sorts a few things out."

"It's good he can go. Did he say anything else?"

"He told me he's an ornithologist. And that he and his wife have four kids."

There's an emptiness to the way he transmits this. As if he's reading the ingredients on a boxed recipe. I don't have any siblings, but I've always imagined, if I did, I would want to keep them close.

———

On a couple of our excursions, he opens up about Hidden Lake. More about the natural wonders than the complex family, though I learn the father is a terror. Or was before he fell so ill. I finally understand that it's been almost thirty years since Paul left. I see how Takeo and I filled that place of family for him.

As much as I need my time alone, I miss Paul when I don't see him for a few days. There's something about our lovemaking that takes me back to the boys I once crushed on. I relish the way the air comes through the open doors of the loft and crosses our bodies, the idea of things unexplored. I'm able to talk with him about my confused feelings. All the while, through the conversations that gain momentum and our playfulness, I continue to mourn.

Takeo's gallery owner comes by the studio that takes up the lower portion of the garage and makes a selection from the remaining ceramic pieces for the retrospective next year. I've held out a few I'll never sell but am happy to see on display. She says I look well, as if she suspects I'm not grieving hard enough. People never know what you go through.

———

"I mean, isn't it better if I'm alone for a while?" I say. My mother has joined me for an early morning run. The hills are damp from a hard rain the night before. I like to take off near my parents' house, the way a long view into the city will suddenly pop up between the houses and trees.

I mention an article I read when I was getting my hair done, about widows.

"I think Takeo would want you to be happy, don't you, dear?"

This is the first time since losing him that my heart has found any light, but I'm still wandering, as if I might find the room where he's hiding and things will go back to the way they were.

"Some days I can't contain it—having feelings for a man who was my husband's closest friend. I cry when I'm editing, in the shower…at other times."

"Does Paul know you'll feel this for a long time to come?"

"He goes through it too. Just tell me this confusion is okay. I mean, you wrote the book. Books."

"All of it. All of it is okay."

This isn't like my mother, this kind of broad statement. Even knowing this, I try to embrace it.

A couple of bicyclists call out, speeding around us on a downhill patch. I feel the breeze they stir. We dip under a low pine branch holding drops of last night's rain and get showered. I hope she's right.

———

I jump into my car and head to the mall. There I flop down on mattresses of every type and roll from one side to the other, trying to imagine which ones will go stiff and brittle and which ones will turn so soft, my body will sink and be barely visible from eye level. My hope is to find one that's firm with a little give. After paying the rush fees, my selection is delivered two days later, along with the new sheets and pillows and a down comforter. I'm too reluctant to give up the headboard, so it stays. It's something Paul made for us. Two men carry away the old mattress and box spring.

Paul and I make love in the new sheets on the new bed. I try not to feel guilty for destroying the mattress Takeo and I slept on. Secretly, I hold on to our old sheets and his pillow, and tuck them into the back of my closet.

When Paul goes away for a few days on a licensure thing, he tells me there's a giant crane on the building across from his hotel.

There are too many crane accidents, and I imagine one occurring as he leaves the hotel for his morning run. Just the thought of losing him boils me down, reduces me to the scent of grief.

———

Curled up in the big comfy chair in the living room the next day, I rest a little before I go back to editing. I've been working on this documentary for a while now. When I sit up to drink some tea, I find Takeo stretched out on the couch. My breath spins in my lungs like a small tornado before it settles.

He's in a work outfit, spatters of fresh clay on his apron, throw pillows behind his head. This is Takeo as his fit and healthy self. There was a moment like this once, when he flopped down on the couch this way and I asked him to leave his apron in his shop. He laughed and used the excuse of removing one layer of his outfit to ask me to remove one of mine. Soon we were in bed in the afternoon's fullness. But this isn't that day.

"I knew it," he says.

"What?" I ask, though I know everything he's about to say.

"He wants you to have his child." Takeo sits up so his whole body is facing me. I hadn't noticed the cup of tea in his hands, but there it is, steaming a little.

"Paul hasn't told me that." I tug at the ends of my hair until I pull out some strands and watch them drift to the floor.

"He will. He's been holding back."

"You sure?"

"He wants to marry you and make a life." Takeo takes a long sip of tea, the steam playing against his glasses.

"I don't mean to cry," I say.

"You're talking to me, love."

"That's what I'm saying. He'll never be you."

"He doesn't need to be."

"What if I don't get pregnant?"

"What if the moon stops turning?"

"And what happens when the baby isn't yours?" I hear Paul's truck. It's midweek, middle of the day. I shift to look out the living room window, just for a second, and when I turn back, Takeo is gone.

I tell my father about this. No one else. Some people are open to things that don't fit a tidy reality. He's one of them. His response? "Takeo will never be at rest where you're concerned. I think he's looking out for you."

———

I'm shocked and not shocked when, three months later, Paul comes through the back door, tugs on the right leg of his jeans, and tries to kneel while opening a ring box. "I'm not sure where you end and…and you end and I…" I think he says our life together will be like a road or a river, though it might be an interstate or floodplain. I'm not sure I recognize the difference in this moment. I barely hear a thing he says as the dear man grapples to find words so I will say yes.

We marry in a dizzy haste. My parents join us at City Hall with a couple of friends and plenty of Veuve Clicquot.

Paul moves in with me and puts his house up for sale. We have sex freely, without the use of birth control. I continue to have conversations with Takeo in my head. In my dreams. After Paul and I say good-night, I say good-night to Takeo, praying for his safe journey, trying to imagine his life after death. Our house settles into a kind of rhythm, and I wrap my film. Paul and I sketch out the plans for the flower beds. Soon spring will be here. We talk of having people over to enjoy the garden.

That's when he gets the second call from his brother, Gabe.

Their parents are so ill, it's time for Paul to drive out. Arrangements need to be made for them. The property will have to be patched up and sold. Everyone will have to think about that lake and how their history sank to the bottom, settling in the silt before rising to greet us.

CHAPTER TWO

Flesh and Blood

U p ahead, the torn pieces of a billboard flutter in the draft from the traffic. It's a woman's face with one eye, half a mouth, one nostril, and ghostlike swatches of a blue dress or uniform around her shoulders and bodice. Then she's gone, swept behind us with all the other signs I look for. I record the details of this place so I can return to film her as she comes apart. She's a few hundred feet from a barn broken at its spine and a rusted flatbed growing into the earth.

When Paul lowers the driver-side window, waves of air pressure tap against my inner ear. The temperature drops, and the plastic tarp securing our stuff in the truck bed flaps so hard, it threatens to fly off. I check the speedometer. We're going eighty-three miles per hour. I wonder if he's rushing to get away from something at home or the thing we're driving toward. We are headed to Hidden Lake with his eighteen-year-old son, Leon.

I kiss Paul's cheek, and he puts an arm around my shoulders.

"You hungry?" he asks.

"Just tired."

He holds me as if he could contain me. But he already has me. I can see the road racing up and back in his vision. *I'm here*, that's what I said before we left home. *We're family.*

Leon, who sits on my other side wearing his noise-cancelling headphones, said we don't need to check with him. He's happy to stop and eat as often as we like, crash if we're ready to find a motel. Tall and sinewy like his dad in his college swim team photos, he has his mother's deep eyes. Her family comes from Morocco, and Leon and his mother visit yearly. He wants to do construction or at least carpentry for his day gig until his band takes off. This is his chance to pick up the skills of the trade. Paul is known for his fine California homes with detailed finish work.

"We'll look for somewhere to stop for the night. I brought some movies if we can't stream," he says.

"Let me guess. *This Side of Eden, On the Waterfront, It Happened One Night*—" Paul is big on classic American films.

"Am I that boring?"

"Reliable. Reliable is good."

"Then I'm in trouble, because I brought a couple Fellini, a half dozen indie films from the pile you haven't seen yet, and all of Kurosawa."

"Aren't you full of surprises?"

Paul signals the intimacy he'll carry into the hotel along with our suitcases. Despite his quiet brooding, he's always affectionate and generous with me. I often hold him and tell him I couldn't do this without him, never specifying what *this* is, though he seems to understand and pulls me in tight, and we rest for a while in our crossed love.

Grateful for the cold air that fills the cab, I watch the sunset turn flatlands into a bolt of color. We're in a stretch of farms with giant combines, their large headlights coming on, chaff flying in the air. Then clusters of Herefords, the occasional stand of trees lined into windbreaks, a new sign featuring a plate of fried chicken, biscuits, and mashed potatoes swimming in a lake of gravy, if only we would turn left in five miles and follow more signs.

The drive out was supposed to be the honeymoon Paul and I hadn't had yet. Leon planned to fly or drive by himself. I thought he'd want to. His parents pooled resources and gave him a six-year-old Volvo station wagon in top condition for a graduation present. It's better than my eight-year-old Honda. Everyone wants him to be safe. We shift about on the one bench seat since this is not a crew-cab pickup.

Stirring now, he reaches into his backpack in the footwell, coming up with a leather case. From this he slips out a six-inch bowie knife and sets it on the dash. Taking his headphones off, Leon coaxes his dad, saying, "Should be good for skinning."

I forget sometimes that Paul grew up with knives and rifles and fishing rods. His father showed him how to track, kill, gut, skin, dress, and scale. I'm prepared to grab the knife if I have to, but Leon is clearly waiting for his father's attention, and this is my first extended time with my stepson. I know he's reluctant about me. He missed our wedding, going to a concert instead. Not his band's but one he told his father he couldn't miss. When I asked on the first day of our trip which CDs he likes, he laughed and said, "Seriously?" as if I was asking him to play license-plate poker. I get it. I know he didn't ask for me in his life. I just don't know how to begin a simple conversation with him. Yesterday, when the sky blackened as if we were having a solar eclipse, and I looked back at the road, we were feet from a hard rain. This mad earthly event was chasing us but never spattered our truck. I tapped on Leon's shoulder and got him to look. He gave it a quick moment then turned away. A whole weather system had failed to reach him. My mother would say a relationship with bad weather takes time.

The knife rocks back and forth, catching the light and sending it into my eyes like a strobe. Paul slips his arm away, but before he can pick up the knife to inspect it, the right front wheel hits the edge of a ditch. Both right tires grab between the asphalt and the earth. Leon and I reach out at the same moment.

Working off its own force, the knife is already midair. As our hands collide, the blade drops in slow motion, cutting my jeans and left calf. It continues to drop and nicks my baby toe inside my left running shoe, where it settles. Pain bends me in half.

Downshifting, Paul secures all four tires back on the road. As time speeds up again, another vehicle honks at our erratic moves. I take the knife by its stupid plastic handle molded to look like a deer's antler and remove the blade. Blood circles my toes and seeps freely around my calf.

Leon says, "Shit, are you okay?"

I give him the knife by the handle, trying not to scold. "Nothing major."

I happen to know something about metals, yet I don't tell him he shouldn't expect the blade to hold up, shiny as it is.

As soon as we find a turnout, Paul shuts the engine off and gets out the emergency medical kit. I pry my shoes off, and he helps me tug my jeans down, somewhat shielded by his body and the passenger door. He dabs hydrogen peroxide on the cuts, gets one of the larger bandages in place and a thick strip for my toe. Despite the evening chill, I put on a pair of shorts so I can keep changing bandages if I have to.

"Sorry I wasn't fast enough," he says.

"Love you," I say.

Takeo once said certain things mark a trip. If the first train starting out was late, he struggled the whole vacation with missed connections. If the first room he rented wasn't anything like the pictures he saw online, he found nothing but miserable rooms ahead. It was probably a bit of storytelling and his way of teasing me about my careful travel approach, but it became this thing we played off each trip we took. In Vienna he pointed out that all the waiters had dour personalities. I laughed but I think he was right. I hope this trip isn't about wounds.

Leon brings me back to *our* travels, handing me an iced tea from the cooler without my asking. He takes the pressure off the cap. "Sorry," he says. "You want to sit by the window for a while?"

It's almost dark, but I want him to feel his gesture means something. "That would be nice," I say. "By the way, I've worked with bands, shooting videos. Editing. If your group wants some help, I…"

"Thanks," he says, as if he's not eager to commit. Maybe he's worried this will shift a loyalty. I know he's awfully close with his mother. He climbs into the middle of the bench seat, and before I get in, Paul comes over and holds me. "It means the world that you're doing this."

I watch the last of the light and think over what *this* is. Paul's father, a difficult man, might not last until we arrive. His mother is having issues with her memory. In whatever condition we find their parents, Paul and Gabe will assess the situation, and we'll make plans.

There is an understanding that I will be shooting footage with a modest-sized digital camera, nothing more. Paul presented this as my contribution to the sale of the property: show the beauty of the camp and the lake with its surrounding woods.

His brother and family are there already. "It might take a couple of months to put everything in order," Paul said after his brother called the second time. "I'll understand if you want to stay behind."

I reassure him this is what families do, and we get back in the truck and drive on.

———

Hidden Lake is so close to Canada, it would be easy to lose yourself on a forest trail and end up across the border. That's how Paul described it. Tall pines, boats to take out on the lake, time to sketch out a film project uninhibited, hours to put your feet up and read. We drive through the poles that once held welcome banners.

The way he had me picturing the campground, I never imagined a property in this state of decay. He didn't either, by his look. But I've learned that once something truly difficult occurs in Paul's world, it can sift so far down in his psyche, he might never see it again. So I don't say anything, just hold his hand.

A wind bites through the valley and heads off. The land is just as beautiful as Paul described it. I think of small milk cartons dropped along the shore when I see the cabins. I was sure there would be other properties, people with docks and boat ramps around the lake, lights going on in the houses across the shore in the evenings. But it seems we are very much alone, twenty-three miles out on a semi paved road suffering from years of heavy rains, thick winters, and some blistering summer days climate change has wrought. There used to be a national campground and a ranger station abutting the property. Both were shut down by the government a couple of years ago.

From the map Paul drew, I know Hidden Lake has a perimeter five miles long. The shape makes me think of an irregular puzzle piece, and it has two coves. Since the house is on a berm, you can see a good deal of the property from there. Two stories tall, the building is U-shaped, the tips of the U facing the lake. On the first floor, the kitchen sits at one tip, the game room at the other, the dining room in the middle. The second floor is all private bedrooms where the family and staff used to sleep. Emmett and Elizabeth built a small upper-level or third-floor room where they sleep, complete with a bathroom, referred to as *Upstairs.*

At the edge of the berm, there's a thirty-degree slope leading down to a set of four sheds, two on each side. Below this, two bathhouses containing showers, toilets, and sinks without mirrors. To the right are eight cottages. To the left another eight. Some cabins have more bunks than others but there are one hundred beds in all. At the lip of the water, straight down from the center of the house, is the boathouse and pier. In the past at least, rafts and floats and water wings were plentiful. Bows, arrows, targets, and cloth numbers for field days were stored in one of the sheds. The central firepit is nestled to the right of the boathouse where the campfires were built.

As Paul turns the engine off, I realize there's an hour or so of light left. On a flat above the parking area, there are paved rectangles where the badminton and volleyball nets were once strung. The house is dark and closed in, with those small windows on the second floor and raw wood siding gray with age. Not a place to make anyone comfortable.

Gabe and his family step outside, not lined up exactly but anticipating us, along with three dogs. The two spotted hounds and a small black dog bark wildly. Chickens make their own racket in a henhouse, their fenced-in yard potent with smells of droppings.

Paul climbs down from the truck first. Ignoring the animals, he shakes hands with his brother. Their exchange is lukewarm, almost flat. Next, Paul gives his sister-in-law, Salish, a kiss on the cheek, introduces me, and lets Gabe remind us of their four children's names. The two young nephews—Timothy, a boy of eight, and Mason, just five—are there for an instant, not long enough to search for family resemblances, though I do note that Mason wears a red cape. The smallest one, Lily, a girl of three and a half, gives me a smile, a kind of enchantment, holding on to her teenage sister, Jones, who has the largest eyes I've ever seen and deep black hair. Lily finally tugs her inside.

Gabe is bigger-boned than Paul and not as tall or straight-shouldered. He's written four books and many articles on ornithology that have a largely academic audience. Their early life is something I'm trying to piece together.

Though I tend to hug family, after an awkward shuffle I meet my sister-in-law's handshake. "Salish," she says again.

"Nora. We finally meet."

"Let's go over the property," Paul says to his brother. Turning to me, he says, "You'll be okay?"

"I think I'm ready for some tea," I say and give him a kiss.

"Mind helping with Nora's stuff?" Paul asks his son. He

knows I'm eager to get my equipment out of the back before nightfall. Leon nods and picks up a stick to throw for the dogs. Only the black dog makes an effort to chase it, but she stops midway and returns to the dining room stairs.

"The wreckage awaits," Gabe says, starting down the hill ahead of his brother.

Salish and I look out toward the lake. Once our husbands walk onto the dock, she says, "It's past the little ones' bedtime. But Jones is in charge tonight." She heads into the kitchen with its bank of windows that face the lake, a vegetable garden thriving in front.

Hurrying to catch up, I find the small black dog at my heels. She waits by the door when I go inside. Salish pours me a cup of strong, cold tea, as if it sat waiting too long in that giant country kitchen. While Leon gets some of my things stacked in the game room, we settle in to wait for the brothers.

My sister-in-law has a face so utilitarian, it's captivating in its plainness, like a well-built Shaker chair. "The children ate already," she says.

I thank her for holding up dinner for us and add, "It's nice to get out of the truck."

When I ask after the parents, she tells me I'll have to meet them tomorrow. She's already taken a tray up, and they too go to bed early.

———

We're seated at one of the larger tables in the dining hall, and Salish brings the last of the roast chickens out, setting the platter on an old, stained trivet. Gabe, whose chair almost touches mine, whispers, "She killed the chickens fresh this afternoon."

It seems an odd thing to sound so charming about, but I can see right away that he's more lighthearted than Paul. I don't imagine my sister-in-law actually slaughtered them, but I'm pretty sure she baked her own bread and four different pies. Fresh Bibb lettuce, radishes, carrots, snow peas, and broccoli are all from the garden near the kitchen. She's an adept cook.

Salish sits directly across from me and next to Paul though she's constantly hopping up to fetch things. Leon is on Paul's other side. Gabe is the one to carve, and he does this with agility, knowing the bones, joints, and meat of a bird in a way most people don't.

"Nice," Gabe says, admiring the first of the chardonnay. Paul and I brought three cases of mixed California reds and whites. As we drop into conversation, Gabe seems willing to fill me in on anything I care to know. I begin with simple questions about acreage and weather patterns so I don't push in too quick. Eventually, I get him to talk about his father. Emmett, it seems, had a need for isolation that often ran aground.

"The management of this place was a constant imposition on his solitary nature," Gabe explains. "He'd go off hunting for days at a time without telling anyone he was leaving, even our mother."

Paul picks up the foil that covered one of the wine corks, twisting it into a hard shape. "And sometimes the only sorry carcass he brought home was his own." He tosses the clump of tin across the table.

"What about your mother?" I ask Gabe this in a quieter tone. "Did she like being so far from things?"

"Not really," he says, "though I'd say she loved nature. Long walks, an appreciation for wildlife. And she was quite a swimmer."

Paul sits back with a clouded expression. Unlike my husband's gray eyes, Gabe's are almost violet. I noticed Lily's eyes are the same color.

"Was it a shock to find yourself in civilization, after you moved away?" I ask.

"More a relief. Never missed this place," Gabe says.

Paul looks pained. Like a tape measure tugged an inch too far, I don't know if he'll snap back or run out of tension, but I decide to wait until another time to pursue family history. I mouth *I'm sorry* to Paul, and he signals back that everything's fine.

I expected the brothers would have more to say to each other after all this time. Paul keeps up on international news and knows a good deal about Civil War battles. He can fix some watches, brews a perfect cup of coffee, and studied philosophy in college before he dropped out to be a carpenter full-time, eventually sitting for his contractor's license. Surely there must be something to talk about. I imagine Gabe has a great deal to say as an ornithologist and father to a large tribe, if nothing else, and I hear he can recall years of baseball stats. Growing up, they listened to games over the radio with their father. It might be a place for them to have a lighter conversation, but I'm not going to be the one to start it. Sports are mostly background noise to me.

When Paul looks at the stranger who shares an entire childhood with him, Gabe smiles broadly as if he's won at something.

I have no idea what that might be. Maybe something was said when they were out circling the property or each other.

We finish the meal, and my husband breaks open a Courvoisier he threw in for good measure. Salish sets down empty jelly jars, four in all. She didn't seem to understand, when I filled a wineglass for Leon earlier, that he's allowed to drink in moderation. His parents have a European sensibility about this.

I spring up and start to collect dishes, one in each hand. "What a meal," I say. "You have no idea what a relief this was after all the fast food and—"

"At least it was an improvement over that," Salish says, almost yanking the plates from my hands.

"I didn't mean—"

"Just relax," she says, as if she might be willing to forgive me in time. She stacks the dishes in armfuls and heads to the kitchen.

In that protective way he has, Paul jumps up and takes a few items off to the sink to ease the tension.

After the food items are put away and another round of coffee is poured, Salish makes a last trip to the kitchen and brings out several blue flannel bags of different sizes and shapes. Some are rolled up with small ties. Thinking of my mother's set, I assume this is sterling flatware, though the shapes are exotic. Maybe Salish plans to finish the meal with fruit and cheese. I almost say she shouldn't bother with such a fancy set—I hate to see her go to the trouble—but then I've had a little too much wine, and surely this will come out sounding wrong.

Paul and Gabe sit back and continue to drink, unable or unwilling to approach a fresh conversation. Leon keeps up with them. All of us watch as Salish goes through the meticulous work of undoing the bundles. When she's finished, there are thirteen knives between us, from a meat cleaver to a butter knife. My cuts begin to sting. Or I realize they haven't stopped yet. In my mind, I check in with Takeo over his travel theory.

"You can pick them up," she tells me, encouraging me to feel their balance and heft, noting how precisely crafted each one is. Cabernet sloshes in Leon's glass as he leans across the table, taking an immediate interest. I watch Paul watch Leon.

Salish explains they're referred to as *novelty knives*, with their unique woods, shapes, and inlays in the handles. Her father and her father's father had a business manufacturing knives.

Leon picks up a paring knife and seems to barely touch the tip with an index finger. Blood surfaces.

"Put it down," his aunt says.

He laughs, and the sound echoes through the large dining hall. She won't let him hold a single blade after that, pushing his hand away when he tries to grip the boning knife.

"Probably best to leave them alone," Paul says. "I'll look for my old hunting knife tomorrow. If I can find it, it's yours."

Leon shrugs, like he's too old to have his father try to fix things for him. Sucking on his finger, he tops off his wine and gets up to wander the house, maybe in the direction of his sixteen-year-old cousin, Jones.

We drove ten hours straight today, except for quick bathroom and drive-through stops. My body feels as if it's still moving headlong through space while Salish talks to me in earnest about the angles of the knife tips and the way the metals were poured or pounded, like we're on a field trip. But I understand, as a filmmaker, what it is to have an unstoppable passion, so I keep my eyes wide.

When Paul yawns across the table, I have that automatic reflex and yawn too. Salish is insulted again. "I thought you'd be interested," she says, starting to gather her knives. I recognize this moment from my early filming days, when someone is about to turn away from an interview. The door can shut fast and lock tight.

"Please don't stop," I say.

Salish looks at me as if she's trying to decipher each small warning that streaks through my head. "Polymers destroyed the business. Plastic handles. If he had been willing to lay off some of the workers...but he knew all the families. His whole life was in knives."

Inspecting those blades gleaming on the white tablecloth, I do what I can to act new to everything. Clearly, this is her way of trying to connect. She has four children. I have none, just the ache of the one I lost with Takeo, unless I count my stepson, who's only here to learn carpentry. Salish doesn't like to read and doesn't care too much for movies. My life is in films and books. The only things I know how to cook are simple stir-fries and broiled items, though I do know how to pop biscuits out of a tube and bake them on a pan in the oven, and I can hard-boil eggs, even if the shells tend to stick like cracked plaster. She's had a series of jobs working in kitchens, from short-order cook to pastry chef. I've seen a chunk of the world on film projects and early on when my mother and I went on my father's research trips. For Salish, travel is driving a couple of states over, she told me, finding a cave with stalactites silhouetted by colored lights, and losing herself underground. Maybe she loves the cool since her father's foundry ran so hot. Maybe she's drawn to bats. The wine has gone into full bloom in my head. I try to reset.

Paul and Gabe look at me, hoping I'll say something more, when this rushes out: "I knew a sword maker in Kyoto, Japan." I add something about his work, keeping my story small and containable, focused on metal. I hope she'll see my effort. I don't say this was Takeo's father. I don't say my first husband's name. Paul and I share an empathetic look.

I have to move now, to stretch after the cramped hours. Following Salish into the kitchen, I'm determined to see that the day ends well. I ask if she has any rubber gloves when I learn there isn't a working dishwasher. "Let me wash."

Salish cinches her apron into place and rolls up her sleeves. "There isn't a thing on earth I want you to do in my kitchen."

In the time they've been here, she's carved out her territory, taken on burdens beyond a casual role as family cook. I can only imagine how hard this has been, moving household operations while keeping track of the kids' educational and personal needs. I stick around to smooth things into place, and when she returns the knives to the kitchen from the table, again I see her pride, the way she lines the bags up in a drawer, adjusting their ties. There will always be one thing she'll be eager to talk about.

Running the water into one of the two deep sinks, Salish adds plenty of dish soap, lowers a stack of dishes, and fills the other sink with hot rinse water.

"The craftsmanship on your knives...it's beyond remarkable," I say.

I hope she never discovers who my former father-in-law was

and what it took for him to make a single blade. But I can see Salish is someone who takes a thick compliment well. This flinty woman with her large, rough hands blushes fully and asks if I'd like some honey in my tea, pointing to a shelf in the pantry. Apparently, Paul mentioned my love of a particular brand while they were making arrangements. In this moment, I hope we'll find a way to push through and she will consider me an ally.

———

Too wired to sleep, I sit nursing a glass of wine with Paul and Gabe, Salish finishing her cleanup. Leon has drifted downstairs to join us again. When it gets quiet, we hear two coyotes as they start to sing, almost in tandem. I often hear coyotes near the Berkeley house. The familiarity soothes me.

Sitting back and shutting his eyes, Leon says, "They have eleven vocalizations."

I know there are greetings, alerts, growls...

The wind picks up. It moves so quickly, it rattles the windows until they seem to bow. Branches hit against the side of the house, and the lights go out. I see a streak of blue in the yard so bright, my eyes hurt. The moon is no longer reflected on the lake, just this rush of blue. I shut my eyes and hold the edge of the table. The wind cuts through the house as if we might all be carried off. Footsteps come and go. Someone puts a hand on my shoulder, and I jump. A low gasp leaves my throat.

The lights go back on. It was only Gabe. The wind calms.

I say, "Did everything look blue for a minute?"

"I'd call that solid black," Leon says.

"The circuit breakers are in the kitchen. Used to happen all the time in storms. I'll show you where they are tomorrow," Paul assures me.

"The color?" I ask.

"It's possible you saw an arc," he says.

I gaze into the yard to see if anything is about to surge again. Just then Jones traipses through the dining room in sweatpants, a pajama top, and unlaced combat boots. She has a flashlight in hand that she hasn't turned off. Leon studies her and her light.

"There are plenty of leftovers," Gabe says.

Jones ignores him and goes into the kitchen. She trudges back a short while later with a cup of coffee and a slice of apple pie. "I'm trying to get stuff done, if you could stop leaning on the power grid." This seems directed at all of us.

Once she's out of sight, Gabe says, "My stepdaughter would tell you your blue light was a ghost."

"Okay..." I say.

He laughs. "She's deeply invested these days, in the spirit world." Leon shakes his head. "Great. The haunted campground."

"According to Jones," Gabe says.

"Has anyone watched *The Crimson House*?" I ask. "I couldn't sleep for three nights after I saw it."

"*The Shining*," Leon says. "But *Sixth Sense* really did it."

"*The Orphanage*," Gabe joins in.

After we run through a list, we ease into silly movies that scared us as kids. I begin to feel a little more myself, and it's possible I've made a first opening with Leon. The three of us talk films for a while, and Paul only listens, the way he does when he's overtired.

Before I bid everyone good-night, I circle behind my husband and put my arms around him. "I'll be up shortly," he says.

Heading into the game room for my smaller suitcase, I note the two pool tables with warped cue sticks, two sagging Ping-Pong tables, and endless board games on shelves. Cabinets are full of crafts materials with dried out paints and broken crayons.

I go up the main stairs. Ours is the largest bedroom down the hall, known as the Wedding Room. I open the door and find it full to the rafters with clothes, dirty cups, books, and papers strewn about. The bed linens and blanket are whipped into a heap, and towels are on the bathroom floor as if they couldn't make it to the bars.

Someone takes the stairs rapidly. It's Salish who follows me as I step inside.

"When we thought of moving, we realized we just have too much stuff." Maybe to stop me from taking inventory, she reaches around, nudging me into the hall while pulling the door shut behind us. "But we left the Quarter Room for you so you could have some privacy. I even got fresh sheets on the bed."

I don't have to study the layout again to know this means Paul and I are stuck directly across the way on the other side of this U-shaped house. The Quarter Room is a small room once used by staff, from the time when this was a working campground. We will have to share a bathroom out in the hall, with Leon.

We had all of this worked out before we came. Salish said, quote, *You're practically newlyweds. It only makes sense that you have the Wedding Room*, end quote. But now it seems I should go along or be known as that new person from the difficult side of the family.

"The kids often get up in the middle of the night and need something, especially Lily. And I am trying to keep an eye on Jones. You understand."

I consider how much there is to repair in this family, and back away from the opportunity to have an en suite bathroom.

Once I'm sitting on the sagging bed of the Quarter Room, I get its name. Four of our room could fit inside one of theirs.

The coyotes sound as if they're fighting now. I don't even bother to get undressed. I hear Paul coming up the stairs before I drop.

CHAPTER THREE
Controlled Burns

P aul sets a cup of tea on the bookshelf. Along with this
he nestles a plate with scrambled eggs, a scone, and apple
slices.

"Aren't you sweet," I say, sitting up. "What time is it?"

"Ten thirty a.m."

"Ah. Early." I reach over and sip the tea then rest the cup
back in its saucer. "You realize I'm conveniently naked under
this sheet, don't you?"

He sits next to me and kisses my forehead. "You didn't even
stir when I undressed you last night."

I tug at his T-shirt. He hasn't bothered with deodorant or
shaving, as if he's returned to a part of his boy life at the lake.
"I'm stirred now."

"We have a couple of things to talk over."

"I know," I say. Sitting up, I kiss him.

His fingertips are a little rough when he touches my face. I
imagine he's been running his hands over old boards, getting a
measure of things. He's not fully resistant, but unlike other days,
he seems slow to accept my heat.

"And we have some organizing to do," he says.

I unzip his jeans. He doesn't have to read out his list to me.
I can see it unspool in his eyes: he needs to set up one of the

sheds with his power tools, draw up initial ideas so he can work on renderings, make a list of items to pore over with Leon, think through a timeline, start a supplies list. He is churning and eager to make the most of each minute, each portion of light that spills over the lake today. He's only half in the room with me, half disembodied with his readiness to go.

"And properly meet your family," I say, "and go out on the lake, and wrestle giant bears in the woods, and…"

My husband and I have congress in that room where the large moths breathe against the window screens, and his love reaches up to meet mine.

Afterward, I lift my hips, and he places a pillow under my bottom so I will retain his sperm. Then I watch as he climbs into his clothes, keeping the day in motion. As he zips up, he says, "Don't go downstairs for a while, sweetheart."

"What?"

"Our sister-in-law."

"What about our sister-in-law?"

"One of her knives went missing."

"Oh god."

"The paring knife, if you should see it. They were her dad's and…"

"Someone probably dropped it in the trash or something. I'll help her look for it after my shower."

"Just let her bring it up. By the way, we're working on a schedule to take care of Elizabeth and Emmett. I'll understand if you'd rather not. With Emmett, I just don't want you to—"

"—take it personally."

"Exactly. We could go up and take them their lunch tray so you could see what you think…or make it another time?"

"I'll go up with you."

———

The bathroom on our side of the house must have stood idle for years. An old bar of soap is coated in insect bodies and wings, and it would take carbolic acid to bring the toilet bowl back from the dead. I find some supplies in a hall cupboard and give everything a deep scrub. From the linen closet, I take a bath towel and washcloth, along with a hand towel to use as a bath mat. Letting the rust sputter out of the showerhead before I step under the spray, I unwrap one of the hotel soaps collected on our drive out. The hot water pounds.

As soon as I'm dressed, I take my Nikon DSLR and start down the back stairs. At the landing, I feel cold air hit as if I'm standing by an open freezer door. I look for a source: a crack in a ceiling beam, a window left open, anything that would make an updraft or downwind in this interior space. If I go back up two steps, the chill dissipates. If I go down from the landing two steps, it warms again, as if this is a game of hotter/colder. I will have to ask Paul. I enjoy it when he talks construction. Joists, transoms, dentil molding. So far, we have taken three historic home tours together, and I got out to his last building site—the one that looks onto the bay—seeing it in various stages. Takeo and I went to a couple of Paul's homes when the work was complete to celebrate with the crew. Chips, salsa, guacamole, and Dos Equis. Those were happy times.

At the bottom of the steps, there are three ways to go: straight ahead into the kitchen; a kind of U-turn that opens into a pantry lined with dish cabinets before it feeds into the dining hall; right out the side door, if it weren't overtaken by foliage. I hear Salish talking to someone in the kitchen and see my little niece, Lily, outside with one of her brothers. This is the eight-year-old, Timothy.

He strikes a match, throws it toward the ground, and lights another. Even though perspective is foreshortened, I'm aware Lily is standing too close to his small fires.

I hurry through the dining hall and step outside. Then I slow. I want them to imagine I'm setting up to film something disturbing in nature instead of something disturbing in my new family.

I study the lake and take a couple of light readings. Timothy continues with the matches, and Lily watches me as the chickens flap and squawk. The two spotted dogs look over to understand what I'm up to. Again, it's the black dog that comes down from the steps and joins me.

Moving in closer, I say, "Hi. I'm Nora."

"We know," Timothy says, as if swallowing a wad of gum.

"What are you up to?" I ask.

He moves the matches behind his back and looks down past the dock and boathouse as I settle onto my haunches. This is definitely Salish's second child, who likes to fish, do archery, and pummel his little brother, Mason. Timothy has become a rather morbid boy, Gabe said. He hopes the time at the camp will pull him out of it.

"I'm Lily," my niece says.

The light shifts, and I consider her silky hair and the strawberry birthmark on her forehead, along with her capacity for delight issued by a single glance. Lily is also notable, I understand, for being a sleepwalker.

"Mind if I make a short movie?" I ask.

Timothy considers this, and by way of answering, he brings his matches out again. I start filming. He focuses on an anthill. As the large beasts come out of their home, he lights a match, moves it around looking for the right target, and sets one of the ants on fire. Lily's eyes go wide, her mouth draws tight.

I don't want him to see me cringe. "Bored much?"

"They like to eat people," he says.

Matching his serious tone, I say, "I understand. You're saving the human race. But…it's possible, just by accident, you could start a fire."

I feel Lily curl into my side. She smells of grass and pine and maybe a note of bubble bath. I lower my camera, wobble on my toes for a moment, and fall back, taking a seat in the dirt. She giggles.

Lining up the image again, I record him lighting another match and throwing it at the black dog.

"It's okay, girl," I say as she backs up and trots over to the steps again.

Timothy stands, looking like a surveyor in a new land. "How far do you think it would burn?"

I sense this is a trick question, that I could ignite an arsonist's career with the wrong answer. "Have you ever played poker?" I ask.

"Mom won't let us play video games."

Lily puts her arms around me, and Timothy bobs in the lens again.

"Ah. I was thinking of cards. Gambling."

"Really?" he says.

"If you promise not to set this place on fire, I'll teach you everything I know about it." This is my bluff. I know how to play the game, but I'm not very good at it. A little better at gin rummy since my dad and I used to play. I can see my offer is a struggle for him. But just as I think I should take off and get Gabe to help, he furrows his brow and says, "If you show me how to cheat."

I have no idea how parents handle these moments. Do they admit to knowing there are ways to cheat to a child this destructively young? "I could show you mountebanks and inveiglers."

"Huh?" Lily says, touching my cheek while Timothy considers the possibilities. He's too bold to ask me to explain.

"Online?" he says.

"That's possible, but you'd have to turn in your matches."

With the heel of one shoe, he levels the anthill, throws me the box, and runs into the house. Lily sails behind him, riding his draft. I begin to worry for her.

———

Hearing the portable table saw kick up, I follow the sound. This takes me to one of the four sheds between the house and bathhouses.

At home, Paul likes it when I go out to his shop to see what he's up to. It was my suggestion he set up his tools in Takeo's studio, the two potter's wheels covered in the corner now, the kiln at rest. I knew Takeo would have approved, though sometimes I still think I'll find him lifting a vase from a lump of clay when I step out back. Paul loves fresh air and keeps the large roll-up door at the top unless there's a downpour. At night, he has to keep at least one window open in the bedroom, in all seasons. So I'm not sure why he has the door to the shed locked. When I place my hand against the center, as if this will give me a pulse, I feel a faint vibration from the saw. The sound starts to whine as if he's trying to cut snakewood or the blade has turned dull. If I open the door, I might startle him, and he could have one of those accidents I try never to think about.

Looking at the lake, I see a Great Blue Heron fly along the horizon, the light moving with large clouds. I wonder if Paul is surprising one of us with something he's building. I wouldn't put it past him to turn out a gift to thank me for coming. He's like that. But I do wonder where he's gotten the wood to move along the miter slots. He hasn't had time to write out a list of cuts yet or order the lumber. The saw finally comes to a rest. I give the door a gentle knock and a second one. "Paul?"

Just then Gabe walks by, heading toward the lake.

"Do you know where the key to this shed is?"

"Sure enough."

His voice has a touch of Southern at times. Paul's voice is slightly deeper and marbled with California tones. Gabe reaches above the doorframe and produces a key.

Inside, it's dark and quiet, and no one is in sight. Gabe goes over and yanks on the chains of the two hanging florescent fixtures. They sputter on, and the metal housing swings up and back, light gliding over the workbenches. "We cleaned the shop up before you came," he says and reaches up to still one and then the other.

I have some idea about the way sound travels, bounces, reverberates. You have to, to make movies. But the sound of the table saw was anchored in the shed. I guess it's possible the hangover is playing with my senses. I take a breath.

It's not a clean shop, not by Paul's standards, but I can see there's some imposed order. No cobwebs in sight or mouse droppings. A Miller High Life clock appears to be dead but wiped down, an old leather tool belt hangs on a hook, and there are screws and nails and nuts overflowing their cardboard boxes. The band saw is cool to the touch. I move over and put my fingertips on the saw's throat plate. It's fully warm. There's sawdust around the extension wings but no freshly cut pieces of wood.

"Careful. Blade's up. And your knee's awful close to the switch," Gabe says.

I draw my hand away. The blade is set so low, I had missed it. I continue to inspect things. I wonder if there could have been an electrical surge. I pull the plug from the socket and straighten, realizing afterward I could have gotten a shock.

Gabe picks up a hammer and lets the head fall into his other palm. "We keep the door locked because of the kids."

I nod in agreement. "Oh, did Salish find her knife?"

"Not yet. We'll keep looking." He rests the hammer on a workbench and starts toward the door. "I'm off for a swim."

As we step outside, we see a group of crows dive-bomb a hawk, out toward the lake. We watch in silence for a moment. Then he locks up.

"Why birds?" I ask before he goes. "I mean of all the careers you might have pursued?"

"I had a biology teacher in high school, sophomore year. I was that obnoxious kid, always cracking jokes in class. And I was raised to hunt. So, one day, I said, Why bother studying something we're meant to kill? All the kids laughed. She seemed to take this as a personal challenge, and the next day she did a slideshow. She had drawings from Michelangelo's notebooks, brought in a couple of wings from large raptors, talked about the number of bones, the real mechanics. Explained that the study of birds is also the study of ecology and so on. She showed us the construction of different types of nests and took us on a field trip with binoculars. Basically, she worked on us until I got hooked."

As I walk up the slope, I think about circling back to find Paul. I'm sure he'd be willing to look at the table saw and the outlet. But I can ask him tonight. He has too much to sort out today. It's enough that Salish has us fretting over her knife. I laugh and tell myself it was only one of Jones's ghosts.

———

My sister-in-law is bread making. I stand in the kitchen and begin to record Jones on video as she watches her mother while leaning in the passageway to the dining hall. On both sides of Jones are glass-front cabinets filled with heavy white dishes, most of them scratched, many chipped. All the tables in the hall are empty, and the mantel of the gaping fireplace in the dining hall is loaded with pictures of the kids who collected at these tables over decades. The windows of the house are in need of a wash, but their filminess creates a decent backlight as she moves into the kitchen.

Jones looks over, into the lens, without changing her expression. She has none of her mother's plainness. I wonder if she thinks everyone should want to film her no matter what she's doing.

When the light from the windows hits her eyes, the gold bands around her brown irises make me think of honey, though I understand there's no pooling of sweetness in Jones. She's dressed in a T-shirt with faded, backward letters I can't read and cutoffs with the pockets hanging out the bottom. Her thick-soled boots are laced up today. There are piercings in her ears and one on the side of her nose. Maybe there are others. Gabe told me she did them without her mother's permission. Fights blew up. This last winter, he said, she became *the girl who no longer obeys*. They were lucky to get her into the van to travel north. Certain remunerations were paid.

I pause the video. Like adolescent rebellion, Hidden Lake is another natural occurrence. It has a pervasive green color today from algae or maybe small luminescent worms. Gabe described this phenomenon last night, and I wondered if I'd ever get in the water until he told me they're harmless and the lake is great for swimming.

The three young ones are playing a game of tag now. Lily looks defeated by her brothers. I would gladly go out there and tag them back for her. But I'll settle for bringing her a cookie and lemonade in a while. Maybe she has a book she'd like me to read to her.

Returning to film Jones, I find she's avoiding eye contact

with her mother. Jones goes over to the sink and stands there like she's expecting something to occur. Salish and I wait to see what she's up to as Jones shifts and takes up a spot by the main cabinets. This is followed by a moment in the center of the room, another by the door to the mudroom, the last just outside the pantry.

"What?" her mother says, tossing a dish towel on the counter.

I focus my lens on her mouth and pull back to catch Jones as she says, "Checking for hot and cold spots."

I say nothing about the cold landing on the back stairs. Or what it's like to swim in Hidden Lake according to Gabe. The whole thing is filled with pockets of hot and cold—a combination of geothermic and solar radiation.

"God, I have no patience today," Salish says. "Take it down to the lake."

Panning to her face, I say, "She seems to be talking about ghosts."

"You think I don't know that?" Salish says.

Jones looks pleased, as if she's wound up boxers in a tin ring. She looms into the lens so she's only an eyeball. "I'll need a contract if I'm going to be in your film."

"I'll print one up." I keep the camera running as she backs off.

"If a picture frame tilts or a board loosens in the floor or a branch grows and touches a windowpane, my daughter says: *Ghosts.*"

My eldest niece is the only one, it seems, with a clear explanation for certain events that take place at Hidden Lake. She stays up late into the night reading ghost stories, along with her share of mysteries and thrillers from a supply of books left by past campers. Her mother often scolds her for getting Timothy going when Jones reports on stories she's read. I'm sure she'd say the cold spot on the landing is caused by a restless spirit.

I feel for Salish, the way her daughter grabs all the attention. It must be hard.

"You probably don't know that Einstein believed in ghosts," Jones says.

In a rare moment, Salish laughs.

I think of explaining that this must be a meme but settle for getting it recorded.

"I guess genius troubles you," Jones says. As if she has a charger with her, the light bulb in the oven hood sputters to life. I imagine this is the confirmation she was looking for. She turns to face us squarely. "It's going to get worse if you ignore it."

"Find *anything* else to do," Salish says.

Jones reaches for the pantry door handle and finds it locked. "What the fuck?"

"What do you need?" Salish asks. "I'll get it for you."

"You locked up the food?" Jones says.

"You know," her mother says. She moves a pan from breakfast into the sink filled with soapy water. I would revisit my offer to help wash or dry, but this seems a bad idea with her temper up. I don't like thinking of her suffering through all the pots and pans. Without looking at Jones, she says, "Go help the little ones organize some educational puzzles. I'll bring a snack up in a while."

"You want us to sit around doing puzzles when we could be flayed alive in the middle of the night?"

"Enough," Salish yells as if Jones has flown to the far corner of the house and her mother must pitch her voice high enough to reach her.

Jones looks at me. "She told you I've been fucking cut, right?"

"Upstairs. *Now.*"

Jones pulls up her shirt, revealing a black bikini top with faded pink flowers. In the center of her chest is a bandage with a blotch of blood. "All of us are in imminent danger," she says.

"Imm-in-nent."

"What on earth have you done?" Salish asks, as if the only explanation is that Jones has cut herself.

The room goes still. "How did it happen?" I ask and continue to film.

Jones smiles into the camera and says, "Like you said, *she means ghosts.*"

When I pull back, Salish looks as if she could stop her daughter's hair and nails from growing. "You took my paring knife, didn't you?"

"Are you serious?" Jones asks.

I say, "You're missing a knife?"

"Yes, as a matter of fact, I am." Salish's face brims red as she addresses the camera for the first time.

"When did you last see it?" I ask.

"Sometime after Jones came down for a snack last night."

"You think I care about your fucking knives?" Jones says.

"I don't think you care about anything," Salish says.

"I'm not the one who brought us to this shithole."

"You sound just like your father."

I don't know what quality Jones replicates in her biological father or what moments in history her mother is stung by. Gabe didn't talk about him.

"Drop dead," Jones says, and runs through the dish pantry, through the dining hall, and up the staircase like a bead of mercury.

It occurs to me that if Salish *were* to drop dead, no one else has a key to the pantry. Most of the dry and canned goods and the refrigerator and freezer are housed in that giant space. We divvied up keys last night. We could only find one for the pantry door. She has become the absolute keeper, the empress of food, with the capacity to plump us up or starve us out.

"Grounded!" Salish shouts after her and pitches a cast-iron pan into the sink of soapy water. A wave rises and splashes over the old butcher-block countertop, slops onto the floor, and soaks her jeans and tennis shoes with a skim of soap and brown grease. Salish bellows from deep within her pent-up life.

A door slams upstairs. Without friends for Jones to get into trouble with, a TV to watch, a mall to hit, or a freaky part of town to invade, this grounding probably means nothing to her. At most she'll lose her phone and computer time. But I'm sure Jones would only break into our room, not that we lock it—it has no key—and hijack my equipment while I'm out walking. Or stay in her own room and read more ghost stories. She has books stashed everywhere. Gabe says they tumble out of linen closets and appear in the bottom of bathroom hampers. They hide behind cereal boxes and work like a layer of frosting between her box spring and mattress.

Turning off my camera, I give Salish a sympathetic look and say, "Why don't I make some coffee and help you look for your knife?"

"Maybe another time," she says and turns away so the lake is out ahead of her.

I leave the kitchen through the back hall and go upstairs. I swap camera batteries to keep them charged and turn on my desktop computer that I have set up on the child-sized desk. There's a message from Hal, a producer friend, who wants me to edit a music video for the new band he's promoting.

The footage is pretty bad. Mostly grainy moments in a smoky club with too many guitar close-ups. I turn the volume off and look for anything salvageable. The lead singer is the one with talent, and he has the least amount of footage. I would have to push Hal to get someone to record more despite the grumblings I'd hear.

I start a note to him but keep deleting it. There's something he's seeing. I know it's best to get curious. That's when I realize the careful attention paid to the bass player. This must be his new love interest. He has a thing for men with brooding faces. Delicate ones who look like they've stepped out of Thomas Hardy novels. He lost his partner a few months before I lost mine. No one wants to have this in common, but I've tended to take him for coffees, see how he's holding up. I'm surprised he hasn't said anything about the bass player.

Watching the footage many times over while I take notes, I realize I've started to scratch my chest, that the skin near my heart feels almost painful. Sometimes I get hives, and then I can't stop scratching. Trying to recall if I brought the right ointment with me, I go across the hall to the bathroom and pull my shirt up.

There's a cut in the center of my chest. A straight vertical line. A bead of blood seeps from this wound and runs down my torso. The skin all around it is red. My hands tremble as I blot it with toilet paper. It looks too much like the cut Jones displayed. Taking a deep breath, I tell myself I must have scratched too hard. There are no other explanations.

Before I get a bandage on, I dash back across the hall, grab my Canon, and stand in front of the mirror to record the cut, then I turn the camera for a direct shot. I take a deep breath and hold it steady. After I put my camera down, I stanch the wound, put on a gauze bandage from the supply we brought, and return to the Quarter Room. When I change my clothes, I record the cut on my big toe and the one on my calf where I've lined up a couple of butterfly bandages.

In an effort to calm down, I scrub my bloodstained bra and T-shirt until they come clean. Going through the events of the morning, I look at things as if I'm a forensic pathologist who considers the way time works. I know this isn't a deep cut. All three lacerations should heal with minimal scars. The liquid vitamin E I brought will help. But as I pace up and back in a room the size of a quarter, I wonder what it is about Jones and her blessed ghosts.

CHAPTER FOUR

Ghost Movies

S alish has gone upstairs for her after-lunch nap, which she forces on the younger kids as well. They must do something quiet in their rooms if they can't sleep. She has *loaned*—emphasizing this word with care—my husband the key to the pantry.

On a tray, Paul sets a bowl of clear broth, a small slab of red Jell-O, an open can of pale mixed fruit in syrup, and a plate of leftovers from last night—mostly chicken and sautéed carrots—along with a weak cup of coffee. The parents get their lunch after everything is cleared away.

"Grab a couple of napkins?" he says.

"I swear she has cabin fever." I open and close several drawers.

"Who?"

"Salish. She's overtaxed," I say.

"Just use paper towels if you can't find napkins."

Describing the morning fight she had with Jones—without the reveal of the cut at the end—I rip the towels off the roll two at a time.

He rubs the stubble along his jawline. "She's a little tense, but she keeps asking if there's anything she can do to make us feel at home. She even wants a list of special dishes we like to eat and—"

"That's what I mean. She has way too much to do and shouldn't feel like she's everyone's servant."

He makes a troubled face.

"What?" I say.

"You sure you want to do this today?" He picks up the tray.

"Yes."

When we get to the top of the stairs, Paul goes ahead of me. Rather than walk down the hall where most of Gabe's family is settled, we take the perpendicular hallway to the left. This is where Jones has her room, placing her at the exact center of this U-shaped house, with a full view of the chickens, the lake, and some of the cabins, the rest flanked to the left and right of the shower houses, nestled behind conifers. The boathouse and dock are aligned with her room.

"Why don't you wait here a minute while I get Emmett and Elizabeth cleaned up," he says. Moving past Jones's room, he takes the steps up to Elizabeth's and Emmett's. Balancing the tray, he opens the door. I don't think I've heard him use the words *parents* or *mother* or *father* when referring to them.

Wandering up and back in the hall, I hear what can only be Emmett's voice as it strikes the rafters with force. Music goes on in Jones's room seconds later. I realize they must be almost above her bedroom. Slumping down on the worn carpet runner, I listen to Florence and the Machine boom over the shouting. When I finally decide I don't want to get involved in an argument—I'll try for another day—Emmett stops. A moment later the upstairs door clicks open, and Paul pops his head out, signaling to come ahead.

The first thing I see is Emmett, looking like a thousand-year-old man, with his rutted face and its system of broken capillaries. His dentures sit in tissues on the bedside table. He lies prone on a single bed, his head propped up by three pillows. The covers are pulled up to his chin. Elizabeth looks much younger, though I understand there's only two or three years between them. Her skin is papery, her eyes a faint blue. She sits in a chair by the windows facing the lake, her twin bed neatly made. One of the windows is cracked open, but the air smells antiseptic. The bathroom is picked up, a supply of fresh linen across one of the dressers. Paul has arranged the plate of leftovers for his mother on a small round table with the juice. Tucking a paper towel under her chin, he places one on her lap, then he cuts up the chicken. The broth is for his father. Paul sets the bowl on his nightstand, fixes a lobster bib under his chin, and pulls a chair up to feed him. Finally, he gives me a smile as if to thank me for simply standing there and breathing.

Jones's music calms down.

Emmett winces. "What does *she* want?"

"This is Nora," Paul says.

I catch Elizabeth's worried expression. Then her eyes brighten. "It's the woman from the travel agency. I've decided on Denmark."

"See what you've done," Emmett says.

"I'm Paul's wife." I sound winded, as if I'm already rushing to get away.

"Who is Paul?" Elizabeth asks, her face full of wonder.

"I'm your son," he says in a patient tone, but I can see he's pained. "This is my wife, Nora."

"Well, I can't help her," she says. "Paul died years ago."

"I'm here," he says.

"If your right hand makes you stumble, cut it off and throw it from you," she says.

"And that would be from the Book of Matthew," Paul tells me softly. His face is drained.

I've read little of the Bible. Despite a certain logic, it's hard to know with dementia, if she realizes what she's just said to him.

We watch as Emmett struggles to sit up but is unable to make it. "Give me the blessed spoon, boy."

Ignoring him, Paul comes back to me and puts an arm around my waist. "Why don't I see you later? This will probably take a while."

"You don't need my help?"

"No, he doesn't need your fucking help," Emmett says.

"Settle down, old man," Paul says and turns to me. "I'm good, sweetheart. Maybe you can get a walk or run in, and I'll see you at dinner."

I linger at the door, wanting to say something to Elizabeth. *I'm glad to have met you.* Or, *I'll be back to read to you sometime.* Or, *I'm sorry things are so rotten.* But nothing seems right. My grandfather on my mother's side went through dementia, so at least I know it's best to pretend Elizabeth's reality is my reality. I open the door, turn back, and say, "I'll work on your tickets to Denmark."

Paul winks at me.

"I'd like an outside cabin."

"I'll bring you some cruise brochures," I say.

As I descend the stairs, I hear Emmett shouting about the idiot Paul has married. There's an impulse to fly back into the room and run the man through with a few choice words, but

I hear my husband come to my defense. This won't be an easy time for either of us, but at least we're together.

———

Lauren, my closest friend, an alum from film school, is engaged in a project involving Tibetans who live in northern India. She is the only person with whom I exchange long emails. Today she tells me how her film is going and the way her new cameraman is flirting with her, which I'm happy to encourage. I fill her in on some of the history of Hidden Lake Camp. I'm lucky I've caught her in her room. Our exchange goes back and forth rapidly.

Paul and Gabe weren't just the owners' sons. They could only eat breakfast after the campers had their fill, and then the boys had to help wash and dry dishes along with the cook. Before dinner, they hosed down the dock, lined up the boats and oars, stacked the rafts and floats so the campers could have their fun. As soon as a camp group left, Paul and Gabe cleaned the cabins of messes left behind and shared latrine duty. They delivered fresh sheets and towels they helped fold with their mother or a housekeeper along with bars of soap to the next group that moved in. When camp was in session, they manned the supply store for an hour each day. Now it's used as a henhouse. Homeschooling was about being too far from the nearest public education, and they read the Bible out to their mother at night, her perennial request.

I'm not surprised Paul left.

Gabe took off a year after Paul did. He was only 14. He found relatives to live with in a different state. Of course, Emmett blames the demise of the camp on his sons' exodus.

How are you handling all of this?

I'm okay. Paul's been very dear and I want to be here as he works through things with his family. Besides, if we're serious about trying for a child, I can hardly go back to California just now.

What if we both found a way to have a child before the windows shut?

You sound serious about this guy.

Yes. Maybe. Who knows?

I would babysit when we're both home, as much as you'd like. BTW, I've started working on a film or working toward working on a film at the camp.

Can't wait to hear. But I must dash. More soon.

In the evening, Paul says he hopes his father doesn't linger, but it's his mother that troubles him. He admits he should have found a way to stay in touch, to see her before her condition went this far. We go to bed early, and I hold him tight.

———

It's easy to lose track of the days. The sky is as dull metal as my brain this morning. Fighting the bitter chill, I cinch the belt on my Irish knit sweater. I feel cramps come on and find my period has started. Another chance lost.

Crawling back into bed, I think about every unfair thing I

can link together until I fall into thick dreams. I finally surface just after lunch when half the house has started its nap.

Pulling my wool cap low and fixing a pair of dark glasses in place, I go out and sit with the small black dog on the stoop outside the dining hall. Her chin rests on my thigh as we watch Gabe drag a heavy picnic table over to meet another in the low grass, making one long surface. The chickens rise and settle.

He spreads out sheets of newspaper and quickly weighs them down with large rocks. The dog and I almost laugh when we see him struggle against a gust as if battling the elements in a silent film. Next, he goes off to a shed, hauls a couple of cardboard boxes over to the tables, and unloads pieces of precut wood onto the surface. He has a full bottle of wood glue and gets a nail gun connected to a long extension cord that feeds out from the game room. We stroll over to inspect his work and stop in front of the tables. I take a seat at the far end of a bench, and my companion slips underneath and rests near my feet.

Gabe seems to understand my need to just sit here and watch. He organizes his cut wood into piles, each containing four sides—one with a hole or entry—one base, one panel for the roof, and a small bit of dowel to make the perch. He spreads the glue in wavy lines along the edges, smears the lines with the tip of an index finger, and fits the pieces together. Then he sets this aside, takes one that's started to dry and uses the nail gun to secure the first birdhouse.

This means two lost brothers who build houses at different scales.

Drawing a pile of walls in close, I grab the bottle of glue. He doesn't say anything when my finished structure looks like it barely survived a mudslide. I begin on the next house, deter-mined to make this one true.

"Let's take Jones at her word," I say. "If there were ghosts, who would they be?"

He wedges a dowel in and sets another small building into the row of new homes. "You'd have to ask her."

"Your parents had the main house built, right? And Paul said they never took vacations. So your family should know if anyone died here."

He motions for me to hand him the start of my second property and shows me the right way to secure it. I realize his hands are similar to Paul's, the way the thumbs turn out.

"I've missed a few of those years. And another family built the place. But there *was* the ax murderer," he says, lifting one eyebrow.

"Right," I say.

"It's a phase. Last year, everything was manga. She got a pair of those black contact lenses and nearly blinded herself, so we had to intervene."

"Not easy being a stepparent, is it?"

"It's harder for them."

"I don't know if Leon wants me to engage him or let him be. One way seems intrusive, the other disinterested."

"It's different when you have your own. Then you *know* you're screwing up."

"That's reassuring."

"He's a lucky man, my brother. Maybe that makes it a little harder for Leon."

"A matter of allegiances?"

"He can't simply hate you."

He's curious, this avian psychologist. Where Paul has always been a little weak on knowing why we do what we do—or at least expressing this to me—my childhood was saturated with underlying meanings. I appreciate the kind of shorthand I have with Gabe.

Looking down at the birdhouse I'm bungling, I decide I'll go make a sandwich and get back in bed with the heating pad. I leave him with a whole village to construct.

"Come back if you get bored," he says.

———

Paul calls for a meeting the next day. He's made a full assessment. The hens have been fed, eggs collected, garden watered. Salish has served the first round of breakfast. The way the light hits the lake, it's more reflection than water this morning. To go out rowing just now would be like moving through the clouds. I'm still in my nightgown and robe as the meeting begins.

"The buildings are in worse shape than you said," Paul addresses his brother. "The roofing alone. Why didn't you let me know? At least send photos?"

I get up and pour a cup of coffee from the large drip machine, not sure I want to sit at the kitchen table just now. Paul could have *asked* for pictures, of course, but in every sense, they're working off a thirty-year gap.

"We're here now, so let's talk about what needs to get done," Gabe says.

Paul hands each of us a sheet of paper. In his funny way, he's handwritten four identical lists of necessary fixes rather than typing something out and printing duplicates.

My eyes go straight to the total cost of repairs. "What about selling it for the value of the property?"

Salish rushes at me like a spillway. "We've yanked our kids out of school, taken a second mortgage on our house to have funds for materials, not to mention the full month of caregiving, cleaning out the cabins, and straightening the sheds—all so you can get someone to buy the land and raze the buildings? And how's that going to get us enough money to take care of the folks?"

"If the national campground were still open," Gabe says, "there would be more interest in the land alone. And we're not taking the parents home to live with us. Are you?"

Salish looks at me as if I better not add sugar to my coffee or even move.

Maybe, if it were Elizabeth alone, but even then, we're all working more than full-time. I think we should move money around and get the parents settled in nursing care before anything else. But this isn't the first time I've brought this up.

Paul jumps in. "No, we're not prepared to take them to California. And he wouldn't make it even if we tried."

"I've talked to a couple of Realtors who specialize in this kind of property," Gabe says. "One of them sells land and camps to nonprofits and corporate groups. The other works with private investors. The corporate guy drove out and gave it a thorough going-over. With the cabins and plumbing already in place for showers, the electrical in, and the size of the lake, we have a particularly appealing spot. The west clearing would be ideal for RVs or a larger central building. We wouldn't have to do the paving. Even at the low range, he convinced me our profit is in renovation."

"Of course, Realtors like to make things seem rosy at the start,"
I say, almost talking to myself. I add extra sugar to my cup.

"How would you know?" Salish says.

I laugh in a full-throated way. "I'm married to a contractor."

"What, for like three or four months?" she says.

Paul gives her a look that shuts her down. I go over to the
pantry, give the doorknob a tug, and the door pops open. Salish
has failed to secure the fort. She starts to get up but seems to
change her mind. While they talk, I make some toast and put a
smear of peanut butter on top.

"Give me the Realtors' contact info, and I'll give them a call.
See what the comps look like," Paul says.

"Sure. Is there anything you can trim off the list?" Gabe asks.
"Like new windows for the cabins?"

"I'll take another look."

"The place has already been deeded to you and me," Gabe
says. "We'll have to reach some kind of agreement."

"When did that happen?"

"A couple of years ago," Gabe says.

"You've seen the paperwork?"

"It's in a file in the office. I'll pull it out."

"Hard to imagine him wanting to give us anything besides grief."
Paul scrapes his chair away from the table and goes off to work.

———

I sleep in most days and burrow into the books I brought.
Among others, this is the season when I will read *A Tale of Genji*,
The Underground Railroad, most of Alice Munro, *My Ántonia*, and

One Hundred Years of Solitude for a second time. The lake is too cold for a swim yet, but I take daily walks around the perimeter and up into the hills.

One morning I hike to the general store, meet the owners, the Brenners, and hike all the way back. I work on the band footage and show a group of gamblers to Timothy, the morbid one. He rapidly loses interest.

I try to imagine what it was like when this was a thriving campground—children running around the cabins and firepit, flying off the end of the pier, short-sheeting, sneaking into the boathouse and kitchen at night. I only went to camp one summer and almost shot another girl with an arrow when she rushed without warning toward my target. My parents came and took me home when the other girls got mean about it, saying I did it on purpose, and I became inconsolable.

It's so quiet now, you can hear the minute anyone pulls up to the house, though no one ever does except the parents' doctor. We have two vehicles: Gabe and Salish's minivan and Paul's manual pickup. I never learned stick shift, and all Paul wants to do is stay put and work. So I am here in a stillness broken only by electric saws and occasional fights. The big sounds come from the storms, the sharp pushing in of wind or animal cries. There are a couple of those at night I haven't been able to identify. I'm reminded of the times Takeo and I camped out in the High Sierra. Gradually, I adjust to the pace.

———

The moon is almost full tonight. I look at the uncovered window and the shape of Paul next to me as his ribs expand

and his diaphragm contracts. His snoring has gotten worse, and I wonder if his breathing sometimes stops altogether. I shake him until I hear that strong in-breath through his nose. He seems to surface, fully awake, but when I try to talk with him, I realize he's still unavailable, which is different from his daytime unavailable—a distinct mood I've started to notice. I don't think it's just the work, and I worry it could burrow in.

I asked him to go to a sleep doctor a couple of months before we left home. I showed him an article on sleep apnea and one on PTSD. Paul laughed and said he doesn't have any conditions. Like a sky that's uniformly cloudless 365 days of the year. If he's the man who stops breathing when he sleeps, he has the perfect insomniac to intervene. But it upsets me that he didn't go.

I pull my laptop off the dresser and return to bed. Here I write to my father—with Leon in mind—and ask for some favorite ghost movies. He teaches film at Berkeley, and neither of us finds it easy to sleep unless we watch something just before we turn in. While I wait for an answer, I put my earbuds in and start *La Belle et La Bête* from 1946 and drift in the blue light. I feel safe for a time, as if my father is in the house and we have stayed up talking.

Waking in the middle of the night a second time, I hear a low animal sound I definitely cannot identify. There's a kind of huffing. I grab my laptop that's about to slip off the bed. I'm not sure if the sound was in my dreams or in the movie or outside waiting to get in. Maybe it was Paul's snoring. But it's quiet now, and I'm in a fresh cycle of wakefulness.

Early in our courtship, Takeo gave me a fairy-tale book that had been his grandmother's. He knew I would love the illustrations. Having retained his ability to read as well as speak Japanese fluently, he translated a few of the tales for me when we read together at night. There was one about a *shiryō*, or a departed soul, who killed his wife so she would join him in the afterlife. There were days after I first lost Takeo that it wouldn't have taken much for me to climb into a boat, row out to the center of a lake, tie a weight to my ankles, and drop over the side so I could be with him again.

Now I do what I've taught myself to do. I take these feelings and roll them into a ball, making them smaller and smaller until I can swallow them like a pill. As soon as I'm done with one, I start to roll the next. Maybe it's the isolation here. Some days it feels as if I swallow more than I should of this kind of medicine. Periodically, I worry I could lose Paul.

My father writes back.

The Shining, Nosferatu and Ugetsu. Can't sleep?

Nah. How are you?

Book goes well. Mom's patients are nicely unwell yet ever improving. I thought you were afraid of ghost movies.

One of the nieces, the older one I told you about, Jones, she's obsessed with ghosts. And I'm trying to reach Leon who, I've learned, has a certain interest in terror. BTW, I'm kind of glad I didn't bring the big camera but I have started filming.

Ghosts?

Ha ha.

You'll tell me next time we talk?

Nothing to tell yet. Just playing around. Love you.

Love you too. Get some sleep.

Going over to the window, I see the lake is in its phosphorescent green stage. The moon is full, and the slope down to the edge looks floodlit. Out of nowhere I begin to see dozens of white moths. This happened once when I was with Takeo outside of Prague. I see his face more precisely in my mind as I watch them.

Getting my robe on, I reach out to grab a flashlight and knock into a glass of water perched on the bookshelf. I throw a sweater on the floor to soak it up. Paul begins to babble sleep nonsense. Avoiding the worst of the creaky floorboards, I thread my way downstairs.

The air is pungent with the smell of fresh baked items lingering in the kitchen. Yeast, dark-brown molasses, maybe nutmeg. Salish spent all day baking again. I go through the dining room and step out into the chill air. The moths come to rest in an arrangement that lights up the trees.

The children have gouged the yard around the house into raw dirt with their trucks, buckets, and shovels. Two giant plastic dolls keep watch, one with a missing eye as if this is the set of a horror film. The dogs are up in the children's rooms. The chickens startle and then quiet.

I hear the sound a second time. It isn't a moan exactly, or a growl. Maybe a sadness. Running downhill over the lawn, past the sheds, and through the taller grass, I head to the dock. I've learned which are the broken boards and step carefully until I reach the spot where I can sit and dangle my feet in the water. Here I listen for Takeo's voice, alert to each small sound.

My father heard his mother sing to him after she died, more than once. I think he told me this in case Takeo comes looking for me. But then, Dad has an intuitive nature when it comes to certain things.

I want Takeo's advice. He liked to do that, give me advice if I asked. In fact, we both did. We wanted the best for each other.

As I turn and look toward the house, I see a light go on in the parents' room. Maybe with the bright moon, my mother-in-law doesn't realize what time it is. Soon their light goes off.

"I don't know that I'm finding my way very well."

I know how voices echo and bounce off the cabins and trees, ricochet against the lake and boulders, sometimes become other sounds. But I can't hear his answer. I think of his hands—the small scars from working the kiln—the way his fingers notched between my fingers.

A slight breeze ripples the water out and out, and no answer comes.

CHAPTER FIVE

Face in the Bucket

The thing is, you come first," Paul says. We have gone back and forth. Estimates and comps from in-state Realtors. Conversations with a good friend who's done quite well as a developer, at least back in California, and is able to access particular inventories. The bank, interest rates, a fair amount of pacing. Finally, my husband says it makes sense to him to remodel or update, but he will understand if I vote against the idea. The work will take six months, and he asks me to be sure I can put up with his family that long.

Looking out at the henhouse, I mutter to myself. We both understand what my gynecologist said before we left town. She spoke with a kind of vigor I dislike. If Paul and I hope to have a child by natural means, there's no room for waiting. I sense I would split Paul in two if we left now.

There are the parents, of course. No one has come up with a fresh answer to how they can be looked after. And as an only child, I worry too much about my own parents now that they're in their early seventies. If something should happen to them, I would hope everyone around them would treat them with kindness, even sacrifice for them, including Paul.

My mind has entered a loop. I return to buildings. Paul has been the contractor on his share of homes and done plenty of remodels. People trust his work, and that's led to a tributary system of referrals. He doesn't cut corners, selects his own lumber for the finish work, has a team he's managed for years, and in time, the debts from the divorce will be paid off in full and he'll be in good economic shape again. He made some money turning over his home, and that goes into the pot to supply materials.

When we decided to come to Hidden Lake, Paul organized everything with his partner, waiting to pack the truck with tools until the right things were put in place. This is his methodical nature I've come to rely upon. And he never complains to anyone about the challenges of working with the highly privileged. Wealthy clients sometimes ask him to rip out the cabinets he has just installed, rethinking the style entirely, then ask for the next set to be torn away, as if they're moving furniture about. He gets paid; it isn't that. But when he actually builds the cabinets, it's the loss of the craftsmanship he laments. Sometimes though, they let him salvage the work. That's how we got our kitchen cabinets. He didn't even charge Takeo and me—said he was happy to see them find a good home.

We stay up late talking three nights in a row. I ask in more than one way, "What about you being here that long, dealing with family, your father barking at you?"

"Maybe it's a small thing if we can get everything we need out of it. I'm not sure how we'd carry nursing home bills at this point."

We consider every option. He never presses. I give myself time to think.

In the end, I sign off on a second mortgage on my home. Gabe and Salish match our funds. Lumber and drywall arrive on big flatbeds that keep Timothy and Mason in rapture. Lily, who is in a state of wonder much of the time, might never remember the big trucks, the unvarnished doors and roofing materials. She is so little.

Since no one can afford an extended vacation, Paul will receive a weekly check for his labors. With Gabe's project on the North American swallow and his agreement to address the bills and other paperwork for a bookkeeper's fee, he can only offer ideas and the occasional construction moment that requires three people. In addition to my documentary work and editing, if I sort through the material culture of the camp with Gabe, this work will also be based on an hourly wage. Paul insists Salish receive a reasonable chef's pay. For two brothers who haven't seen each other in decades, and seem far apart on many subjects, arrangements launch well enough. We all know our jobs and are eager to get on with them.

But, for some reason, settling things produces a restlessness in me. I try to work through this with camera lenses. I spend more time documenting this family, consider the possibilities, dig into a curiosity about why I haven't seen the brothers hold a single personal conversation yet. If they've done this out of sight, Paul hasn't brought it up.

———

A funny instinct keeps clutching at my intestines. One morning, when the kids are still asleep and the adults are seated around the kitchen table for breakfast, I creep up the main stairs, enter the Wedding Room, seal the door, and start to film.

Panning over the rumpled sheets and the ornithology books on the floor, I imagine Gabe sitting up in bed at night, sketching swallows or the signs of swallows that he spotted that day. I can see Salish looking through recipes as she sits next to him. Or she drops to sleep early after the little ones are tucked in, complaining about the light he keeps on.

Mostly he's known for his work on the condor and other birds of prey. But he began to move his focus a few years ago to the swallow population. He told me something about the impact of climate change and the big shift in farming practices—the way the numbers continue to diminish.

I record his clothes and shoes and boots along with the supplies in the bathroom, the sad douchebag draped over one towel rack, a bottle of vinegar. No one has seen to the mold around the tub or bothered to clean the sink much or the yellow-black ring in the toilet. There are a couple of erotica books on the floor near the tub, pages with water stains.

As I gaze out the windows, I'm aware Gabe might look over when he's sitting in his desk chair as I turn my light on or move about or lift the shade in order to see the lake. It's possible he thinks of me on the other side of the curtain after I close it. I am the only woman here, other than his wife, but maybe there is something more in the way he pays attention to me. Our work is different, but we both understand what it is to capture things or at least hold on to them long enough to study them. I shake these thoughts from my head.

His desk is crowded with books and papers. I don't have time to explore his computer files. But I do slide the drawer open. Coins, pens, open pack of gum, loose papers, sticky notes, paperclips. I'm about to close it when I see the edge of a photograph. I slip this out, and realizing what it is, a sharp pain hits my back. I quickly put it in the side pocket of my camera bag.

Takeo's mother, Satchiko, had sent a few black-and-white images of family members and friends months ago. They were taken on the day before my husband's cremation. When the envelope arrived, I saw one of me in the black dress I haven't worn since. This was shot at her house, though I don't recall anyone taking photographs.

There was so much to do before we came to Hidden Lake. I'm sure I locked up this envelope with the other photographs in the storage closet. That Paul would send this to his brother or bring this along, leaving it about—I don't know when I've felt this violated. I hurry and look through dresser drawers and closets, but there doesn't seem to be any more of me hiding here.

Stepping out into the hall, I know I've already been in their room too long. If I confront Paul about the photo, I will have to explain why I've been rifling around. After going through the delicate process of moving quietly down the stairs, I sneak through the dining hall, and see that no one's looking my way when I dash past the kitchen and up the back stairs until I reach the cold landing.

I'll have to capture Jones on film talking about the way the cold air—what does she call it, neutrinos or ghost particles?— can take over on a warm day. I've looked outside, inside, asked Paul to look. He had no idea what I was talking about. Patient as he was to consider the insulation and window seals, he shrugged at the temperature difference. He couldn't explain the table saw in the old workshop going on and off either. Paul made clear, however, that it will never start up under its own will and there isn't a short, but that noise has a unique way of moving about in the valley. After a while, he grew impatient.

Turning my computer on, I consider the photograph from my wedding with Paul on the home screen. I used to think I looked happy in this picture. Now I'm not as sure. The temperature has risen a good ten degrees around my desk, the air thick with the buzz of insects. I hear Salish's voice rise as I open my camera bag to see if I need to switch batteries. I pull the black-and-white photograph out first, turn it over to take a second look, and startle. It falls from my hands and spins to the floor like a seedpod, slipping under the bed. I get down on my hands and knees and fish it out from the thin coat of dust. There's a figure in the foreground, but it isn't me. I don't know who it is. Short blond hair, stiff-looking dress that might be a uniform, shadows in the background. I check under the bed again, in the camera bag, look everywhere in case there were two photographs.

The only explanation is that I looked at it too quickly in the Wedding Room. Yet this is what I do, study quick images strung together. My mother said I shouldn't be surprised if I have small, momentary shifts in perception at times after losing Takeo. They could happen on and off for some time. She didn't ply me with articles or ask me to read books that would make me dwell on those shifts, but she assured me that dealing with a sudden and profound loss can untether us in unanticipated ways. She said below these outcrops, I am solid bedrock. I don't think she meant to use a line from one of her lectures—sometimes she forgets herself and does this—but I feel reassured thinking back on what she said.

I've taken something that doesn't belong to me but decide it's best for now to hide it in a file in the bottom of this small desk. There will be an opportunity to return it.

———

Heading downstairs an hour later, I get Salish's latest report. "Last night, when I was checking on things, the slicer—the one that looks like a freshwater fish?—the slicer was gone." She sits at the kitchen table, bewildered. Her mood is more dilute today, without accusation. I know she has an edge on that blade capable of splitting the pages of a letter falling through the air. And the steel paring knife with a bloodwood handle hasn't turned up.

"That's odd," I say.

"I set booby traps over the kitchen doors."

There are three doors in all: one to the back hall that I take to go upstairs; the one into the dining hall with the dish cabinets lining both sides; and one near the vegetable garden where the dinner bell hangs just outside. The first two are left open most of the time.

"How?" I ask.

"I was in the kitchen and opened the doors just a crack and balanced a half bucket of water between the doorframes and the doors—three in all."

Looking up to the places where she points, I try to imagine what this balancing act would take.

"But the thief must have seen me up on the ladder. They pulled all three buckets down without spilling a drop and left them by the sink."

The ladder is propped against the wall near the pantry. "Wait, how would a thief get into the kitchen with all the doors rigged that way?"

"That's what I'd like to know."

"And how did you leave?"

"I didn't."

"You stayed in the kitchen all night?"

"Yes."

"So you were in the kitchen and someone came through one of the doors without the bucket knocking over, stole a knife, went back through a door, and you didn't hear or see anything?"

When Salish expresses the full measure of her concern, she gets deep vertical lines in her forehead like exclamation points. "I don't want Jones to know."

"Did you fall asleep?"

"Just for a minute."

I go over to the sink and look down into each of the buckets, where my face floats. Then I go through the trash and the many drawers, check the refrigerator and the large freezer case, thinking she could be turning absentminded if she hasn't completely lost her grip. The cold billows out of the freezer in shapes that hover and fly off. I look under the ribs and shanks, the Popsicles and frozen waffles. I release the lid and the brittle rubber cracks as it shuts.

I sense her vulnerability, that she feels quite alone in her troubles. "I'm sorry you're going through this," I say.

The kids are halfway down the hill with the two spotted dogs, and soon enough they cluster near the trailhead close to the thickest part of the forest. This is the place where the kids go when they're told not to wander into the woods. They have been known to slip, one at a time, behind the cathedral of trees at the edge and disappear. It's not just the worry over stray animals and knives. All around the perimeter of the lake, it's shallow, but there's a sudden drop twenty feet out. None of us wants the kids to wander into the water alone, and I worry especially about Lily. I'm eager to help her with swim lessons as soon as the weather is right. Naturally I will stay with her every minute. We often talk to each other through her dolls now, and she has appeared in the Quarter Room during a few of her sleepwalking episodes. She likes to tuck in next to me until she wakes fully in the morning. She's such a love.

I heat some water and drop tea bags into two cups. I keep thinking there should be neighbors and other dwellings within walking distance. In our time being stuck here, it's easy to get lost in things like missing utensils, misread photographs, signs that aren't signs at all. Everyone thought Salish misplaced the first knife. With this second disappearance, she shows me scratches where a small, sharp tool was used to pick the lock on the pantry. If she didn't do this herself, I'm guessing it was Jones or Timothy.

I grab the honey.

My sister-in-law has ongoing rows with Jones, and I've heard Salish and her husband go at it down by the lake. I rarely see signs of affection between them. Now she talks of marching the three younger kids into the kitchen and lining them up to quiz and scold them. She might even hide the honey.

To keep my head above this twisted water, I come up with the following: "If I take enough footage with one of my handheld movie cameras and review it a few times, I might see something we miss in the moment."

She closes the pantry door and opens it again, considers the lock, then squints at me as if I'm going out of focus. "Like Zapruder's film?"

Salish doesn't do cynicism well, but she's trying. I guess everyone knows this one-minute wavering image of assassination, but it seems to hold special meaning for her. She brought it up when she learned I'm a documentarian.

"Never mind. It was just a thought." I turn to go upstairs.

"You think I'm making this up."

I would never say this to her face. In fact, I do the opposite. I've tried my best to assure her. "I've been helping you look."

"In the freezer?" she says.

I grab my tea and start to leave.

"Go get one of your stupid cameras."

Takeo said I push until I get what I want. Maybe he was the only one who understood that my way of pushing is to walk away. It's a bad habit, but I can't stand blowups.

I head up to the Quarter Room and pull my Canon off the top shelf of the closet. Before we left California, I mounted a mic on the side. My parents are storing most of my camera bodies and lenses, along with some of my archive, in their spare room.

Pausing on the cool landing, I begin to understand that the knives are the gift. This is the simple frame I've been looking for. I feel almost cruel in seeing this. I probably won't solve Salish's knife problem, but I can film a woman unhinged by this loss. I can take shots of the lake and the children running toward the lake, and a marriage that might dissolve like spoonfuls of bromide in water.

"Stand there," she says when I return to the kitchen, as if I'm a member of her crew.

This would place me directly in the sun's path, making her a sunspot in the lens. "What am I shooting?" I move around as she peers into the dining room, checks outside, and tucks herself into a corner of the kitchen where two countertops meet.

"Go ahead, start it."

I take a reading, turn the camera on, and zoom in just enough. Salish unfastens the buttons of her blouse and pulls it open. On her chest there's a gauze bandage with a spot of dried blood. She tugs this off, and a thin cut begins to run. Between the cups of a frayed cotton bra, just below this fresh cut, there's a new scab. Both marks are about an inch long, but they vary in width. Together they begin a ladder up the center of her chest. She reaches into one of the cabinets where the first aid kit is stored. Cleaning the new cut with alcohol, she winces. Then she applies a fresh bandage.

I learned from my college friend who cut that it's a bad idea to overreact. I move until I get the right angle of light on Salish's face, her wet eyelashes.

"Just before a knife goes missing, I wake up with one of these," she says, indicating her marks. "I'm terrified, and I'm certain Jones is mimicking this."

I think about calling my mother to ask what she knows about this disorder. There must be a name for Salish's condition or combined conditions. I think she's the copycat. It must be one of those long names that ends in *proxy*. What I've not been able to sort out entirely is my own mark.

"I know they'll take another knife. What's to stop them?" she says.

Panning over to the windows, I focus down the hill, the children like no-see-ums flying about, too close to the forest again.

"I'm concerned for you," I say, thinking again of my school friend, though her mercy was having a plastic surgeon for a father who had plenty of doctor friends to fix her up from mind to scar.

My sympathy has Salish fastening her blouse. "Where are you setting up?" Her tone is impatient.

"What?"

"You're going to leave the camera running all night, aren't you?"

"I'm sorry, Salish. I don't loan out my cameras. And I wouldn't bait a thief with one." I can see her disappointment. "We'll figure this out," I say. "I promise."

———

Before naptime, Lily asked me to read to her. But first, we must root out a few lumps. When she made her bed today, she pulled a thin blanket over her stuffed animals. I kick off my shoes, nudge them aside and plump a pillow so I can stretch out.

"We have to make them cozy again," she explains, nestling her animals around me. Going to her bookshelf next, she hands me a Little Golden Book, *The Color Kittens*.

"My mother read this to me when I was your age," I tell her, running my hand over the cover.

"You used to live here?" she asks.

"No, no, this is my first time."

She gives me a puzzled look.

"We had a copy of the same book."

"That's funny. Are you going to read?" She crawls around me and settles in.

We go through *The Color Kittens* and *The Poky Little Puppy* and almost finish *Babar Visits Another Planet* before she drifts off. I shut my eyes and feel my breathing twin with hers. Takeo and I lost a girl. Stillborn. I know it won't be good if Lily wakes up and finds me pinned to this thought.

I slip away, returning to my side of the house. It seems there should be enough grace in this world for me to have one living child before it's too late. In order not to dwell on this, I wash my face, brush my hair into a fresh ponytail, and head downstairs. I get one of the extra thermoses down and make coffee the way Paul likes it. Heading out in the cool air, I almost reach the cabin he's working on. That's when I hear him shout, "Goddamn it!"

"What's going on?" I say and step inside. I hand Paul the thermos, and he takes it as if it's a bomb to defuse. There isn't any furniture yet, other than the built-in bunk beds that are bare of old mattresses. "Did you hit your thumb again?"

"Gabe's been taking my tools. When he does bother to return them, he puts them in the wrong places."

"That's no good. Have you talked to him?"

"Just tell me what it would have taken for him to bring a few basic tools of his own? He could even use the old ones on the property to make his blessed birdhouses."

I almost correct him with the proper term, *nest boxes*, now that I understand it. But Paul is actually yelling at me, his face reddening. I say, "Is something missing?"

"That's not the point. He throws hammers in with screwdrivers, wrenches with clamps. I spent an hour straightening everything up after dinner last night—you should have seen the sockets—and he's at it again."

Part of this is the way Paul keeps his shop. There isn't a tool that shifts out if its designated home or even considers relocation. I've often wondered if this is a response to his family's chaos, the endless swirl of the campground, something his father imposed. But the first time I asked about his early years, he said he didn't have a lot of memories from that time. *How old were you when you had your first memory?* I asked, and he said, *Eight or nine.*

"Maybe he's trying to get your attention," I say, taking a last approach.

"God help me if I have to analyze my brother while I'm trying to save this place."

The word *save* steeps for a minute.

"I wasn't bothered much by not having a sibling when I was young, but now, with my parents getting old, I wouldn't mind having someone who understands. I'm sorry if Gabe isn't that person for you."

I wish Paul would let me hold him. Or at least let me point out that he's exposing his heart while asking me not to look at it. But he's freezing me out.

He struggles with the cap of the thermos, and some of the coffee dots the floor when it comes off. He wipes the drips up. I thought he'll refinish the floors eventually, but maybe he's thinking about ants.

"You're not going to sort out everything," I say, "but you could get to know each other a little."

"Maybe when he starts taking the work as seriously as I do."

"I'm sorry—that it's so hard."

I've only seen this monolithic side once before. I learned if he digs his boots in, there's little to do except let him line up his sockets and match up his clamps or work it out behind a band saw.

———

To make the four-mile trek to Brenners—often referred to as *going into town*—I assemble a peanut butter and jelly sandwich, an apple, and two snack bars while Salish rushes to put the breakfast things away ahead of me. I fill two reusable bottles with water and bring my baseball cap and sunglasses. The other things I throw in make me feel like someone planning for an injury.

With no cars to flag down, it's possible I could lie out on the road for a long time until Paul or someone in his family understands that I'm not hiding out but actually missing, if something should happen. I can't count on phone reception.

The road is cut into a hillside thick with poison ivy, and the drop is steep on one side. If I fell off the edge, I would roll like a speeding tire until I hit a tree or boulder. Even in the backcountry of the Sierra, I rarely entertained this kind of rushing thought. Despite this, the idea of being adrift from the house exhilarates me.

There are no homes or commercial plots on any of the federal lands. Gabe worries it will be developed or drilled or strip-mined eventually—the trees taken out for lumber, a number of species threatened along the way. He studies land management reports for his work. Gabe is the one who has conversations with the county about repairing the road. I've heard him on the phone, and he's quite good when he's playing diplomat—along with offering ways for the county to be environmentally conscious so they might line up some grants from a private foundation. A surveyor is scheduled to come out to have a talk. For now, the forest lands are deep and quiet without the feeling of expansiveness like so many of the places I've been to in California.

Once I get moving, a certain peace gathers during these walks. At the half-mile section of road that's pure washboard, I step from ridge to ridge, barely touching each crest, arms out like a young girl set free.

Following the last of several hairpin turns, I arrive at the short road to town just past the abandoned ranger station and the national campground, with its locked gates, warnings to stay out, threats of fines. It feels hotter here, and my boots and calves are coated with dust, but I'm glad to arrive in the heart of this small civilization. Stopping by the tiny clothes and souvenir shop, I peer inside. It shut down years ago but was never boarded up. I don't know why the inventory was left in place. The sun has cut through the cotton dresses on the mannequins in the display windows, literally shredding them. I am often surprised that no one has broken in or thrown rocks at the glass. One day when I walk past that store, I expect to see the dresses burst into flames.

The one open business, Brenners, a general store and gas station across the way, sits by a narrow stream. Mrs. Brenner is nearly deaf due to a congenital disease, and she reads lips. Mr. Brenner is partially blind from macular degeneration, the center of his vision almost gone. They are about the same age as Paul's parents, and at one time, the four of them socialized weekly, played gin rummy, and drank late into the night on weekends. Their three kids have all moved away.

Brenners does no business except to order our groceries and receive our deliveries now that the national park is closed. They plan to shutter the business at the end of the year and move in with one of their daughters a few states over. The shelves are mostly full of things with past due sell-by dates that radiate out from the cash register like tree rings. Brenners is also a postal substation, and they weigh and stamp my infrequent letters. We're more than lucky Sunoco hasn't dropped the store from its route.

Inside is the churn of the cooler with its distinct pitch, separate from the grating noise of the freezer unit. Smells of ice cream Drumsticks gone bad and soured milk spilled on the shelves are ever present. The Brenners live in the back of the store, so I don't like to startle them. I call, "Hello."

Just then, Mr. Brenner appears and goes over to slice a roll of turkey on his machine. The equipment is slowly breaking down, and it sounds as if he is sawing through a tree. I worry about him on that contraption with his sight. Mrs. Brenner slips behind the main counter and waves at me. She keeps her thin yellow-white hair plaited in one long braid sometimes wound at the back of her head. Preferring slacks and twin sets, she keeps everything neatly pressed. I begin to feel as if she sees me coming for miles.

"How are things?" I shout.

"You made it." Her voice carries across the store.

"You look well."

"Hold on." She calls to her husband. "That's enough, dear."

He flips the switch and rests the last slice of meat on the

small mound atop the scale. This, I imagine, will be their lunch. I wonder if he would have built a giant mountain of slices if I hadn't appeared. He rarely talks to me. I say hello again, but he doesn't respond.

"Nora said hello, dear."

As with most things I say, she shouts to her husband as if he's the one with a hearing problem to let him know exactly what I've said. And the room goes still. He puts the roll of turkey back into refrigeration and goes off to do some shelving. This is a task in which he often places things in odd arrangements. Pudding cups by detergent, sanitary napkins next to boxes of rifle shells. I wish he'd put the ammunition behind the counter, knowing Timothy courses through the aisles at least once a week. All I can do is keep an eye on him when I'm around.

I pull the letter I've written to Satchiko from my pack.

"Perfect," Mrs. Brenner says. She seems to enjoy using the small bronze weights in the pans of the old postal scale and selling the kinds of stamps that travel to Japan. I watch the way she looks this up in her official book, though my letters are all to the same address and have the same weight, a single folded page, in which I have struggled to say something appropriate as the widow and daughter-in-law who has remarried. Satchiko doesn't like to use email.

I ask about her other son and his wife and their child; how the weather has been in Kyoto; if she's getting translation work she enjoys. This is the first letter since my new marriage in which I admit I wish Takeo and I were traveling this fall to be with them. We always went in the fall. I don't know how she will take this, so I think of asking for my letter back.

But Mrs. Brenner affixes the stamps, and I let it go. "You say hello to that sweet husband of yours," she shouts as I go out the screen door.

It's a beautiful day, and maybe I did the right thing by letting my mother-in-law know how I feel. Going down to the stream that runs by the back of the store, I eat my sandwich, watch the water travel over the rocks, and save the other food in case I need it for the walk home.

———

Salish moves onto the dock with a bucket. She wavers, as if one of her feet has punched into a rotten board. Righting herself, she proceeds to the end. There she sits for a while, soaking her feet. The wind stirs the beech trees and roughens the surface of the lake in patches. Patterns of light travel over the outcrop of boulders in the distance. I wonder where I would be without this lake in this desolate place. Maybe it's the same for her.

When she returns to the house and sets her bucket on a kitchen bench, I realize for the first time that her eyes are almost the color of the lake, the way they change. I watch them shift now as if a storm bears down. Those strong eyebrows make me think of a bird of prey. I laugh to myself wondering if this was why Gabe was drawn to her.

The bucket is full of fresh carrots. We've had a chance to enjoy more of the garden thanks to the replacement of wire netting Paul and Leon put together, along with the nasturtiums that defeat some of the insects. Gabe is out in the yard working on a project. I turn the camera on.

"I asked him to tie a line of noisemakers around the perimeter," Salish says as if answering this to an audience. She is one of those people who turns into someone she imagines she might be if a camera followed her around for a tour of her home and all her thoughts were succinct. Something like Jackie Kennedy at the White House without the charm. "He found a ton of monofilament in one of the sheds."

Gabe ties bells and bits of glass on this filament along with empty tin cans. All that will do is annoy the coyotes and the occasional mountain lion. His wife might even trip on one of the lines when she goes for a late walk. Touching the downy hair at the back of her neck, she studies her husband as he gets the stakes into the ground, no doubt with one of Paul's hammers.

"We're going to sleep with the axes and scythe beneath our bed, starting tonight," she says.

It seems the knives have grown into giant blades in her mind. I wonder if there's a possibility of losing a toe when she makes the bed. I don't say this, only a vague, "Huh."

Salish goes into the pantry, and I stop the camera, turning to look outside. Gabe is also taking a pause, resting his eyes. I can't tell if he looks exhausted or defeated. I think of bringing him something cool to drink, but I know this might incite his wife. When I turn back, she's holding one of the two chef's knives. The grips were designed to fit perfectly in her hands. Knives are her hard currency. She's trying everything she knows to hold on to her fortune.

Checking the edge of this blade, she adjusts her apron, soiled red with berry stains. At the sink she draws a hard brush over the carrots. Then she lines them up on the block. We hear the cries of the children running toward the house as Salish brings her knife down and starts a line of steady chopping.

"Mom! Mom!" The children rush headlong as if the trees are on fire. A flock of starlings takes off from the ground with the stampede. The dogs yowl and yap and circle the kids. Timothy is the first to reach us.

He hurries into the kitchen out of breath, one of the young spotted hounds by his side. Mason, the five-year old with the droopy eyes, stays outside, where he huffs his breath against the glass door, making a serious face in his steam. He is dressed in a homemade pirate outfit and raises his eye patch to get the full view of his steamy artwork. Jones moves slowly in the distance. Lily comes in and curls into my side, sweaty and panting. I pull the damp curls away from her forehead. She smells of pine and moss. I never have to zoom in with Lily. She likes to push in close, gazing with affection into the lens. I would steal Lily away for my own if I could.

"She hit her head," Timothy splutters. "Jones…Jones was the wolf…and when she chased us…she fell. And hit a giant rock. It was so cool."

"All right," Salish says, undoing her apron.

Timothy runs back to see what his father is doing, and Lily motions for me to bend down, gives me a kiss, and trails after him. Mason lowers his eye patch, leaving his steam to disappear, and takes off to run ahead of Lily.

Washing her hands with a cake of antibacterial soap, Salish looks in the direction of Jones, who makes it to the yard in her torn jeans and hard boots. Gabe speaks to her, but she just shrugs. I notice Leon down by the cabins, watching to make sure Jones is alright.

My impulse is to run over to her, but I recognize the order of things. This is Salish's girl. We wait until Jones comes into the kitchen. She fills a cup with water from the sink first, drinks, fills, and drinks again. Her face is speckled with dirt, her hair knotted with bits of leaves and twigs, but there's no sign of blood. To get her to sit and have that bump on her forehead looked after, Salish talks about the latest knife that went missing—the cleaver.

I don't recall hearing anything about a cleaver.

Jones laughs and takes a seat on one of the stools. "You're losing your entire arsenal."

After checking for signs of a concussion, Salish holds her father's butter knife under cold running water then tries to place the flat of the blade against the hard bone of Jones's forehead. I've never seen anyone attempt to calm swelling this way. Jones straightens her spine and forces her mother's hand away.

"Something pushed me from behind. I hope you get that. The kids were in front of me. Something pushed me really hard."

Turning on me, my sister-in-law says, "The bread isn't going to remove itself."

It's never a simple thing to know if she will scold for helping or not helping, but I can check the bread. I put my camera down and work on the pair of singed mitts. Opening the oven door, I see the loaves are golden. They won't, however, have the crust she can rap against the cutting board to hear a particular sound that makes sense to her.

"Soon," I say and latch the door.

Her second territory is unlicensed medicine. She can stitch a wound, set a bone, and probably start a heart or deliver a baby—even her own. If one of us is bleeding heavily, we are picked up and carried to the kitchen table. We sit on chairs for the minor injuries, the little kids often squirming to get away from her rough hands. When I had a toothache, she offered to remove my molar. I took the long drive with Paul to a dental office instead—our one getaway—spending a night in a motel. I learned I was experiencing some gum trouble where a bit of seed had lodged in the soft tissue.

Jones is the bravest during procedures and the most resistant.

In her awkward affection, Salish says, "Give it a couple of days, monster." Sometimes she uses pet names for her children. Maybe she thinks these are like home remedies. But I'm uncertain over what she concocts. Or whom she likes. Her words often feel like affection without heart. It's easy to see Jones doesn't appreciate this and might still be mad at her mother from the other day.

"You better keep checking the oven," Jones tells me as she leaves for a rest. "Or she'll push you inside."

Salish ignores this and calls through the dining room, "Are you going to be down for dinner, or should I bring a tray up?"

Jones doesn't answer.

Outside, Gabe drops a handful of bells on the ground. My breath thins watching him. The old mitts sag on my hands as I stand there reading the temperature of each family member. I wonder if he measures out his anger toward the brother who left, or if Gabe feels no need for extended family life and its concerns.

"They're done now," Salish says, as if she caught my gaze and it means something.

I open the oven door again, and she's right, of course; the bread is done to her liking. I pull the hot metal pans out, set them on the cooling racks she's arranged at one end of the table, and remove the gloves.

She takes the bread knife and begins to sharpen it against the whetstone as I turn the camera on again. Salish will make this blade so sharp, it could skin the paint from a house. When she's done sharpening, she goes back to the carrots with the chef's knife and cuts them in a deliberate way. She looks at me from shoes to skull as if I'm a rodent and she's ready to slice off my tail.

"When I find out who's doing this, I'll gouge their eyes out."

I learned about timing from my father. He likes to watch old Laurel and Hardy movies and Burns and Allen shows from his shelf of comedy duos. He said it's not about two people meshing but creating a tension. One line strikes the other, sometimes with physical comedy or a facial expression thrown in. There are many things I could say to use the tension Salish has set up, but I imagine with her, this would fall flat.

"I'm sorry about the cleaver," I say, wondering if she'll fill me in.

"If this keeps up, there won't be anything left to butcher the chickens with," she says.

Or slice the cheese or divide the rope into usable lengths or slip the eyes out of the fish she cooks. She can't stand the eyes staring at her when she fries the bass and trout, so she cuts them out with her paring knife faster than Gabe and the kids can catch the fish—or she did until the paring knife went missing.

She goes silent, and I head upstairs thinking about cleavers.

———

It's not that I believe in ghosts, but after listening to Jones for weeks on end, I've become curious. After lunch, I ask Paul if anyone has ever died on the property. He looks at me as if I've pulled my head out of a volume of *Ripley's Believe It or Not!*

"Indulge me," I say.

"You could ask Emmett."

Of all people, his father. There's no reason for Paul to be like that. Does he imagine I'm asking a hostile question? I turn away.

I've asked Jones if any of the kids go up to see the grandparents. "Not really," she said. She feels badly for her grandmother, but Elizabeth has no idea who Jones is, and Emmett just gets worked up and yells at her. Sometimes the little ones knock on the door and run, making the old man roar at them. They shriek and squeal, and sometimes Timothy boasts he's going into that room one day. This is the ghost in their machine.

CHAPTER SIX

Locks and Keys

The knives go missing one by one. Two days ago it was a butcher's knife with perfect heft and almost no roll when it cut. Each night, as the wind drags across the lake, I listen for sounds of squatters, criminals, tricksters—or anyone in my husband's family looking for knives to steal in the cover of dark. When I wake, it's hard to imagine I've gotten any sleep.

To clear my head, I go for an early swim now that the weather's started to shift. Fish dart in and out through my strokes as if they are tugging me into the center of the lake. I feel wrapped in cool sheets of water here. From this distance, the house and its ghosts look small and smaller.

When I return to the dock and towel off, I give a fresh eye to the cabins. The one side looks particularly run-down with so much progress made on the other. Each cabin has the name of a flower. Daisy has gone through roof repair, and there are drop cloths inside. Scaffolding is set up to clean and prime the ceiling, tools returned to their boxes with a lock on the door. In Tulip, shelves have been added, and they've retrimmed the old windows. Six original bunks in all, the old mattresses heaped outside waiting to fuel a bonfire or be hauled to the dump. The interior of the cabin is painted a cheerful yellow, closets designed without doors. Eventually there will be a table with six chairs and a hanging lamp. This was Gabe's idea. He'd like to promote a sale to the science community or an environmentally friendly group. The badminton net will be replaced, new Ping-Pong tables ordered. The list grows with so many family ideas. The money will wear thin at this rate.

Violet's door is ajar. It's not like Paul to forget to lock up. This is what he always does at the end of the day, along with unplugging the power tools, cleaning out brushes, capping turpentine. He worries the young ones could get into something. Leon likes to come down to the lake to get high at the end of the day, when he thinks no one sees. Maybe Leon was inspecting Violet, fell into a pleasant drift, and forgot to push the pin on the lock.

The walls seem more lavender than violet, but then Paul is a little color-blind. In any case, they've done a beautiful job. Too beautiful. They will be working deep into winter, and they haven't even started on the main house. And where will any of us be for gas and supplies when Brenners shuts down at the end of the year?

As I turn to go, my eyes catch a mark in the closet. There's a cut in the back wall, as if someone dragged a sharp tool or knife tip into the wood, over and over, making the letter *W*. I know how pissed Paul will be with this vandalism. I touch the letter and catch a sliver in one of my fingers.

I get out my pocketknife and work at the sliver with the hidden tweezers. Once it's out, I secure the door and head back.

Salish is in the kitchen, and when she goes into the pantry, her safety locks threaded through the open latches, I decide not to bother her. I try the game room door, but it's fastened shut, and I left my keys in my room. All I can do is wait.

Coming out of the pantry, her arms loaded with breakfast fixings, Salish suddenly sees me at the glass door. She clutches her chest and drops the bread and eggs. Once she realizes it's actually me and not a specter or stranger, she stands there for a long time, scowling and catching her breath. She steps around the broken eggs, tightens her apron, and comes over to the door.

"What are you doing?" she calls through the glass.

"Open up, and I'll explain."

"Why should I?"

"Because I live here, Salish. For now, anyway."

"I told your husband when the first knife went missing, *Look to your wife.* That's what I said."

"Stop."

Just then Paul walks into the kitchen, takes everything in, and I think he asks Salish, "What's going on?"

"Would someone please let me in?" I shout.

He comes over and opens the door.

"There's something in one of the cabins," I say.

"Which one?" he asks.

"Violet."

His face shows his full annoyance. "I'll look after breakfast."

"You should see this now."

He turns to Salish. "Go ahead and lock up behind us. I have my keys."

Leading the way down the hill, I look back at him. Maybe he's determining the weather as he glances skyward or looking for somewhere to float above the things that delay his routine. Our bodies riffle the tall grass, the sky expands, and the water appears to travel toward us.

I wonder where he used to hide as a boy, away from his parents and brother and the droves of campers. I could see him taking one of his father's guns, running into the woods, and shooting squirrels and birds, his father upbraiding or thrashing him on his return. Emmett didn't like to waste ammo on anything small. He used to drive his pickup over steep terrain, use the hoist at the back, and haul the large animals he shot on pallets. Heading back to one of the sheds to skin his kill, he cut up the meat for the freezer.

When we reach Violet, I tell Paul to look in the closet.

"Never leave them unlocked." His tone is gruff.

But I had locked it when I came up to get him. "I found it open, Paul."

He goes in first, and his body fills the frame of the closet. Taking his time, he examines the wall as if he's a doctor studying a cadaver. He's clearly troubled, and he stands there arrested. I think if he had his tape measure on him, he would ask me to record the exact dimensions of the cut as he calls them out like a surgeon. But when he moves to the side, I see that instead of the single letter, there's a name etched into the wood.

Now it's my body that feels hot then cold, then hot again. My breathing quickens, and my head goes light as if it's filled with helium. It would be impossible to cut the letters in this fast. And I know what I saw the first time, what I touched, how I got my splinter. This can't be a grief-related moment. I'm not stumbling in a hallucinatory maze. I ran my palm over the smooth surface around it and traced the single letter *W* with my finger. I took my time.

Looking at Paul, I wonder if I should tell him this. He seems as breathless as I am. Finally he says, "Goddamn it. I'll have to replace a couple of boards."

"Walter?"

"One of the kids is screwing around," he says.

"Okay but why Walter?"

"Probably some game. What were you doing up so early?"

"No sleep."

"Maybe until the knives stop vanishing—"

"They will when she stops hiding them."

"Who?"

"Salish."

He almost laughs. "But they're her knives."

I don't understand his unkind temperament in moments like this, his distance. "Maybe she wants to stop cooking," I say.

"I wish you two would find a way to get along."

"Your parents' light went on this morning."

"I'll check on them while you get dressed."

"What if your mother starts wandering?"

She's the one I feel sorry for. Last week I pressed again that we should get her into assisted living, but everyone said she'd be too unsettled if she were moved. Then I suggested Emmett could be placed in a nursing home with her. But no one thinks he'll last that long, and it's not like checking into a hotel for a month. Paul insisted there are deposits, long-term agreements, and so on.

I read to Elizabeth once a day now, though sometimes Emmett makes my delivery impossible.

Paul shifts. He softens. "You've been remarkable. Have I told you that?" It's as if he's trying to find his way by looking at an outdated map. He hugs me loosely.

If we went through this back in California—both of us temporarily pulled in different directions and trying to reset—he might remove the tie of my robe or draw the fabric up from the bottom hem. Those were his overtures. And I would shut my eyes and kiss his face or neck, sometimes as if I were kissing Takeo's face or neck before catching myself.

I have to calm my mind as I work through things.

When I get back to our room, I open a blank document on my laptop and type this: *W. Walter. Animals. Bonfires. 1-inch cuts like ladders. Bowie, paring, slicer, cleaver, butcher's knife. Marriage. Ghost marriage. Coyotes. Broken doors, locks. Sleep, no sleep. Woods, lake, cabin fever. Childless. Lily. Ghost movies. Ghost stories. Campground. Tropes. Hot and cold, life and death. Documentary. Truth. Lies. Keep batteries charged. Something is terribly wrong.*

This is what I learned from my mother. Put everything down. Patterns will form on their own. I just don't see them yet. I think I should leave, and I think I should stay. I have become very protective of Lily, and I don't know that her mother has this instinct.

Separately, I list everyone's names in my husband's family, at least the ones I know about. My place on this tree has me so far off to one edge of the paper, I can only use my initials, as close to Lily's name as I can make them. I give Leon one direct line to Paul, knowing he wouldn't want a line to me.

I tuck this file into a larger one with editing work where I have the black-and-white photo of the blond woman, stolen from the Wedding Room. As I study the image again, I begin to see the possibility that in the background, there might be one corner of the game room. But it lacks the sharpness that would make for a clear determination.

Writing to Hal, my producer friend, I ask him to send more band footage, giving him some possibilities.

It's hard to know who to talk to. I could tell anything to my friend Lauren, but with her intense work and travel just now, I hate to trouble her. I pulled away from some of my friends after I married Paul—so I wouldn't have to see them pull away from me—and I can't imagine writing to them about what's going on. I could get my parents on the line, but I can't stop seeing my mother as fragile. She had a heart attack four years ago and has a stent now. If I spoke only to my father, she would read his face, and that would make for a different kind of worry.

———

Salish spent another whole night in the kitchen, keeping watch in a stiff-backed chair, with one pulled up for her legs. She wouldn't take a pillow when I offered one before I went up to bed. "I'm on full alert," she said.

I've gotten her signed release to be filmed along with one for Jones, Paul, and Gabe, and I work on the other permissions.

I start my camera.

"They took the boning knife." Her hands shake as she folds her throw blanket. "I had at least six cups of coffee and never, not once, did I fall asleep."

I did witness the way she placed her knives on the counter in a wheel shape last night, handles out, each tip overlapping the next. I see where one of the spokes—the boning knife—is missing now. The early light touches her brow and cheekbones where her face has started to break out, and the deep hollows under her eyes.

She tugs her stringy dark hair out of a rubber band and it falls in uneven lengths. I wish she'd take care better of herself.

"It was quiet last night," I say. "You're sure you didn't nod off for just a minute? Sometimes a hot cup of black tea will actually put me to sleep."

She goes over to the sink and runs the water as hard as she can as if to drown me out.

I wonder if taking an interest in her cooking might get her on better footing. "Do you use a boning knife often?"

She lets the water run into her cupped hands, splashes her face, and as she tightens the handles, she straightens, and the water drips and soaks into her blouse. "That and a hatchet. You've probably never had a better chicken sandwich."

I don't want to get started on fresh-killed things again, but it's hard not to ask. "So you really slaughter them yourself? You must do that when I'm out or—"

"Are you struggling, that a woman can butcher a chicken?"

"God, no. And I can't imagine Gabe would want to do it if he's trying to save the bird population. I just thought the chickens were here for the eggs."

"*Studies*. He *studies* swallows. That's all. You have some funny notions for someone rooting around looking for the truth."

I don't remember saying anything about the truth. Maybe I got carried away when I drank too much the first night and forgot, but people do have their assumptions about what I do.

I film her slipping the knives back into their flannel bags—the remaining eight of the original thirteen. Next, she arranges the bags in three empty tackle boxes she must have found in one of the sheds.

"You hope to keep a thief out that way?"

"You should be worried like the rest of us," she says, snapping the first lid shut. "More, if you ask me."

We're all a little worried. But it's about the way she's let this thing take hold. If she isn't doing this herself, it's probably one of her kids messing with her. I bite. "More?"

"The dream I told you about. Where the woman skins you alive."

"Jesus Christ, Salish."

My mother has always shown an interest in dreams, so I tend to ignore mine and everyone else's. It's possible Salish said something once while I was working or just working in my head. Paul likes to point out that he can speak in his loudest voice when I'm concentrating, and sometimes I don't even hear him. Though other times, I actually do but keep working.

The light in the room shifts. Her face darkens and quickly illuminates. "Then she ran after the children." Glowing with sorrow, Salish looks out to her three youngest.

"Okay, too upsetting. Let's just search for this one like we always do. Then I can keep an eye on the kids if you want some time to rest."

She locks each tackle box with its small key and tucks the boxes into the pantry that's large enough to hold supplies to feed over one hundred people for a full week.

Coming out of the pantry, she drops the three keys onto a long string and knots the ends together. She puts this over her head like a necklace. The boning knife has landed us in the tyranny of tackle boxes, and I'm not sure what I'm supposed to

do if I want to slice an apple. The camp must have a collection
of dull blades somewhere. But maybe she threw them out.

Salish looks at the linoleum she will never scrub bright
enough to find her own reflection. "I'll be right back. Stay here.
Don't take your eyes off anything," she says.

Opening the screen door, she steps outside.

———

Their shoes kick up a cloud of dust. I turn my camera on Salish
and Paul as they walk up the dirt path toward the house. The
way she leans into him, they look like director and actor consult-
ing on a set. I'm not sure who has which role, and I have no
interest in being in their movie. Reaching around, she clutches
his arm and seems to study the ground.

My husband's face looks overly weathered, pink where he's
started to peel the burnt skin around his hairline. When he got
up this morning, I saw how cut up his hands have become, one
thumbnail still blue from hitting it with a hammer last week. At
home he does basic framing when he has time and occasional
finish work. His crew handles demolitions, drywall, concrete
pours, window trims. He works with the architect and subcon-
tractors, does the paperwork, estimates, ordering, permits, and so
on. Now he and Leon are doing everything down to the marrow.

Paul peers at me as if he's gone through a vision change. I
don't know why he doesn't wear hats and sunglasses. The reflection off the lake has me squinting today.

Leon takes up the rear, carrying a toolbox. He looks even
more like a young Paul these days with the way the sawdust

collects on him. His hair is light from bleach, and all the T-shirts he wears make a statement about death. I keep a running list. There's *Death Metal, Death Piggy, Dr. Death...*

They let the screen door smack shut behind them, and Leon places the toolbox on the cutting block. Salish loves that old heavy block and plans to haul it back to their home when this place gets sold—at least that's what she says. She doesn't comment on the box sitting on her clean surface, though I see her chafe.

"How high do you want the locks?" Paul asks and gives the camera an annoyed glance. He's shy around my cameras, but he might also be worried about the film I'm making. It gets harder to know the source of his irritations. He takes the level from Leon and fixes it against the pantry door as Salish looks on.

"So the little ones can't reach them. Even if they stand on a chair."

For some reason, Paul spares her the kind of questions he has started to ask me like, *How high a chair?* Questions meant to sharpen me, get me to be specific, accountable. Increasingly at the camp, Paul likes it when I'm accountable, even if he misses when I am. He stands on one of the upper rungs of the ladder. I had a friend who died falling from the top rung of a ladder when he hit his head.

Leon hands his father the drill, the latches, then the screws, all the while staring openly at the lens. It's different with him. Leon has that easy look now that he's seen samples of what I do, as if he's thinking about how many people will see this clip. It's about promoting a band, a platform, a viral identity. He finally signed a release form.

The business of the locks is a one-man job. But maybe Salish made it seem like they were both needed. Once all three latches are screwed in place, Paul comes down off the ladder. Salish climbs up and hooks brand-new combination locks into each latch. Leon makes a snarky face toward the lens. My stepson must think, the way I do, that his father shouldn't indulge her.

While Paul fills his thermos with coffee, I think about signaling to him, coming up with some excuse to talk to him privately. But he gives the camera another uncomfortable face. Then they head back toward the cabins to the rot he has to fix there instead of the rot no one knows how to fix here.

"So what do we do if we get hungry?" I ask Salish.

"I don't feed you enough?"

I laugh. "Why would I suggest—"

"I need you to record this," she says, stepping down onto the linoleum again.

There's something about this moment. It's like being called onstage to watch Houdini before he descends headfirst into a cabinet of icy water. I don't know if a drowning will occur, but I can't imagine any of this will go well.

The light shifts, but before taking a fresh reading, I look away to count the children again as if they are marbles scattered outside a chalk ring. Their voices echo up to the house, and I have that sense perception I get when driving through a tunnel, their rhythmic sounds fluttering against my eardrums. The clouds start to move rapidly over the lake, and all I can think is this: if it isn't her doing, who on earth would keep taking her god-blessed knives? Anyone can see how worked up she's become. If this is a prank someone's playing on her, it's turned especially cruel.

I hold the camera steady on her face and record her as she picks up the tiny white scraps of paper with the lock combinations printed in black ink. One by one, she puts them in her mouth and gobbles them up.

"Isn't that a little extreme?" I ask and keep the video rolling.

"Four children. *Four*," she says, holding up the fingers of her right hand to express her level of fear where four is the highest number.

I want to call the three little ones up to the house and get them to hang out around the yard, but I'm afraid this would only increase her agitation. Salish doesn't spend a lot of time with them that I've seen, but she bristles if any of us intrude. I think about Timothy, the eight-year-old, how uncoaxable he is—in some ways his own man, in others a skim of toughness over a vulnerable center.

"Is that still running?" she asks, tilting her head toward the camera.

"Just cooling off," I say.

When she saw one of my cameras the first time, she asked if it has to cool down the way a slide projector does. I guess it was mean to say yes, but I thought she was kidding. It seems she and Gabe don't take videos of their kids. Or many still shots for that matter. As if they had invisible births and disappearing lives.

We have all been at this campground too long.

I put the camera down and pour her a glass of cold water so she can wash down the last of the numbers and gather her wits.

"You going up to rest?" I ask.

"Not with the dough rising. God help me, the bread knife better stay put."

"Okay, I'm getting a shower and then back to work."

"Thanks for, you know," she says, nodding toward the camera.

"My pleasure," I say.

———

The towels never dry out entirely in the bathroom, and the rugs smell of mildew even after they're newly washed and hang in the sun for hours on a clothesline. We share this smell with Leon.

As the water in the shower heats, I tie my hair up, strip my nightgown off, remove my bandages, and study the cuts again—the absolute precision in the mark on my chest that has started to scab over. Drawing the shower curtain back, I'm about to step on the tiles when I realize I left my shampoo in our room. I kept it in the bathroom at first, but I think Leon used it at as if he were tipping it upside down in the shower and watching the bubbles fill the drain and spread across the floor just for fun. I know it wasn't Paul. Hurrying into my robe, I pull at the door handle. It's met with resistance.

"Paul?"

When there's no answer, I say, "Leon?"

Usually he knocks. One time he moaned so I'd understand his urgency. There are five bathrooms in the house, and all he'd have to do is go downstairs. He could do that easily. But Leon seems to wait until I've just settled in. He delivers a single blow to the door. All the muscle he's built hammering nails, scraping, lifting, sanding, hits the thin center.

"Hey!" I can't even pull the door open. "I'm trying to get out to let you in." I turn off the water and wait.

Ever since the trip out, there are moments when Leon behaves as if he knows me well enough to act something out with me.

He pounds again, harder this time. The panel in the center of the door vibrates, cracking open a seam in the wood. I worry it's going to fly apart. The hairbrush poised on the glass shelf above the sink drops and clatters against the floor.

"Leon, quit!"

I let go of the handle and wait. Finally, I hear him run down the stairs. I go out and stand in the middle of the hall in my robe and shout loud enough for him to hear me in the kitchen, "You little shit!"

This is followed by Paul's voice calling up the stairs, "What the hell is going on?"

Hurrying down, I push past him. Leon sits at the table eating a bowl of cereal. Salish rolls dough onto the pastry board, her eyes narrowed. Paul comes up behind me.

"How long have you been down here?" I ask Leon.

He shrugs.

Paul says, "What's this about?"

"Just someone tell me." I realize my robe has fallen open and Leon is looking at my mark. I quickly cover up.

Salish raises her hands in the air, white with flour, as if she's gloved up for surgery. "He's been down here about a half hour, helping with the chickens and the compost. He hasn't troubled anyone. Are you satisfied now?"

I feel my shoulders drop. "You heard someone on the back stairs, right?"

"No, not on the back stairs," Paul says. "I heard Gabe go down the big stairs for an early swim. What's going on?"

I don't recall a time in California when he raised his voice to me this way. I look out and see his brother's even strokes as he heads across the lake.

"Seriously," Paul says with a calmer voice, this side of tender. "What?"

I describe what happened, assuming no one will believe me. But Salish wipes her hands on the nearest towel and says, "I'm counting heads, and then I'm counting knives."

Paul pours a cup of coffee, adds some sugar, sets it down in front of me, and returns to his half-eaten breakfast.

I say, "I'm sorry, Leon," and get the same shrug.

"I'll check the swelling on the door. Now that it's turning humid—" Paul begins.

"Swelling doesn't pound," I say. "You heard the pounding, right?"

"We thought you were having a moment," he says.

"A moment?"

"What if somebody came in through the side door?" Leon says.

"Did you hear the door open?" Paul asks his son.

"Did you hear me when I was twelve and snuck out of the house at night?"

"What?" Paul says.

"Maybe it's the old man," Leon says. He sits back and crosses his arms behind his head, pleased with this idea.

"Emmett can't even get out of bed," I say.

"But what if he can?" Leon says. "What if he just likes being waited on?"

"Where did you go?" Paul asks Leon.

"The park, the 7-Eleven. With friends."

"Someone was pounding on the door," I remind Paul. "And I was trying to get out. And I don't have *moments*."

"The kids are fine," Salish says returning to the kitchen. "Elizabeth and Emmett are awake. Whose turn is it?" She looks over the schedule taped to one of the cabinets. But we all know it's my turn. "I'll make up the tray as soon as I finish my count," she says and lines up her remaining knives.

"I'll be back," I say and go upstairs.

When I shower, I keep the door propped open. I really would leave this family to its machinations if it weren't for Lily and the film that gains momentum.

———

I put my camera on a dresser and set the tray down. Elizabeth is already up, sitting in her chair. She makes small comments about Frank Sinatra, who was her father's favorite. I am relieved to see her in a happy mood. This must mean Emmett, who is still asleep, rested well. Fine wisps of hair that have come loose from her bun lift and settle in a quick breeze. She wants to see the water even on the still and overcast days. She used to press flowers, collect butterflies, go on hikes.

I see Gabe is still out on his long swim.

"They've sent the maid," Elizabeth tells her husband.

I never correct her but simply follow each stream branching off from her dementia. "I'll start with your husband's side of the room, if that's okay with you."

Paul has already been up, put on latex gloves, removed Emmett's adult diaper, washed him, and applied ointment. This is another task Paul takes over, along with turning Emmett's body and going through the small battle of teeth brushing. I only have to wash his face, comb his hair, and feed him soup.

When I'm halfway done, Emmett says, "You think anyone wants you here?"

I've been told repeatedly he'll only get meaner if I respond. His mind continues to be sharp despite the way his body breaks down, so I know there's nothing random in his question. Today he appears to be in worse pain than usual. I give him an extra half tablet of medication and mark it on the chart we keep for the doctor who drives out once a week now.

Elizabeth asks, "Is he sick?"

"Yes, a little sick," I tell her.

"I've got cancer," he says in his harshest tone. His wife appears to take this in as if she's learning it for the first time.

"What if he dies?" Elizabeth says. "Frank Sinatra died."

"Try not to worry," I tell her.

"From the tree of the knowledge of good and evil you shall not eat, for in the day…for in the day you eat from it, you will surely die."

This one has to be Genesis. She does have her share of warnings.

I'm aware she will look out at the lake until lunch when someone arrives with another tray. She never wants to go anywhere, though she's physically capable of doing so. I caught her walking around the halls upstairs only once, commenting on the art. I didn't realize at first that she had done the watercolors of local flora.

Elizabeth can eat a sandwich or pick at things on a plate without help. Her favorite food is cheese, though this constipates her, so Salish doles it out sparingly. Emmett needs spoonfuls of broth brought to his mouth. He has been known to spit it out intentionally. I sit to one side, practically behind him, since it's hard for him to turn his head. It makes the process messier, some of the soup dribbling down the lobster bib I tie around his neck, sometimes sliding into his pajama collar. But I remain mostly dry and I always change his pajama shirt if this happens. Today Emmett fumes.

When they're all set, I read a little from a Bible passage until Elizabeth seems at ease. This is the only book she wants to hear. I read from John 1: "The light shines in the darkness, and the darkness has not overcome it..."

After a few minutes, I put the tray by the door and get my camera ready. Propping it by my side, I angle it so I can film without making it seem as if they're being filmed. Taking the seat next to Emmett's bed again, I ask, "Do you know someone named Walter?"

"What business is it of yours?" he says.

"Walter the maintenance man, or Walter the dead man?" Elizabeth asks.

"What are you stirring up now?" Emmett says to me.

I shift my body around so the camera is trained on Elizabeth's silhouette. "Either one," I say.

"I felt bad for him," she says.

"Why?" I ask.

She begins to sing an old song I recognize from my one camp experience. I can even remember the hand gestures that went along with it. "Little cottage in the woods, little man by the window stood, saw a rabbit hopping by, knocking at his door. Help me, help me, help, he cried, before the hunter shoots me dead. Come little rabbit, come with me, safely to...safely to..."

"Abide," I say.

"Now you've got her going. She'll be singing that all day," Emmett says.

I turn back to him. "So Walter was a maintenance man."

"Get the hell out of here," he says.

I put the chair back and note that Gabe is no longer out swimming, but Paul is paddling hard in one of the rowboats toward the dock as if he's gone into training, preparing for a race. I wonder what this is all about, this sudden fit of exercise. Usually he saves the lake for late in the day and rows less deliberately. But today, with the clouds gathered in the south and the sun striking through, the movement of his boat sends red rings traveling across the green surface.

I remind Elizabeth to use one of the bells if she needs us, and I check the windows' safety locks. Tomorrow should be easier since I'll have lunch duty. I give her a kiss on the forehead. I don't want this kind of isolation and confusion to ever hit the people I love. Taking the tray, I slip downstairs.

———

Wandering outside with one of my cameras, I find Gabe sitting in the campfire circle with Lily on his shoulders. Mason is dressed as Spider-Man today. I wonder how many costumes he owns. Timothy, Jones, and Leon all sit on tree stumps. Gabe lifts Lily down, and she goes over and climbs into Jones's lap.

"The call of the sharp-shinned hawk," Gabe continues.

"That's a funny name," Lily says.

"It gets its name from its short shins." He runs a hand over the front of his calves. Jones copies this on Lily's legs.

"You can see dark bands when their wings are spread," Gabe tells her. He picks up a pad of art paper and quickly draws this hawk. "They're quite fast, and they're the smallest of the hawks that glide through the forest. One way to identify them is by their long square tails. When they're mating or sending out an alarm, they make a high-pitched sound like, *kik-kik-kik*."

Lily gives this a try, and Jones accompanies her. Even Leon joins in to encourage the boys. Mason gives it a try.

"This is stupid," Timothy says.

"Because you can't do it," Lily says.

Immediately he shows her that he can do the best hawk call ever. Gabe goes on to the high-pitched sound brooding females make. I take some footage, and then I let my camera rest and join in. I've rarely seen him miss a day spending some time with the kids. He's the one out in the lake, tossing them into the air. He's the one setting up relay races and baseball games, organizing kite flying, once his work is done for the day.

Just then Paul emerges from the cottages. I point out the empty tree stump next to mine so he'll come over. But he frowns and goes up to the house. I begin to feel like a small outer building he might get to when all the other buildings are put in order.

"Do a vulture." Timothy peers at Lily. "They like to eat hawks."

"Actually, it's the other way around," Gabe says. "A hawk might eat a young vulture."

"See," Lily says.

"So let's talk about vultures," Gabe says. "Mostly they're silent." He begins a second drawing.

"That's why they're the scariest," Timothy says. "And if you die out in a meadow, they'll tear you apart and eat your guts."

Lily buries her head in Jones's chest, and Jones scolds him. Gabe reminds Timothy that his sister is too young for such thoughts. The lesson proceeds.

CHAPTER SEVEN

Dressing and Undressing

When I look at the footage from Hidden Lake, it feels like an anthropological moment. I wouldn't call it *An American Family*—the documentary in which the Loud family bled for that first moment of reality TV—but I'm aware of confessions and the troubles tucked inside confessions.

I also note similarities in Paul and Gabe's mannerisms and the way heredity plays out in the family. A look Gabe has manifests in Leon. Leon's way of scratching his right ear is present in Timothy's left, and so on. I am the only one not related by blood to any of them.

Midafternoon, Jones knocks on my door, telling me to take a walk with her; I should bring a camera. She doesn't explain or wait for a look from me but takes off in that large, galloping stride of hers. I grab my equipment, wondering if she's going to make some type of admission—if she'll confide in me on or off camera.

Both of us tell the dogs to stay, and though the small black dog follows me for a while, eventually she goes back to the house. The spotted dogs have a sense of discipline that is unyielding. The black dog seems lonely.

We go past the boathouse, several cabins, and the outcrop of boulders before I realize we're not strolling to be away from the house so we can talk freely. We are taking a hike. She adjusts her day pack and heads uphill on one of the steeper trails. I enjoy exploring the ridges and meadows, but I would tend to take one of the gradual, sloping paths and always bring water and a snack. If Jones weren't one of my main interests, I might suggest another way, but I think it's best to go along. I realize she has my yellow bandana tied in her hair, pilfered from my laundry.

The light is overly saturated. I keep my meter and camera tucked in my bag as we ascend. There are gaps in the trail where the earth has eroded. Without anyone to maintain it, we have to jump over those places or find ways around them. We work our way over a large downed tree. She keeps the lead, pushing branches away in some spots and holding them for me so I can go through without being whipped in the face. She can be so different when she's away from her mother. I watch for poison ivy.

Stopping halfway to the ridge, we rest for a while on a flat that provides an aerial view of the property, the buildings laid out in a cross design. Gabe tinkers with the noisemakers again while the kids run around. Salish is out of sight, no doubt locking and unlocking something. I consider the roofs that have been patched and the ones that haven't, the patterns the new materials make against other patch jobs like crazy quilts.

Jones unscrews her bottle of water, and we each take a drink.

"I'll probably die before I turn seventeen. Because of this place."

Lowering my sunglasses, I study her squint. Even when her face is still, it takes up all the energy around it. But I am having trouble reading this particular expression. I don't know if I should ask if she's depressed. Bringing up the wrong concern or becoming too concerned over the right one will bleed into her mother's territory, and Jones might evaporate before my eyes.

"You should get your camera out. Pan the lake, the buildings," she says.

I smile broadly rather than try to educate her about documentary filmmaking.

"I can drop that in later," I say, though I get my camera set up.

She considers this as I begin with a close-up of her face. Repeating what she said about her death when I prompt her, she adds, "It's not that I think I'm possessed. I mean, look at Marie Antoinette."

"Okay."

"She lived in Versailles, and Versailles was haunted by lots of ghosts, and she died a young, tragic death."

"Madame Deficit was almost forty when she died. She beat the average life expectancy. At the time."

"She was like twenty. That's why Sofia Coppola cast her."

"You mean Kirsten Dunst?"

"Exactly."

"The real world and film blend in interesting ways, don't they?"

She gives the lens an accusatory look. "What I'm saying is that the property's haunted, not me. I know the difference, unlike my mother. But the consequences can appear the same."

"How do you know the difference?"

"I've made a study of it," she says, touching the thin silver ring that divides her right eyebrow. This piece of jewelry and its perch are new. I wonder if Leon gave it to her. It's possible she made her own incision, or he did it.

"Is the entire property haunted?" I ask.

"I have equipment and charts on order so I'll be able to start pinpointing things scientifically. But I know it loves the house. The kitchen, of course."

"Have you figured out who *it* is? And why *it's* taking knives instead of Frisbees or beach towels?"

She fills the entire frame with that naivete and lack of innocence she's so good at expressing in one look and says, "There was a man who made fun of his wife every time this ghost appeared to her in the back hallway of their house. The husband decided to take photos to show his wife she was an idiot. One night he stayed up extra late. With his camera hanging from his neck, he waited. Standing in the passageway where his wife had reported seeing the ghost at this exact time of night, he felt the camera strap begin to tighten. He tried to remove it, but he couldn't. The leather got tighter. And tighter and tighter until finally, he was strangled to death. When the detective on the case developed the film in the husband's camera, you could see the apparition."

"Pure Midwestern gothic."

"You're such an odd person," she says and gets up to continue the climb. "You should look up the word *allegory*."

"I'll get right on it," I say, nesting my camera back in its case.

"I said the same thing to my mother the other day, and she said she didn't like funeral songs, like she thought I meant *elegy*."

"They do both end in a *y*."

I see something of my younger self in Jones, though I never went off on how I would die young. Of course, I couldn't with my mom around. She would have dragged me to some psychiatrist for twice weekly sessions. But I liked to upend things, throw people, especially her. We're very close, best friends now, but sometimes that's the problem. My father busts me in sweet ways over the sparring my mother and I do. They adore each other. That's what Takeo and I had. Adoration.

When we get to the top and we're on even ground, I feel the temperature drop into a more comfortable place. Some of the oak trees are permanently bent by the wind. The meadow has small purple and yellow flowers. It's harder to see the family and their activities from here, only the cross pattern formed by the campground, the shimmer off the lake. We are still too far to see cars in the distance or Brenners, the way it's tucked into a hill. Just trees, the old ranger station, and the washboard road leading away from the house.

"Look," Jones says. She points to one of Gabe's nest boxes. I don't know how many he's put up, but each one is marked with a number and sits on a pole. We walk through the grass to inspect it.

"He's studying swallows, not to be mistaken for Vaux's swifts," Jones says.

She joins her stepfather sometimes when he's out in the field, and he pays her well as his assistant. This is one of the finished houses, with its sturdy box, sloping roof, small opening, and a perch. I begin to reach out to feel the way he sanded the hole.

"Hey. You'll screw up the science."

"Right," I say, withdrawing my hand.

"Water?"

I take another drink and look out to the road again. "You hike here often?"

"I've walked miles in every direction."

"Can I see your map?" I ask.

She shows me her compass.

"So you like exploring."

"I can walk slowly if you follow me with the camera."

"Just go at your normal pace."

We move along the perimeter, where the land has a long descent on the federal-land side. Just as I begin to feel I'm wasting battery, we reach a wide granite ledge covered with orange and yellow lichen. She circles this and stops at a spot with a downed branch. She pulls the branch away, brushes the leaves off, and exposes a large rock embedded in the ground. A name and date have been crudely worked into the stone, and the lettering is so worn, it's hard to read. It appears to be a headstone.

Jones pours some water, and it fills the letters. I am too aware of the ritual in Japan in which families come with buckets and dippers to wash the bodies of gravestones, something I should be doing this summer.

"Walter Jackson." Reading his name aloud, I feel light-headed. The dates appear to be 1955 or 1956 to 1989. She sweeps her palm over the rock again.

"Walter was a maintenance man at the campground," I say.

"You think he's buried here?"

"It would seem so, though it might only be a monument."

She gives the camera a conspiratorial look. "There are shovels in one of the toolsheds. I've even seen a couple of the collapsible kind."

I could just see Jones out with a collapsible shovel, trying to dig up the dead to make a forensic point. I tell her about the conversation with Emmett and Elizabeth as I crouch down. "Do you really believe in ghosts?" I ask. "I mean, it's fascinating, but—"

"You don't?"

"No, not in the way you might think. But I went on a ghost tour in Prague once." I turn the camera off for a moment to say, "You understand I was a widow before I met Paul, right?"

"You're so tragic," she says with reverence. "Did you see his ghost?"

"Takeo, my husband, and I went on a ghost tour underneath the Prague Astronomical Clock." I explain it was built in the thirteenth century. "The guide wore a top hat, had a full dark beard, and reminded me of a painting by Hodler."

She furrows her brow. Jones has several expressions to convey impatience.

"Sorry. I'll show you a picture sometime. Anyway, no matter what room we stood in, there were dark passageways leading off in different directions. He showed us a deep pit where people were thrown when there was torture instead of jails." Jones listens, wide-eyed. "I asked if he believed in ghosts, and he said he was an agnostic, so how could he believe in an afterlife?"

I don't tell her everything. I convey the chill that rushed through the hallways but not the feeling as Takeo slipped his hand into mine. This was the first time I understood he wanted to make something of us. He rubbed his thumb over the back of my hand in that way he had of freighting love. I've considered this moment many times. He wanted me to see the future. I don't mean moving to Berkeley, or the wedding in my parents' yard, or the day I found out I was pregnant. This was not like going into a kind of tunnel in which your life or death flash ahead or behind you. It was simply Takeo holding on to me in the dim light with that sense that we were a couple and would be for a long time to come.

"But our guide went on to say that a colleague of his spent a lot of time in the underground passages and had spoken with a ghost—well, a supposed ghost—named Victoria a week ago. Our guide pulled out this electric monitor—"

"That's what I'm getting. An EMF meter. Did it light up while you were there?"

"He asked Victoria two questions, and each time the buttons lit up right away. Then he said it made him nervous, and we moved into another room."

"You didn't talk to her? God, I would have."

"I wanted to ask her a question, just to debunk the thing and—"

"Maybe I'll travel around the world taking ghost tours. Or giving them."

"You could. If you aren't planning to die when you're seventeen."

She makes a face. "It would help if we had a cat instead of all of these dogs."

"You're fond of cats?"

"Not necessarily. But they can see ghosts. You can tell when they get really still and wide-eyed and start hissing and you can't see anything around. Were you filming a movie in Prague?"

"I was on the crew."

She asks if I can show her how to operate a movie camera, as if she's done with all other conversations. "I don't have the kind of camera you're talking about," I begin, but it feels important to stay open to Jones. "I could give you some idea though, with one of the cameras I have on hand. Listen, why don't we take the longer way down?"

What I don't tell her is that after that tour, I woke up in the middle of the night in our hotel room, feeling as if someone was standing by our bed. After I settled down, I wrote the whole thing off to having a nightmare. We left Prague the next day.

On our way back to the meadow, Jones stops so abruptly, I run into her.

"What the fuck?" she says.

I think she's snapping at me until I see the nest box. This is the same one we stopped at earlier. A bird is pinned to the front. Its head is pointed upward, and the two long prongs of its tail point down, the wings spread out. It's held in place by Salish's paring knife. Maybe through the heart. I get my camera out, and I'm about to make a recording of this event when I hand the camera to Jones, telling her how she should hold it, where she should stand, and what to adjust and how. Maybe it's a silly thing to do, but it seems to calm both of us. I want a close-up as I pull the knife out and catch the bird. And I wouldn't ask her to get the blood on her hands.

"Ready?"

"Yes," she says.

As I slip the knife away, the bird drops. A little blood leaks from the wound into my palm.

"They're communicating with us," Jones says in awe.

I go over how she can pan smoothly. Placing the bird on the

ground, I turn it over, inspecting both sides. The eyes are just slits. I drop the knife and hold my palms out, suggesting she get a recording of the blood that fills the lines of my hands.

I tell her how to put the camera away properly. Then I wipe off as much of the blood as I can on the grasses. "I don't know if we should tell your mom about this…communication, right away."

She bends down to look at the bird. "She'd so freak."

"I'll hide the knife for now. You know it's one of hers," I say.

"I hate her stupid knives."

Jones pours some water in my cupped hands so I can wash up. We both take sips from the bottle of what's left. I wipe the blade off and ask her to hand me the bandana. She hesitates—as if this has become her permanent possession—until she gets why and pulls it out of her hair. I wrap the blade in the cloth and slide it into a side pocket of my camera bag.

As we reach the path that skirts the perimeter of the campground, we see Salish coming from the lake. I realize she would have had enough time to spear the bird and run back to the camp.

Jones and I don't talk much until we approach the water. And as we get near the house, I begin to feel claustrophobic. It's like watching a long close-up of someone, the kind that doesn't allow you to breathe. It has to be worse for Jones.

"Your mom's going to be all right," I say.

"I don't see why," she says.

I had planned to circle back to other things, but she's off before I can give her another false affirmation.

"There's a room inside your room," she calls.

"What?" I shout back.

"A room. Inside your room."

I wait, hunkered down, while she goes through the game room. Reaching inside the bag, I touch the wrapped knife, as if I need to make sure it's still there. Paul is out rowing. He's just a speck from where I squat. The sun will set in the next hour or so, and with each meter he covers, he will pull a little further into himself and the full expression of the things he left behind.

The noisemakers are spread evenly along the monofilament that surrounds the house. This is tied from one stake to another a couple feet off the ground and conveys something about the insanity that encircles us. The children have gone in, and I see Lily and Mason through the kitchen door, probably hoping for an early taste of dinner. Mason is dressed as the Dark Voyager.

With each new costume, I'm envious of this five-year-old and his ability to hide in plain sight.

Salish turns from what she's doing, claps her hands twice, and they scatter. I step over a low point where the filament is slack but manage to catch it with my other shoe. Bits of glass and tin clank together as I right myself.

Salish looks out the window and shakes her head at me.

———

The wallpaper in the Quarter Room is embossed with a basket design. Over and over, the same basket filled with the same poppies set in a diamond pattern. I run my fingers along the seams. Since there's no lock, I prop my desk chair against the bedroom door, pull up the rug, and rap lightly on the floorboards looking for a hollow place where another room might exist. I flatten myself in the corners of the bedroom looking both ways along the length of the walls to see if anything stands out.

Climbing up on the bed, I inspect the ceiling. There are a couple of long cracks and various dark stains. Things spilled or seeped out probably from the pipes since there's no attic, only a crawl space. I move the dresser. Pulling the bed away from the wall, I inspect the bookcase and the window. It's more than possible Jones was messing with me.

A room within a room. A case could be made about films working this way when they're done well, the things that nest inside images and stories. I make a note to have a conversation with Dad about buried and mirrored things, though Mom would having something to say about how they work in people.

———

Paul gives me a short kiss as the morning light fixes the room then hurries off to the bathroom with his work clothes and boots. I put two pillows under my bottom today, hoping again for conception.

The first time we made love, he unfolded a safety net. Lately, it seems more obligatory on his part. At least sex keeps me from falling back to earth in a permanent childless state. I hold on to each chance.

Once he has a quick wash, Paul will go downstairs and feed the dogs. Leon will get up, take a long piss in the hollow drum of the toilet, and follow his father downstairs. Salish will have platters of bacon and eggs, hash browns, toast, and sliced fruit waiting for them despite the knife deficit. As soon as they go out to work on the cabins, the dogs will bark, and the spotted ones will follow them down to the cabins on command. Paul likes their company, sometimes taking a short break to throw sticks or old tennis balls out into the water. I'm surprised when I don't hear them knock into the noisemakers.

The small black dog typically stays on the front steps waiting for someone other than Paul, so we have to move around her until she chooses one of us. This is often me, though she doesn't go on my longer walks or runs. Sometimes the children make up names for the dogs, but Emmett won't tell us what he calls them, and Elizabeth can't or at least hasn't been able to yet. Paul said his father probably never bothered to give them names. I asked him if this is what it felt like to grow up around Emmett, and he responded by saying he had to go drive some nails. *Sorry!* I called after him.

The time spent around his father has gotten to him, I know. But reading the degree of his affliction is tough to gauge. I'm aware that I pry too frequently, but it isn't healthy to keep so much corked, especially when things are shaken up.

Routine keeps Paul rushing ahead. Salish is the same way. She feeds the hens and collects the eggs, wipes the sweat from her upper lip with the back of her hand, and talks to the hens about their slow laying, as if their fertility is part of her purview. She scrambles, fries, boils, poaches, or whips those eggs for us when we wander downstairs, though most of the children sleep in beneath torn and somewhat repaired mosquito netting. If they don't arrive before ten thirty or at least ten forty-five, they find themselves in the land of lunch preparation, and then they simply have to wait. Lunches are a little overdone and include pickled foods they push away. Maybe she thinks it's a matter of time until they acquire her tastes and learn that breakfast selections must be repurposed. Dinner is always the best meal of the day, where she tries out new dishes and sets out at least one favorite.

The light goes on across the way, and I see Gabe standing by the window near his desk. He's the one who rarely looks bothered about stuff unless he and Salish have a fight, but he seems to blow those off quickly, heading out for a swim to readjust. Things have been quiet between them lately. Maybe something isn't going right with his ornithology work.

As soon as he realizes I'm there, he gives me a particular smile. I raise my hand, almost waving, though I won't mind if he reads this as *stop*. I don't know if he flirts because of his wife's state of mind or if it's the other way around, but he does give me the occasional look when others are turned away. If he weren't so easy to talk with, I'd take him to task and wouldn't talk with him at all. But I do need conversation, and I never encourage his foolishness. Even with eleven of us, this can be a lonely place that echoes too easily in my head.

When we met for the first time at an arts residency, Takeo and I had private rooms directly across from each other. He was doing sculptural work, not yet settled on ceramics. I was in film even then, though I did some still photography. One morning we stood in front of our windows, back far enough so no one else in the house could see us from their windows. I slipped a nightgown strap off one shoulder then stopped, telling myself this wasn't really me. Quickly, I pushed the other strap off. The nightgown dropped around my feet. It felt, in that moment, that there was nothing I could do that would be more logical—just to stand there naked as if I were exposing a birthmark no one else was allowed to see. He undressed right away, and together we were like a time-lapse of things that have an urgency to open. Mouths, flowers, hands. I became aware of the sound he would make against my chest, a sound wholly different from Paul's, which has become that of a man running to catch a bus to avoid being late to keep from missing work and losing his job.

I try to return to the present and the realization that Gabe is still watching me. He has a look as if he might need to set fencing around land he would rather roam freely. In a confused rush, I hear footsteps on the stairs.

Paul is typically down near the cabins or boathouse this time of day. But now he slips into the room holding a cup of tea out while looking past me toward the window. Glancing back, I'm not sure if I see Gabe move out of the frame or if it's a shadow made by the movement of my hair. Maybe Paul's looking at the gutters that need to be cleaned out and repaired, or he's so lost in his own thoughts, it's difficult for him to know what he sees. His shadow creates pools of darkness where he steps. Eyebrows pinched together, my husband indicates my robe. I don't get it at first, and then I realize it's inside out.

"You sick?" he asks.

I take the cup and set it on a dresser. "No, I'm good. Just a little groggy."

He notes my chest with a nod. "How'd you say you got that cut again?"

"Walking through the woods. A branch." I kiss him on the cheek. "What does the weather look like?"

Paul's good at predicting turbulent weather, dangerous weather, earth-ending weather, and he seems to enjoy doing so—always hoping to stay ahead of things. But all he can say today is, "A few degrees hotter than yesterday. Just as bright."

"The kids will want to spend the afternoon in the lake."

"We should talk," he says.

I notice a buzz in my ears as if I've gotten too close to a transformer.

Paul sits on the edge of the bed. This means he's about to impart something of significance. "One of the rowboats was pulled from the boathouse last night. Someone took it out on the lake. There were empty beer bottles in the bottom."

"Huh," I say.

"And a used condom."

"Was the boat put away?"

"The bow was barely clinging to the shore, unanchored. I got it back in the boathouse, and I haven't told Salish or Gabe, but I'm putting a stop to it."

"You think Leon…?"

"Who else?"

"What if a squatter took the boat out?"

"The beer came from our stock."

"You're counting beers?"

"So I'll know when someone steals them." The fatigue, the strained nerves, they're all lined up in his face. He's entered the world of crime victims and their inventories.

"I'll have a talk with Jones," I say.

He laughs. "She's not going to talk with you."

"She might."

"Would you do that? Sleep with your cousin?"

I don't know if this is just about his son and niece anymore. He knows I'm not big on hypotheticals. But I try to think like Jones.

"If I were sixteen, and he were the lead singer in a band and I had never met him," I begin, "and there was no one else to crush over and…" I see he's worn thin and stop. "Probably not."

A faint blue light appears in my vision. It's still there when I shut my eyes. Maybe Jones would say I've seen a ghost. Maybe Paul is becoming a ghost of himself. In any case, it's happened a couple of times since we've been here. I add *eye doc* to a mental list of appointments I'll need when I return to California, though I had a full exam before I left.

He eases the hand with the bashed thumbnail against my thigh. Eventually, the nail will fall off, leaving an ugly place he'll forget to bandage. He told me a few days ago that it's past the hurting stage.

"Not only is it wrong but then I'm dealing with my brother," he says.

This repeats in my mind like ripples of water that have no shore to push against. And just then the light from the lake shimmers across one wall and touches our backs.

Paul looks as if I've said something in response. The unease returns to his face. He withdraws his hand.

"Maybe if you talk with Leon. I mean, really talk."

"I'll take care of it," he says and gets up.

"Does that mean you'll talk with him?"

He holds up at the door but doesn't answer.

"Should I…be worried about us?" I ask. There's a sense of free fall now that it's out of my mouth.

He gives me a troubled look. "Why would you ask that?"

I don't know what to say if he doesn't understand.

"I realize I've been distracted," he says.

"All the memories must be hard."

"When I was little, I used to make drawings of the houses I was going to build around the lake. Boat ramps, a big water slide, a schoolhouse and store… This place is still in my bones. I never wanted to leave."

I get up and go over to him. "At fifteen. I can't imagine."

He lets me hold him briefly. Then he pulls back and takes my hands. I'm about to remind him that I'm here to listen—to anything, always—when he says, "It's going to be a beauty when I'm done. We might just find a way to keep this place."

I did think for a moment he was ready to open up. "It will look great in your portfolio," I say.

He gives me the oddest look. I know it's easier for him to think about the physical world than the one that brews inside. But there's no way he could be serious. It would mean selling my house altogether—something I'll never do. I decide to let the subject go for now.

Once Paul has returned to his sanctuary and I'm sitting at my desk, I begin a note to my mother. I don't bring up the knives. She would worry in an overblown way—or maybe a more appropriate way than I do. With the intuition that can move back and forth between us, I wouldn't be surprised if she wrote back to say she's been having dreams about knife sharpeners.

I ask her to send me a jar of honey from the farmers' market, another bottle of shampoo from the salon we go to, and to see if she has a free morning to talk when the house is quiet so I can speak with her privately. I consider where I will hike. For all the reasons I will be ready to leave, I do understand Paul's attachment to the beauty of Hidden Lake.

———

The days get hotter, and the poison ivy thickens. Rather than take off into the woods, I decide on Brenners today. It's a little longer to walk the distance in the thick air, but it's a good respite to have a destination, and I enjoy browsing their funny stock.

I'm halfway through their front door when I hear Mrs. Brenner shout, "You look concerned."

Her husband turns around, holding a stack of cake mixes.

"She looks concerned," Mrs. Brenner repeats.

"Okay," he says and turns back to the baking supplies. The store is filled with flies buzzing about, trying to avoid the flypaper tacked to the ceiling like strips of photographic film.

"I have something I'd like to ask. Alone."

"She wants to ask me something alone," Mrs. Brenner calls out.

We move through the store and she clutches my arm. Outside, we sit on the weathered bench. Pulling the bill of my cap down to deflect the sun, I take another drink of water.

"The pregnancy test kits are underneath the register," she says. Her voice seems to bounce off the plate glass in the abandoned shop across the street. This is a subject I've never addressed with Mrs. Brenner. I haven't asked for a pregnancy test or told Mrs.

Brenner about my strong desire to be a mother. All she knows is
that I'm turning thirty-nine soon and that I'm childless. She also
knows me as someone who buys useless items in appreciation of
their remaining open for us.

"Yes, I was going to ask. About the kits. I was also curious to
learn more about the history of the camp."

In the few times we've talked, I've been impressed by her
memory regarding the groups and individual campers. She likes
to provide an adoring picture of Paul and Gabe as boys helping
out at Hidden Lake.

"I thought I'd make a couple of scrapbooks. So I was hoping
to learn something about the people who worked at the camp."

I often find in my work that a circle is the straightest line
to get what I'm after. I set my pack down and get out a water
bottle, taking a long draw as if I'm preparing for a revelation.
Adjusting the brim of my hat again, I signal that I'm in no hurry.
A strong breeze picks up, and a dust devil appears at the far end
of the street. We watch it sweep through and dissolve against
the hillside.

As she rattles off names of people along with their jobs, she
provides a few anecdotes. I think about that specific itinerant
life, what it must have been like coming here for the first time,
expecting to drop into a life of quiet but intense physical labor
only to learn about Emmett. When she gets to the cooks, I
express my astonishment that they were able to feed so many
kids in a day, let alone a week.

"The last real cook was Catherine. She swam in the lake
every day until it iced over, and she kept her hair short so she
wouldn't be bothered by anything. We talked about the campers

who demanded special dishes made this way and that. Eighty or a hundred kids and counselors, and a few of them came into the kitchen wanting soufflés or tortes like their cooks prepared at home. Catherine knew how to listen and then made the simple hearty meals she had planned. Your mother-in-law appreciated her diplomacy and gave her all of her hand-me-downs and sometimes an additional afternoon off if she was willing to cook extra the day before."

"And there was a maintenance man?"

"You have to look my way when you talk."

I apologize and ask again.

"Yes, Walt. Walter Johnson."

"Ah."

"He could fix anything, build anything from a bedside table to a whole house. Helped with our car more than once. Ordered a fan belt for our washer and saved us from buying a whole new machine. He had a membership to a history-book-of-the-month club. Good sense of humor. Then Catherine arrived, and gradually they fell in love. Elizabeth in particular didn't want the staff dating, so they had to sneak around."

"That's pretty Victorian."

"Say that again a little slower."

I change speed and enunciate.

"Elizabeth wasn't that bad, but the times were different. And she had her beliefs."

"How did he die?"

"Who died?"

"Walter?"

"I had no idea. When?"

"Sorry, I must be getting him mixed up with someone else. What happened to Walter and Catherine?"

"They ran off together, and Elizabeth and Emmett had to replace a cook and a handyman all at once. Emmett complained every time he and my husband went out hunting. Even when they got other people in and things began to run pretty smooth again."

I am suddenly more than hungry, and I've always been a little hypoglycemic. I get out my sandwich, unwrap the waxed paper, and offer her half. She shakes her head. "I'll get lunch with my mister."

"Do you think…maybe it's a silly question…but do you think you could have loved anyone other than Mr. Brenner?"

She takes a moment to consider this and says, "Try not to let your husband's mood bring you down."

She has noticed the change in Paul too. It seems disloyal to press on this topic. When she returns inside, I listen to the screen door smack against its frame. The question that echoes is the one about Walter and Catherine.

The volume on the TV in the Brenners' apartment goes up, and I imagine them eating a lunch of deli meats with a touch of flies' wings. I pack up my things and go inside to make several small purchases: another pair of sunglasses for Paul I think he might like, a lanyard for my keys, a package of bubble gum for Lily, a Zorro mask for Mason, a chocolate bar that could be turning white from age, and one of the pregnancy tests. I leave the money on the counter.

CHAPTER EIGHT

A Room Inside a Room

The camp feels too empty, too still when I return from the store. The lake's edge holds no salty-skinned children about to dive off the pier. I can't see Elizabeth in the upstairs window. Salish isn't in the kitchen punishing dough into more bread meant to fatten us up. No music comes from Jones's or Leon's rooms that I can hear from the bottom of the stairs. There are no stud gun pops or rolls of tar paper dropping off the side of a cabin roof. The chickens are tucked away in their house, and the dogs are off somewhere, even the small black one. The two vehicles are visible in the upper lot. I look up the hill on the other side of the valley, thinking of the nest box and the stone with Walter's name and dates, and what I've just walked into.

Using the keys I've worked onto the lanyard, I go through the dining room and find the chairs pressed so close to the clean tables, they might fly backward at any moment by kinetic energy. All the lights are out, and it's not yet dinnertime. Nothing is on the stove. The counters are wiped down, and the pantry door is locked.

I call out three times, but no one answers. I ring the bell outside the kitchen and listen as the last of the sound echoes around the lake. I've not known even five minutes when the camp has been this motionless. My mind leaps ahead wondering what I'd do if I were abandoned here, if the phone wires were cut and there was no electricity to charge my phone that's almost dead. But it seems a silly preoccupation when I could always hike back to Brenners if I had to.

And the light switches work.

I heat a pan of water on the stove and fill a cup for tea. They must have gone for a late Saturday picnic. Surely Emmett and Elizabeth are in their room. Despite my guilt, I decide to catch my breath before checking on them. The idea that they could be gone is absurd.

Nights no longer cool the house down, and the cold spot midway up the back stairs feels welcome despite its eeriness. I call out again, but no one answers. The temperature on the second floor is particularly swampy. I consider the idea that someone could be hiding behind the Quarter Room door waiting to jump out at me. It would be easy to make a list of films with those moments.

I push against the door with my right foot until it slams against the dresser. Going a little way inside, I find a nice, empty room. But I still check the closet after I set my cup down, pushing the coats and pants, shirts and dresses aside. I look beneath the bed. I make a mental note to talk with my father about how long they should wait to do something if they don't hear from me. and then I realize how distressing this would sound.

Surely, he has a list of films where a group of people gets unhinged in close quarters. I'll want to avoid those.

Clicking on the overhead fan, I pull out the stash of tea bags I've saved from each meal so I'll never run short. Once the computer is up and running, I get my feet up on a stool. This puts me at an odd angle to the keyboard and screen, but I have a clear view out the window and can easily pivot toward the door.

The noisemakers were only moved, I see. They're strung up in one of the elms now. It's such an airless day, they don't shift or send glass and metal tones into the air. Maybe Salish decided her thieves are birds and she hopes to catch them in the branches, and maybe this has something to do with being married to an ornithologist.

A noise moves through the pipes, probably from Emmett and Elizabeth's room, reminding me that I need to check on them. I only let this thought travel so far. Again I wonder how there could be a room inside this room or if this is Jones-code for something.

I go out in the hall and consider the length of our room, the length of Leon's room, the amount of space in between and any space left over. Returning to the Quarter Room, I tap on the walls, try to find a hollow spot, any opening. I've often seen the narrowest crack of light along the baseboard in the mornings. This is on my side of the bed underneath the bookcase. I remember asking Paul about this after we first moved in. He said something about sealing it up when he gets to the work on the house. I thought nothing of it at the time, but now I understand, with the angle of the roof, it's impossible not to consider another space behind this wall.

Removing the condensed *Reader's Digest* magazines and book club editions of bestsellers from the 1950s, '60s, and '70s, I stack them in the corner. The bookcase is fixed to the wall. I've seen Paul use this type of bolt to anchor dressers to provide earthquake protection in California, but here it makes little sense. Growing impatient, I kick the shelves with one of my hiking boots.

The bookcase and a section of wall pop open like the magnetized kitchen cabinets we have at home. I peer at an entry that's maybe three feet tall and a little wider. Crouching down, I look inside.

There's a bed, not unlike the bed we sleep in, with a bare mattress and a small table to one side. Maybe I shouldn't, but I crawl through the opening. A wardrobe sits against the wall adjacent to our headboard. I can't imagine how they got the furniture inside, but I'd have to tear into a wall or two to find out. The room is comfortable, almost cool, even with the window shut, yet it's musty. There are no doors, only the opening between the rooms. The one window in this room looks into the courtyard and provides a slightly different view into the Wedding Room. Unfastening the latch, I raise the window. I have a full view of Gabe and Salish's bed with its light quilt and pillows in a disheveled state.

I'm about to open the wardrobe when I hear someone on the stairs. And just as quick, several someones head my way. As I hurry back to the main room, I scrape my spine on the upper edge of the opening. I seal the wall again, and get some of the books back in place just as the bedroom door is pushed open.

"Doesn't anyone knock?" I ask and put the remaining books on my desk. But Paul never knocks. Why should he? He comes in first, stepping aside so Salish, Gabe, Leon, and Jones can enter. Dropping onto the bed, Jones stretches out, grabbing the two pillows for her head and placing her dusty boots on our comforter. Salish takes the straight-backed chair. The men settle where they can in the room. The only one treating this moment as a joke seems to be Jones. I hear the children in the yard, and I go over to the window. Lily looks up at me. We wave.

"Take a seat," Paul tells me.

"Are all of you here to help me pick a book to read, or is this an inquisition?"

Jones laughs. I nudge her to move over, and I take one of the pillows from her so I too can prop myself against the iron headboard.

Looking at the comforter as if we're ruining *her* bedding, Salish notes my boots next to her daughter's and says, "Something has come to our attention."

"That's not what we agreed to," Gabe intrudes, giving me a compassionate look.

"I'll handle this," Paul says.

I squeeze my eyes tight and say, "You've been huddling somewhere."

Leon yawns. "It wasn't my idea."

"This was in your camera bag." Salish removes my bandana from her front apron pocket, unfolds it, and reveals her paring knife.

"And you've been going through my things?" I say to Paul.

"Not intentionally." He leans against his dresser as if he might hide in one of its drawers.

"What does *that* mean?"

"They were curious to see what you've been working on," Jones says, as if she would gladly trip all of them up.

"I'll make this expressly clear," I say, sitting up straight. "No one is to go near my cameras."

"That's kind of evasive," Leon says.

"Leave her alone," Jones says.

"Who are you defending?" Salish asks.

"Maybe we could have a conversation about boats that leave the boathouse at night," I say.

Jones kicks me in the leg, and her mother notes this. Paul shakes his head.

Leon laughs. "Go ahead."

"I'd be happy to explain the knife if the vigilantes are willing to listen."

"See," Paul says.

I tell them about the nest box up on the plateau. I don't mention Walter Johnson or the fact that Jones was with me. "I didn't want to frighten anyone," I say, looking at Salish. "More than they already are."

"That's number seventy-eight. I'll go up and check," Gabe says.

"That should settle things," Paul says, appearing eager to drop it now.

Salish looks at my desk. "Where did you get those tea bags?"

Getting up from the bed, I say, "Everyone out."

No one moves.

"Show's over," Paul says, holding the door open.

Once they're gone, he says, "Next time just tell me." He comes over and tries to take my hand, but I move away, bumping into the bookcase. I freeze. But it doesn't come open.

"Your name's on the chart for Emmett and Elizabeth, but I'll fill in," he says. "I know you have work to do. Maybe tonight we could sit and talk, get things back on track."

I look through him. "What track would that be?"

He knows why I left the comfortable rhythms of Berkeley,

the closeness of my family, the film community, the swimming pool where I do laps without muck and fish, the coffee shop with its lending library and giant picture windows where I sometimes work, the farmers' market, consignment store, hair salon, the way knives are used for cutting bread, cheese, fruit, and vegetables and then go back into a wooden block when they've served their purpose. The tiny cotton and knitted outfits and blankets I've collected—hiding them in boxes with tissue on the upper shelf of my closet—to replace the ones I gave away in haste. This seems like an awfully large expression of love to me. I don't know what he wants.

When he shakes his head, I'm unsure if he means he's sorry he can't say anything or there's no getting through to me.

The minute he's gone, I'm in the bathroom using the pregnancy test. Once I set it aside, I take a shower and brush my teeth, only to lean over and see the way the kit fails to produce even a moment of mistaken good news.

I leave by the dining room door and hear Salish rushing to throw dinner together in the kitchen. Gabe stands under the large oak threaded with noisemakers looking up and shaking his head, as if he wonders why his wife would do such a thing. He sees me and mouths something. Maybe he's sorry about the invasion. Timothy wrestles with one of the spotted dogs, and his little brother, Mason, piles on, the other spotted dog barking madly. My girl comes running over and throws herself against my leg, hugging me tight. I decide to let Lily join me as I go down to the water and along the perimeter.

"Where?" she asks.

"You'll see."

We take the path away from the last of the cabins to the right. Letting her climb onto my back when she tires, I keep going until we reach one of the broad, flat boulders half-submerged in the lake. I hoist her up, and we find a cluster of tiny rocks to toss into the water.

"I miss my best friend," she says.

"I miss my best friend too," I say.

Lily throws a fistful of pebbles, creating pockmarks in the water. Small fish dart about. Her friend is Andy, and I say Takeo's name, pronouncing his three syllables with care.

"Does he live around here?" she asks.

"Not exactly."

"Can I meet him?"

I skip one of the flat stones. I get seven skips out of it. "I wish."

"Do you love him?"

"Yes, very much."

"Are you going to marry him?"

I gather her hair into a ponytail. "I'm married to Paul, silly."

"I want to be a bus driver."

"You do?"

"Then I can pick up all my friends and we can drive to camp and we can go swimming and we can have a sleepover every night. And your friend can come too."

"Can I drive your bus?"

"If you bring the snacks."

"I can do that."

"I'm getting hungry," she says.

"We'll go back," I say.

"I'm too tired to walk."

Lily climbs onto my back again, and I feel her warmth pulse against mine.

She squirms down when we're close to the house and runs to catch up with her brothers. Salish rings the dinner bell, and I go out on the pier. Stripping down to my undies, I dive into the water. Sunset glimmers at the other end of the lake, and I do a backstroke for a while and circle toward the alcove where Lily and I pitched rocks.

I'm surprised and unsurprised when I see Gabe walking along the path as if we had planned to meet up. Swimming away before he gets to the water's edge, I turn and see him strip down and dive in. I think of a delicate fly attached to a hook, monofilament winding out in an effort to reach me. When he catches up, I stop and dog-paddle for a moment over this deep point of the lake.

"You were right. About the nest box," he says.

I let the easy turbulence move me about. "You found the bird."

"I saw where the knife went through, the mark on the box. I'm sorry. About everything."

Bits of pond dirt catch the red light as it moves around his neck. He comes closer as if I need to feel his acceleration. Paddling backward, I say, "What's it like knowing your wife is probably stealing her own knives?"

The second it's out of my mouth, I want to take it back, but I don't. It's important to know if he's only a temporary ally and if he sees what I believe is occurring.

He doesn't flinch. "I suspect Leon."

"He's too absorbed in his own world…like every other guy who wants to launch a band."

"I mean, he *is* his father's son."

"Paul feels bad about leaving you," I say. "You understand that, don't you?"

He goes quiet and looks back at the house. I don't imagine Paul has stated this to him the way he has to me, so how could Gabe know? Trying to shift topics, I get him to tell me about the range swallows cover, knowing he studies migratory patterns in particular. He explains that swallows are everywhere around the globe except Antarctica. "They're like a universal language."

"Do you feel anything about them on a personal level?"

"I guess you could say I'm drawn to their precision flying."

"Ah."

"You understand precision. I see the way you film."

There's something off about his delivery, like he's fishing.

"I have been at it for a while," I say, antsy to swim off.

"You're quite beautiful…when you hold a camera."

At best, it's a clumsy form of flattery. I have looked at ten thousand moments on film where people are about to unhook themselves and their relationships. Perfectly nice people who think they understand the parameters of their lives. Then their eyes get dreamy, maybe their mouths open a little, and they fly out of themselves as if a barrier has been knocked down in a storm.

Swimming away, my arms cut an angle toward the dock, and my mind spins in watery thought. I'll have to find a way to get some footage of his boldness and the way it diminishes him.

———

By the time I shower and dress, most of the family is at one of the larger tables eating supper. Gabe looks up and quickly back at his plate. Paul seems lost in one misgiving or another, maybe some detail of the remodel. Lily blows me a kiss, and I return this despite Salish's glower when I do. Exchanging kicks under the table, Mason is dressed as Santa Claus today, his beard made of glued-together cotton balls. Timothy, who strikes back with greater force, goes at it until their mother snaps at them. The only two sitting at their own table are Leon and Jones, who split a pair of earbuds, listening to music or a podcast. I go into the kitchen, fill a plate from the pans on the stove, and hurry upstairs.

I set the dish down on the desk, rush over, and prop a chair against the door, waiting to hear if footsteps will follow. I shut the window curtain, turn on the overhead fan, and push against the bookcase. With a third try, a couple of paperbacks hit the floor, and it pops open.

I crawl into the disappearing room and go over to the wardrobe. It's a cheap piece of furniture like the headboard and the side table. Maybe a set of catalog items from decades ago. I look at the old mirror and the black mirror rot that mottles my reflection. I begin to feel along the walls and find the outline of an old door that opened into the hallway. Most of it's covered in plaster then wallpaper.

When I open the door to the wardrobe, wire hangers clang together, and I grab them to calm them down. There are a few dresses, a couple of plain blue uniforms, and a woman's coat. Three scarves, an empty purse that smells faintly of oranges, drawers filled with underthings, nightgowns, socks. I feel certain this is Catherine's room. The cook who loved Walter. I turn around to look at the bed where they must have lain and see those small white moths again. They might be flying through a hole in the window screen. One settles on my shoulders.

But it isn't a moth at all. It's ash.

I shut my eyes and look again. I'm staring at flecks of dust. This has to be more than a trick of light. Maybe a new temperament in my vision. I decide to continue my exploration.

Glancing at her shoes, I find one pair of boots with traces of mud, one pair of awkward heels in need of repair, and a pair of flats. There's something stuck in one of the boots like a white lining. I tease it out and find it's a single piece of paper written in a language I don't recognize. A number of words have been badly smudged. Bringing it back to the other side, I seal the bookcase shut.

Typing individual words and phrases into my computer, I learn that the language is Danish. I turn up the following scattered words: *cursed* or *cursing, man, loved, wife, chased, hard,* and *union.* I type these into my computer on a Word document and start moving them about.

A man loved the woman he cursed, and chased her into a hard union.

A man cursed the wife he chased hard until their union undid them.

A cursed woman chased her man into a hard love without union.

But the words aren't lined up in a single sentence—they're scattered over the whole of the sheet. It's impossible to decipher. I try to figure out how I can hide this letter from a group of people willing to go through everything I own. I decide it's best to keep it in the open, as if this is nothing I would even want to hide. I place it in a memoir by Nora Ephron, *I Remember Nothing*, sitting on my desk. I make sure the top of the envelope sticks up beyond the pages.

———

As if it will split us in two, the house cracks with lightning tonight. Paul sleeps on.

In elementary school a friend lost the attic of her house to lightning. It was the family's game room, and luckily no one was up there playing Foosball. My friend and I crept up the attic stairs a few days later, snuck under the yellow warning tape, and saw the blackened wood, the melted games, window openings where the glass had blown away. We were punished for walking on floors we might have fallen through. Ever since, I've had a great respect for this kind of weather event.

Taking my Nikon off the closet shelf, I move to the window to film the lake. I get the screen up just as a lightning bolt hits the water. I see Gabe by one of the Wedding Room windows. Turning my camera off, I set it down on the desk and go back to bed. Eventually I drop off.

Sitting straight up, as if I'm about to fly through the air, I see Lily standing by my side of the bed. Usually she doesn't startle me this way. Feeling for Paul to get him to move over, I have a hard time calming my heart. I turn the lamp switch several clicks. I see there's no light coming from the power strip. The electricity is down.

Lily tugs at the thin cover.

I touch her arm. "What's up, buttercup?" I push over so she

can tuck in. She's just a slip of a girl. "Did something scare you?"
I know she will only answer in silence or disconnected words
since she is asleep.

Salish will scold me, of course, if I wake *her* to say Lily is
in our bed again. Maybe it's different when your last child
wasn't exactly wanted, as she told me one afternoon. It was
the emphasis on the word *unplanned* as if this were a mark her
daughter would carry throughout life, more prominent than
the small port-wine stain on her right brow. I can't imagine
feeling this toward a little one but especially her. I almost said,
Lily is a perfect child. I have worries for her Salish doesn't seem
to possess.

I curl around my girl, determined to stay at Hidden Lake, no
matter what, to keep her safe.

When I wake again, it's two hours later. Maneuvering around
her, I grab my camera off the desk and slip back into bed. I have
to nudge Paul to roll over and stop overheating me so I can
think. I consider Lily with her milky breath and snarled hair.
Paul tugs at the top sheet in his sleep, and I grab hard to take it
back in order to cover her. Only then do I look at the footage
with my headphones on. It rained heavily in the early hours of
the night, the lightning dancing on the screen.

I pause the footage and remove my headphones. Salish is
shouting for Lily. Her voice amplifies along with her footsteps
on the stairs.

"She's here!" I call back.

Paul sits up. Our bedroom door flies open. Lily is still fast
asleep. Salish stands in the doorway, her hair splintering out from
her head as if it's charged with current. Getting my glasses on,

I see the way the hall light plays on her hair, the otherworldly effect this produces. Her wild look.

"Thank god," she says. "Hurry. Bring your camera." She leaves our door wide open, and her feet drum down the steps.

"I'm losing track," Paul says. "How many does this make?"

Grabbing my robe, I let Lily sleep. To listen for her, I leave the door open. Paul is already in his jeans.

The dining hall lights are ablaze. It's still dark out. Salish directs us to the large, gaping fireplace with its thick wood mantel. The hearth is so tall that Jones, who's five foot four, can stand inside it without bumping her head.

There's a line of framed photographs that stretch from one end of the mantel to the other. Mostly pictures of camp groups. One of Emmett and Elizabeth on their wedding day in front of the house. She wore a light-colored suit and held a small bouquet. There are a couple of Paul and Gabe as young boys in Sears studio shots. They look overly tidy, but there's that quiet stare of Paul's and that almost mirthful look of his brother's.

One of Salish's knives is embedded in the mantel below the wedding photograph. Considering how deeply it's driven in, someone must have stood at the far end of the dining hall to throw it.

Salish trembles. I put an arm around her shoulders, surprised she doesn't knock it off.

"I was there when he forged it. It was the only fluting knife he ever made."

"Maybe we should take the idea of a squatter more seriously," Paul says.

"Or someone young and bored," Gabe says.

Paul is quick to fly off. "If you're suggesting Leon…"

"Did you hear me say Leon?"

"So you think it's one of your own kids?" Paul asks. "One of the boys?"

"I wasn't saying—"

Stepping between this snarl, I say, "Did anyone check on the children?"

"First thing. The dogs are with them, keeping watch." Gabe says. "I also checked upstairs." He reaches for the knife handle.

"Fingerprints," I say.

Paul looks at me as if I've raised my voice at a funeral.

I turn the camera on. The knife doesn't budge under Gabe's grip, but I don't see how it could unless the wood was soft as balsa.

"Hold on," Paul says and goes into the office where he sometimes drops his tool belt at night. He returns with a hammer.

I record this and the pained sound that comes from Salish's throat. "You'll ruin it," she says.

"If I had my cat's paw with me… The drill press will stir the kids, but it's your call," Paul says.

Salish relents.

Just as I say, "I'll remove the pictures if—" Paul strikes, and this broken family and their campers fly in a wide array. Glass shatters. Why he thought this would cause less noise than his drill press, I'll never know.

Salish picks the knife handle out of the mess. I see a cut open across her right index finger from a piece of glass. She elevates her hand. The blood comes slowly, trickling over her wrist and down her arm as I hurry to grab paper towels.

None of the kids appear, and soon Salish is bandaged up. But we're aware of the things that have changed. The knife in the nest box, the one in the mantelpiece. This is no longer about knives that are missing. Considering Salish's behavior this morning, it's getting harder to imagine she would do this kind of act.

I sweep the broken glass into a dustpan and toss out the frames and photographs, even the ones still intact—since no one speaks up for them when I offer to clean them off—holding out one of Paul and Gabe as boys. In that Sears background, with their stiff shirts and slicked-back hair, I try to imagine Gabe's eventual feeling of betrayal.

Paul stops me on my way up to our room. "I'd feel better if you went back and stayed with your folks for a while."

"If anything happened to Lily—"

"I understand. But I told Salish she should take the kids and go as well. Leon too. Gabe and I can sort this out."

"I don't know about that, but what did Leon say?"

"He laughed. He said he might do a ghost podcast."

"Right. And Salish?" I ask.

"She said she isn't leaving until she gets all of her knives back."

"Great."

"Then she told me she feels like she's supposed to be here."

"What does that mean?"

"She has a strong affinity for the place," he says.

"I'll never understand her."

"Some of us do. Anyway, what do you think? Head home?"

I can't imagine him more eager to see me leave.

"As soon as I see Salish pack up the kids and go."

He turns away from me as if I am a traitor.

———

Dad will be back from classes by now, cognac in hand. Mom has just pulled into the drive. She'll have her chardonnay, they'll watch the *New Hour*, then they'll start dinner together. The house is mid-century modern, long rather than wide, an impressive amount of rosewood, elevated rooflines and ceilings, and a series of picture windows looking onto a backyard they've spent thirty-five years toiling over. There isn't a season in which the flower beds are fallow. Mom and Takeo often discussed their gardening plans and shared starts. Dad created a koi pond that grew in size, and his favorite perch is in the cluster of chairs where he talks to the fish without a self-conscious bone.

He answers the phone on the third ring.

"Know anyone in the Language Center who speaks Danish?" I ask.

"Not a soul."

"I need to translate a one-page letter."

"Wait. What about Professor Madsen?" Dad says, noting his friend from the film department. "He's emeritus now, but I'm happy to reach out."

"Thanks. I'll scan and send. Give him my email so he can write directly to me?" I move the mouse around on my desk and wait.

"Is everything okay?"

"All good. Can you put Mom on for a minute?"

When she picks up, I ask if I can get a read on someone. "It's Salish again. She has this collection of objects her father made, and they keep disappearing. She might be hiding them and activating her own drama, but she blames everyone else for taking them."

"I have to see a patient at the hospital, so we'll have to make it quick. What kind of objects?"

My mother is used to stories that take many sessions, months, or even years to unfold, so I know she won't press when I skip ahead. "Nothing valuable."

"If I were doing simple, long-distance triage…"

"Yes?"

"I'd suggest she has an urgent need for attention. Beyond that, I'd have to talk with her or learn a good deal more from you. Give her a wide berth, sweetheart. You know how to walk away."

"Paul's become even more distant."

"I'm sorry, love. It will probably get better once you're away from there."

"No, I just…"

"His affair was at the end of his first marriage, after things had already fallen apart. That doesn't make for a pattern."

Sometimes I hate it when she hits on the unease beneath the unease with that pinpoint accuracy of hers, much as I invite it.

"Besides, who would he cheat with? Salish?"

"If he wanted to have sex with a dresser."

"Exactly. And remember, he's not only your husband but a good friend. Give him time to get through this."

"Love you."

———

It's an hour before sunset, and I go down to the boathouse. Lining up two matching oars, I nestle a bottle of wine and one of the old orange life jackets under the seats of a boat I've taken out before. I tug it into the water, climb in, set the oars, and row.

When I'm out toward the middle, I want to scream until the sound bounces off the hills and boulders. But someone would only run down to the dock, thinking this is a call for help, and pull another boat out. I push my face into the stinky life jacket and shout full-throated into the crusty fabric then pitch it over the side. It's so decomposed it bobs and sinks. Uncorking the bottle, I take a long draw. Then I pull the seats up, and throw them overboard. Lying down in the inch of water at the bottom of the boat, I drink. A trace of cloud speeds above. A pair of mating dragonflies appears. They brighten and hurry off as the sky shifts colors. I drink harder.

When I shut my eyes, I see the Old Jewish Cemetery in Prague. Takeo and I held hands tightly from the minute we entered it and didn't say a word. My father's side of the family is Jewish. We're not sure how many of us were lost to pogroms. My husband and I stood there with the gravestones pushing out of the ground in every direction. Layers of broken stones and crushed skeletons below. Someone in my family might be there. I placed small rocks on some of the headstones. Takeo once told me a few of his family had been lost to Hiroshima. He took a rock from my hands to add to a marker.

The boat moves at a quickening pace now, the rush of the valley all around me as I fall inside the boat, fall through wood and water and layers of a life. The sky reddens.

I ask, "Are you safe?"

"You're the one I worry over," he says.

This is the same thing Takeo said before he died. I sit up and look around. I'm still in the center of this deep, hidden lake. Standing in the boat now, I feel the hull rock. The bottle tips over and the rest of the wine floods the bottom.

I dive into the algae-filled water in the direction of the camp, compelled to push through the alcohol and fatigue. Doing the crawl, I barely open my eyes on the strokes where I gather air. When I have to rest, I see I'm halfway there, and the lights of the house have gone on.

Moving again, I feel fish glide past. I turn my head to the side. The sky is almost black. But I travel without rest until I reach the dock. My arms are covered in bits of green slime and black flecks. Leon looks down at me from his spot on the dock where he's having an evening smoke.

"You going to leave it there?" He looks out over the dark water to where the boat drifts in a slender band of moonlight.

I pull myself up onto the dock like a fish drawn from a hook, waiting to see if some force will toss me back where I can breathe.

"I'm testing it out."

"For what?" he asks.

I reach for the pipe, and he lets it rest in my hands. "I was thinking if I got some fireworks, I could load up a boat and push it out in the lake and watch the show."

He lights the bowl for me. I take a draw, hold it briefly, and slowly let it out.

"Who would set off the fireworks," he asks, "if the boat's that far out?"

"There it is. Your father's pragmatism. By the way, he mentioned something about you and Jones."

He takes the bowl out of my hands and knocks the ash out. "Then he should tell me himself, don't you think?" He's not acting icy or clever when he says this. It's more about a pervasive sadness gathered at the camp—the way Dutch elm disease or locusts gather.

"He should talk to us about a lot of things," I say.

I know the dock is fragile and nothing like common ground. I stand, water trickling down my legs, and wish him a good night. I sense he's become a man trapped in a consulate, pacing in his mind, wondering why he ever came here. I know I should have stayed home.

CHAPTER NINE

The Children
Will Be Taken

Not a single knife has disappeared in the last ten days. I imagine the scythe is still under the bed in the Wedding Room, but I don't ask about this or if Salish feels the tip of the blade poke up through the mattress.

I've shot a great deal of footage, interviewing everyone in turn. I have all their signed contracts now, including ones for the children signed by their parents.

Not surprisingly, Paul is the most reluctant to open up. But there's a lightness, a new feeling around the camp. Jones and Leon start to organize outdoor games for the little ones, and everyone is spending more time in the water, often in groups. On two different nights, I project family movies onto one of the sheds, showing some of the footage I've made, presenting the cheerful side of life at Hidden Lake, the natural wonders. I even allow myself a certain optimism when Paul makes a point of asking about my basal temperature.

On my way back from the dock one evening, my calm is disrupted when I find Salish on her hands and knees, digging in the earth. I catch sight of one of the tackle boxes, and realize she's making a hiding place for it near the narcissus, hyacinths and tall grasses that edge the garden. Stopping cold, I back away and turn off my flashlight. Her body dips up and back in the kitchen light where she makes her burial ground. The keys she keeps on that string jangle against her breasts as she scoops the earth out with a spade.

"As soon as I'm done," she calls with her back to me, "we can both go upstairs. We have to change their sheets tonight."

"That's fine," I say and leave her to imagine that a knife burial will stop a thief who has a sustained need for attention.

Coming out of my room an hour later, I start down. Salish is at the bottom of the stairs, her foot on the first step. It is the household custom that whoever is below waits for the person descending as if this is a narrow mountain pass and we are driving cars. But she hurries like a stubborn goat to meet me on the landing. She has a full tray in her hands, and she thrusts it into my solar plexus. I grab the handles, and the glass of berry juice tips, soaking the bologna and bread, splashing my shirt and jeans.

"You'll have to do it. Emmett is overdue for a shave, so you can do that too. And we've run out of the good soap. You'll probably hear about that from Elizabeth, if she can remember what soap is."

"Be nice," I say.

Salish's hair appears to thicken and twist in the humid air. She pushes it away from her face as if the act of talking with me is the hard labor of her life. From her apron pocket, she removes a cake of soap and a barber's straight razor. She places them next to his plate. "Elizabeth doesn't like it when you go up, but I have bread in the oven, and I have to..."

"We all *have to*," I say, despite knowing things get worse when I meet her squarely. "What are you doing with your endless loaves of bread? Feeding the multitudes?"

"Better than having no one to feed." This is the way she has begun to scald me, bringing up my childlessness. By itself it's a fairly benign sentence, but this is one of a series of comments that point to what she imagines is my selfishness.

My grandmother on my father's side had an expression for a self-absorbed person, and I finally use it on Salish. "Your eyes are inside out."

Swinging around to get past her, I barely graze her with one edge of the tray, and some of the juice that's pooled on the surface spatters against her chest and neck. We look like surgeons back from an operating theater, bright red pulp dotting the stairs.

"I really don't have time for you," she calls after me.

Our temporary respite flies off.

———

Upstairs, on the radio, a piano concerto goes in and out of reception. Sometimes the only consistent music comes from the sick bells placed on tables and shelves around the room in case Emmett and Elizabeth need help. Or something Leon or Jones plays takes over.

My mother-in-law studies me and gets out of bed. In her nightgown, she sits by the windows that face the lake. "Don't forget to empty the trash," she says, confusing me again for a maid.

I fetch the cans and place them by the door. "I've been sent to shave your husband," I say.

Her pale eyes follow my movements. Sometimes it seems

her troubles with short-term memory work in proportion to Emmett's cancer. Things have accelerated quickly for both of them. He eats so little, he has become almost weightless. I understand he's refused treatment from the first, other than pain meds.

Every time I come upstairs I burn a little from the times he's told me to go to hell or called me names, including *cunt*. I can only imagine how he treated Elizabeth. Now I don't know if he can talk anymore or simply won't. I've asked Paul and Gabe separately, if there ever was a time when Emmett was less horrible. Both thought about this for quite a while and supplied roughly the same answer: *When he was making his care packages*.

He had been an army officer in Vietnam, and a couple of times a year after he retired from the military, he wrote personal letters of encouragement that he sent in boxes with socks, candy bars, books or magazines, dusting powder, crossword puzzles, powdered lemonade, and baseball caps to troops serving overseas. He spent hours on end in his office, selecting the items, working on the notes. *They were his real family*, Gabe said.

I try to imagine Emmett finding moments of peace inside a series of small boxes, each one addressed to a kindred spirit, as if to his younger self. The journey over to Brenners, the unstated pride at seeing the military postage label fixed in place. I sense that even if he were willing and able to talk, he would never entertain a question on this subject.

I set Elizabeth up with her food after wiping up the red juice, and she begins to pick at her meal. Going into a soft patter, just below the sound of Elizabeth's voice, I say to Emmett that he might feel a little better if he had a shave. He barely opens his eyes in response.

"This morning he put my bags down to carry me over the threshold and introduce me to Gabe and…what's the other one's name?"

"Paul," I say.

"That's right. The little sandy-haired one. Such a serious boy. He kicks me when he gets mad."

"Really?"

"Did I tell you, when Emmett asked me to marry him, he said Hidden Lake was brimming with life?"

I pour warm water into a pan with a little antiseptic, get a pair of disposable gloves on, and dab at Emmett's face. He has a sore on his chest that looks like a small crater.

"But it's filled with cancerous fish. Even the air over the lake makes me sick," she says.

"I'm sorry," I say, instead of going into how the fish appear healthy, that we eat some of those fish. I wash Emmett's face as carefully as I can while Elizabeth stares out. He makes small, high sounds of pain.

"I tell him I want to go home to see my parents. So you know what he does? He sneaks out like a fool in the middle of the night and catches those fish and tells me he got them from the store. He would have done anything to make me stay."

"Maybe he feels regretful now." Rubbing the soap until I whip up a lather, I apply it to his cheeks and chin. Slowly, I scrape at the sharp white bristles with the razor. Both Paul and Gabe think Emmett won't last more than a few days now.

"He cut out the lumps and the tough portions," Elizabeth continues. "Some of them had extra eyes and double tails. Oh, and the ones with strange fins. Then he skinned those fish and fried them in heavy oil so the real flavors and smells would disappear. He insisted on cooking. I thought he was spoiling me."

"I know," I say though I have no idea. It's become increasingly difficult to understand where her reality begins and ends.

Despite my care, Emmett continues to utter sharp sounds until I'm done. Not a single nick.

"He never gave the boys any of the fish—said he was saving it up for me, so I could build my strength to have our first child. I fed the boys early, and we ate the fish after they had gone to bed, with ale and brown bread. Imagine if I had had that child. How misshapen…"

Hidden Lake is drowning her. When she goes quiet, I say, "We'll probably have to wait until tomorrow to change the sheets."

"Are you the barber?" she says, squinting at me. I'm aware I should also wash and re-braid her hair.

"Sometimes I'm the barber. Oh, I meant to tell you, I found a letter in Danish."

"Hide it quickly."

"Why?"

Emmett makes a muffled noise. Maybe he wants to use a curse word.

"Why should I hide the letter in Danish?" I ask.

"It's full of sins," Elizabeth says.

When I see how tired she's become, I turn the bedside light down. Emmett's face appears smaller, his mouth ajar. I adjust his head on the pillow and try to feed him a spoonful of broth that his tongue doesn't want. I try again and stroke his throat so he will swallow but get nowhere.

Elizabeth turns the radio off, and I sit as she washes herself with a fresh washcloth and dresses in one of her nightgowns. Sometimes she does this all over again, maybe three or four times, because she's forgotten she just did it, and that's the only time I intrude. But she does this just once tonight and slips into her bed.

I've rarely seen her wander after she tucks in. One time she thought she was in *my* room, and we had another type of funny conversation. Taking another look to see that things are in order, I make a last effort. "Someone has been stealing things from the kitchen. You haven't seen any knives, have you?"

"Someone's taking knives?" she says.

"A cleaver, a slicer. Even a boning knife."

"She is."

"She?" I ask, washing my hands and drying them on a fresh towel.

"That scaredy-cat who married Gabe. What's her name?"

"Salish."

"That's the one."

Elizabeth has her lucid spells. I try to use this currency wisely.

"Have you seen something?" I ask.

"I've seen her out there burying things like a dog. But you can't control all the controlled burns. She forgets that, that things can get away from you."

"Do you want me to turn the radio on again for a while?"

"No, Emmett likes it quiet now. See how peaceful he looks."

We listen to the sound of his labored breathing. Drool runs down his neck from one corner of his open mouth. I blot this and place a soft pad under his chin.

"I was thinking about Walter the other day. How did Walter die?" I ask.

She crooks her finger, and I come close to hear her whisper, "He died the same way I did."

———

There's a consistent knock on the door, much too early in the morning. Almost a pounding. I'm not ready for this again. Paul is already up and out of the room. I rush to the door shouting, "Stop that!"

Leon answers, "Dad says come downstairs."

I open the door. "Sorry. I thought... Is someone hurt?"

"It's a fucking mess," he says.

I grab my robe and one of my cameras.

What I can't record is the bad blood that stirs the air when I enter the kitchen.

"You must have heard something last night," Salish says, turning to me.

It doesn't seem necessary to talk about the thunderstorm that rolled through. I begin to film.

"What's wrong with you?" she demands. "Come get me if you hear something. Get any of us."

Paul intervenes with a frown. I watch as she goes quiet. I can't figure out how he does that. It never works for me. Not even Gabe has this kind of persuasion over her.

We have all been at this campground too long.

The lid to one of the tackle boxes she buried in the ground has been twisted and torn off. I think of the way a bear went through a campground I once stayed at in the Sierra. He ripped the side mirror off my car and clawed at the door. It was my own damned fault. Though I had wiped them off, I had left unwashed dishes inside, planning to take care of them in the morning.

The remaining knives—at least the outlines of knives—are still tightly wrapped. She uses the recovered paring knife pulled from the swallow.

She goes over to the back door and stands there as if she plans to let something out of a cage. Maybe her wildness that's become harder to contain. The smell that floods the kitchen has me gagging. But I go through the door when she signals to me, as if this is a test of bravery I plan to win.

I see three or four at first until I realize that all the chickens are dead. There must be twenty or more. Blood and bodies pooled in the mud. All with their heads chopped off. Not neatly and evenly. Someone hacked at them. Flies gather in mad numbers despite the early hour.

In the grocery store in Berkeley where I go once a week, there are far more chickens than this in the display cases, cut and cleaned, cellophane wrapped, and date labeled. Packages with words like *free range* meant to assure us that something humane occurred to these body parts. I rarely think twice about my purchase other than considering how I can cook it without fuss—using the easiest, shortest method. The hens Salish fed and fed had their own small range, settling into their home at night. The dogs were trained not to trouble them, and the fencing was strong.

I cover my mouth, turn away and go inside, shutting the door.

Takeo and I found a dead possum on our back steps once. Eventually, we discovered the teenage boys who lived next door wanted to do something ugly or maybe, they thought, cool.

Starting to breathe again, I plan to put water on for tea and maybe talk over what to do, when I see Lily has come downstairs. Her hair is rumpled from sleep, and pillow marks crease her face and brighten her stain. She comes over and wraps herself around me. Just then Gabe comes through the door and Lily sees the massacre. "The chickens." She begins to cry. I pick her up and hold her, turning so she can't see them.

Our ornithologist puts on his rubber boots and goes out with a couple of giant metal washtubs that once held icy beverages for events. He gets a shovel from the toolshed and a pair of work gloves—which I'm afraid are Paul's—and begins to fill the tub with chickens, constantly batting flies away.

Paul and Salish come in, and she suggests I do the morning routine with Emmett and Elizabeth while they sink into plucking and gutting the chickens so they can get some of the meat into the freezer. Lily hasn't stopped crying.

"They've been out there too long," Paul says. "We'll have to build a bonfire."

As I rock Lily back and forth, I say, "I'll take her up to her room and get her settled."

"Hush, Lily," Salish says.

"The little chickens are dead," Lily says through her sobs.

"I'm sure they're in heaven, sweetheart," I say. She presses her face against my neck. I feel the tears and snot and puffs of breath as she holds me tight. I don't know if I believe in heaven, but it's something I pull out to comfort her.

"Get yourself dressed and brush your hair and wash your face," Salish directs. "I'm going to make you pancakes today."

"Only if Nora carries me."

———

Black smoke coils and breaks apart. The bonfire down the hill is going strong. With my camera in hand, I walk through a trace of white feathers that lift off the grass as I move to where the air is sweeter. I take a seat in one of the two Adirondack chairs.

Paul tosses the chickens in, one at a time. He will always be there for the things that need to be nailed, burned, screwed, or replaced. He is a man good at doing.

The screen door slams, and I turn to find Gabe, who takes the other chair facing the bonfire.

"You okay?" he asks.

I turn my camera on him. "Break it down for me. What's going on?"

"Got me," Gabe says. But he looks evasive.

"It's time to call the sheriff," I say.

"If he drove out here over a bunch of dead chickens, he might feel some duty to write the place up for campground violations."

"But it's not a functioning campground."

"It's licensed that way," he says. "And we need that license in order to sell the place as a camp. If something appears to be wrong… You probably shouldn't be filming this part."

I set the camera down in my lap, leaving it on so it will

record the same static view of the fire and pick up his voice. My husband drops the bodies and heads with bright red combs into the fire at a slow pace to avoid too much sizzle and pop. I can see Gabe noting the LED. He asks me again to shut the camera off. After doing that, I turn it back on as I nestle it into its bag where he can't see the light. It's possible I will pick up a little audio that I can enhance later. I put my feet up on the footrest.

"Paul told you he left home after Walter was killed, right?" Gabe says.

I take a breath. "I don't know the whole story," I say, without knowing any of it.

"But you know Walter did maintenance at the camp. That was his shop you stopped in when you thought the saw was on. His tool belt up on the wall. He's the one who showed Paul everything he knows about carpentry. For years, Walter wouldn't let me come in, because I was too young. *Tool's a dangerous thing, in the wrong hands*, he'd say. He was a big man, almost too tall for the table and band saws. I'd watch him hunched over, his giant hands working near the blades. He left the safeties off, even when Paul used them.

"Anyway, after the place had emptied out for winter holidays one year—just the family and Walt—Emmett picked a fight with him." Gabe sucks on his lower lip and looks over at his brother. "There was a rifle shot. And in the morning, I found out Walt was dead."

"Emmett shot him?"

"That's what I think, but I was up in my room at the time."

"You had a cook too?"

"Yes. Catherine. But she had gone to Denmark to be with

her family for the month. When she got word, she stayed there. Left her things."

"Was there a trial?"

"I think Paul got some doctor to say he was unfit to give testimony. Elizabeth didn't have to testify against her husband. And I hadn't seen anything, like I said, so the jury hung and the DA dropped it."

"And the camp?" I ask trying to read the way he taps the arm of his chair as if he's sending Morse code.

"Groups started to cancel. A few families, who hadn't heard the news, came to take advantage of lowered rates when Emmett started to offer those. Eventually they had to shut it down."

"Mrs. Brenner said Walt and Catherine left the camp together."

He stops tapping and gives me a measured look. "She's loyal to Elizabeth and Emmett. You understand."

"What was the fight about?"

Gabe rubs his face as if the smoke has dirtied him. Then he stands, appearing to be done with his story.

"Paul was there. He could tell you. All I heard was yelling. But then, Emmett was known for hollering and picking fights. I turned up my radio like I always did and tried to go to sleep."

"That's funny. I think of Paul as the one who would tune out."

"You don't have to make a lot of noise to keep your hand in."

"I'm an only child, so what do I know? But did you and Paul get along well growing up?"

"About the same as Timothy and Mason."

"So you fought all the time."

"It was a long time ago. The important thing to keep in mind is that you'll be driving away from here when this crazy dream is over."

———

Sitting by myself in the empty dining hall, I tap the number in, cancel the call, try again, and let it ring through. A deputy sheriff answers. I introduce myself and say I'm just calling for information.

Deputy Sheriff Lennard's voice has a somewhat humanized tone. "How can I help?"

"I'm staying with my family at Hidden Lake Camp."

The stench is still in the air. One of us will have to go out and rake the soil.

"I'm familiar. You family?"

"A daughter-in-law of the owners. I'm not sure how to approach this, but there might be someone who wishes us harm."

"Has someone been injured?"

I explain about the chickens. There's a long pause at the other end.

"And my sister-in-law has a collection of novelty knives that keep disappearing. We found one driven into the mantelpiece."

I hear a garbled response, reception going in and out. "Is she willing to come over and register a complaint?"

"I'm not sure."

"And you say no one's been hurt, except for the chickens."

"Yes but—"

"Are there any kids staying with you?"

I tell her their ages.

"I recommend you lock up the guns and the rest of those knives."

My heart loosens in my chest. "Have there been any other reports of troubles at the camp? In the past couple of years?" I see Paul on his way up the hill and get ready to end the call.

"I'll check with the sheriff and let you know if I find anything out."

I give her my name and number, thank her for her time, and disconnect just before Paul walks in. The smell of smoke and blood overpower as he stands by my table. I squint up at him.

"Who was on the phone?"

"Mom."

"Saw you talking with Gabe," he says, hunching over and pressing his palms down on the table.

"We were talking about birds. I didn't realize how many types of swallows there are."

"Don't take anything he says too seriously."

"About swallows?"

Paul straightens his back and brushes a couple of feathers off his clothes. "We'll catch the person doing this."

"What will you do when you catch them?"

"What anyone would do. Just don't be too worried, okay?"

"What would anyone *do*?" I don't ask this harshly, yet I see he's lost patience.

"I hope your folks know I'd be happy to let you go until this business is settled."

As he heads upstairs, I consider the odd phrasing, as if I am a package that can be stamped and sent for a quick return. I hear the shower pounding, the water working its way through the pipes like a long, deliberate message.

Going into the office, I look at the guns racked in a glass case. Emmett has an awful lot of rifles, including a couple of smaller ones from when the boys were young. The old case is locked tight. Paul has the key on his key chain. This is the first time in my life I find myself taking a gun inventory.

As soon as I'm done, I escape outside and walk past the empty henhouse. The hinge of the door sounds in the breeze. I go out for a swim like I'm not coming back.

———

This email comes from Professor Madsen three days later.

Dear Nora,

Your dad asked me to have a look at your document. I've been happy to do so. As you know, film is my first language. I grew up in Copenhagen, moved away 35 years ago now, and return frequently. I'm mostly fluent in Danish and English though the chair of our department at the time always begged to differ on the latter. From my imperfect perspective, I have approached your page.

Without a greeting it's hard to think of this as a letter necessarily, yet it has a somewhat conversational tone. With the damage, the blurred and unreadable letters, I don't feel I can do it full justice. I know with modern equipment you could bring more to the surface and I realize you can look up individual words as you have done. Let me instead give my impression, rather than imagine I can give you anything close to a translation. I'm sure someone trained in the field will offer a good deal more.

One thing that stands out to me is: en forbandelse. This means a curse not cursing. I hope it won't unsettle you that I think of this document as a kind of curse on someone. Maybe this is an aspect you will embrace if it's for a film project as your father indicated. It's the repetitive phrases and a few words that have fallen out of popularity in the last few decades that add to this impression.

Here's a string of words somewhat chipped away at that also signal what I'm indicating: Mennesker vil parre sig forkert. This means: People will pair off (or mate) badly (or incorrectly). And then the toughest of the lot: Børnene vil blive taget. The children will be taken. It might imply that spirits take them. Whoever wrote it seemed to be in some type of rage unless it had a purpose I haven't imagined. It could be a page from a manuscript, a work of fiction.

You're correct that the following words are also present: man, loved, wife, chased, hard and union. But guessing, at this point, would be too far flung.

I'm always happy to talk by phone if you'd like. And I could probably find a professional translator if you'd like me to pursue this further.

It's good to know your dad will start his phased
retirement next year. The department has always
undervalued him and I know he has books he needs to
write, that all of us deserve to read. He is truly one of
the best and smartest men I know.

On a last note, I hear you have married again. I
hope you have found happiness.

With warm regards,

Jakob

The words he highlights repeat like that pattern on the
Quarter Room walls until my vision blurs. *The children will be
taken. People will pair off badly.* It's possible I'm putting mistaken
things in the weighing pans, but I feel certain Jones and Leon,
those first cousins, had sex in that boat. And if there is a wrong
couple on earth it is Elizabeth and Emmett. The Brenners seem
wrong, but they could be too far outside the circumference
of this curse, or too many people are inside of it and I should
expand my thinking. I would never want to judge the couples
I've known and be responsible for deciding which ones are right
and which ones wrong. But I worry Paul and I will end up in
the wrong pile if I can't reach him fairly soon.

Catherine might have penned this note before she fled. She
might have sent this after she returned to her homeland. But it's
odd to think someone would stuff it in a boot in her room and
that no one lived in that room again.

CHAPTER TEN

A Simple Casket

I'm looking for someone to film. This is more about camera as medicine than something specific I need to record today. Timothy is out with his archery set. He has painted a bull's-eye on one of the sheds and has a dozen or so arrows in his quiver, the kind with sharp metal tips. The lake is particularly blue right now, providing a good background. The leaves barely move, but now and then, a breeze picks up. I try to put him at ease by making a little conversation.

"We used to use straw targets."

"Anyone can do that," he says.

"May I watch?"

"I guess."

He's his own amalgam of his parents, with big bones and a plain face. He's often expressionless or what I take to be expressionless. I watch him draw the first arrow out, and fix it in the bow and wait. His long bangs flop into his face, and he doesn't move. I know a filmmaker who works this way. He never just lets the camera run. He only wants shots that are curated, timed, controlled. His documentaries leave me wanting. There's no spontaneity or heads lopped off in a frame or anything unanticipated, but he always has plenty of work, more than most. He takes on a lot of corporate assignments.

Timothy pulls the arrow farther back until he looks like a plastic action figure, designed for this one stance. When he lets the arrow fly, it hits dead center in the target, the tip deep in the wood.

"Impressive. Mind if I film for a while?"

"Get too close and you'll get nailed to the shed."

"Okay, then. I'll be careful." I'm reminded of what I don't know about young boys and how they intimidate me a little. I can't help but think about the mantelpiece, the way the knife was driven in with such precision, though throwing a knife and shooting an arrow are such different skills. I crouch and get my camera out of its bag.

He leaves the first arrow embedded in the shed and repeats his careful motions to prepare the next release, seeming to wait longer this time. He doesn't split the other arrow in two but wedges the second alongside the first, knocking it to one side by a couple of millimeters. It would be hard to say which one is exact center.

"Who taught you how to do that?"

"I did."

"Can I ask you something?"

"Maybe."

"Do you believe in ghosts?"

He gets the third arrow in the bow. We both go quiet. He pulls the string back, and the arrow flies into the target's center, knocking the other two out. We watch them drop to the ground.

He tries to bury a smile and says, "Yep."

"Like Jones," I say.

"I know a bunch more than Jones."

"So you really believe in ghosts."

"Who doesn't?"

"I know, right? Do you think this place is haunted?"

"Yep."

"Do you get scared?"

"You ask a lot of dumb questions."

"Just one more, and then I'll stop."

He has an arrow in the bow, arm back, string tight. He turns so his aim is straight at my lens. Everything stops, including my lungs. He could put a dozen arrows in my head before I could take my next breath. "That's kind of dangerous," I say.

He turns away so the arrow points toward the bull's-eye again. "What's your question?"

I inhale. "Who's haunting this place?"

"You are."

I'm not a performance artist willing to ask more to see if he'll face me down again. Grabbing the handle of the camera bag, I back off without turning, as if I'm leaving a monarch. When I get enough distance between us, I maneuver toward the house and hear one arrow after another drive into the shed, each one making my shoulders jump.

Later that day, I see Timothy coming out of the downstairs bathroom where he's pretended to wash up for dinner. He complains to Jones, who's next in line, that he's starving to death now that the pantry locks are back in place. She says she'll steal rolls, apples, cheese, and pieces of pie for him. I have a feeling they have many such bargains.

During the meal, I watch her save out food beneath the

table, tie things in napkins, and fill her pockets while her mother chatters away.

———

A low, fluttering noise comes from the courtyard. Drawing myself out of sleep feels as if there's one heavy blanket after another to throw off. I get up and go over to the window, surveying the lake and the noisemakers in the tree, the empty yard, burnt patch of ground where the bonfire grew and broke the fowl down to their smallest bones.

In a bright flash, I see a ball of blue light.

Shutting my eyes, I wait a few moments. When I open them again, it's gone. I take several deep breaths then head down to heat some water for tea. That's when I hear that noise again, this time from the kitchen, and seize up on the bottom step until it dissipates. I stand in the doorway, not far from the stove, and I'm about to turn on the ceiling light when I see that luminous shape at the other end of the room. Dizziness hits, and I clutch my stomach. Something flies toward my right eye, kisses my face with a sharp pain, and triggers a headache that already feels like a migraine. I look at the empty kitchen, the low light from the moon touching the cabinets, and I sink to the floor.

The room shapes and reshapes itself in my vision until I'm able to get up again. I go through the dining hall and slowly up the main staircase, holding on to the railing. I recall the semester my father taught a course called Beastly Films. He showed movies like *Pan's Labyrinth*, *Godzilla*, *King Kong*. We watched them together before he gave his lectures, talking about myths they're based on, the psyche, the shadow self, the racism and misogyny seeded in some.

Creeping down the hall, I find Jones curled on her bed. Fast asleep, she has one earbud in, the other out. *The Blair Witch Project* plays on her iPad. Her window is wide open, not across from Leon's but within view of it, his light on. Heat has pushed past the thick and deliberate stage. She has broken a sweat. I turn off the movie and say, "Jones, wake up."

She sits bolt upright. "What the fuck?"

I describe what happened, and as I do, I'm not sure what I expect. But I'm telling an adolescent, in the middle of the night, in a barely anchored house about a ball of blue light. She turns on her bedside lamp and says there's a red mark on my cheek. When I touch it, I feel the kind of raw, tender skin I get with a bruise.

"They like you the way mosquitoes like certain people," she says.

"Maybe it was a small bird or something."

Jones reaches down to the side of her bed close to the wall and hauls up a box, setting it on her sheets. Pulling the equipment out, she clicks off her light. We see Leon standing by his window, smoking.

I feel more than silly, but we make ourselves into faint breaths of air and go down to the kitchen. She holds the EMF meter near a light switch—its panel of four red lights turn on—demonstrating the way it reacts to electrical current. When she backs off, the lights disappear like notes down a scale. She does this again near the bulb over the sink. After she makes sure to remind me that the sensor picks up the electromagnetic fields of ghosts, she says, "Show me where you were."

I walk over to the spot where I crouched by the cabinets that hold old pots and pans Salish never uses. When Jones moves the EMF meter over this area, the lights are cold. It is an interesting trick.

"And you saw it where?" she says.

"By the sink at first. Then it seemed to rush across the room. I'm sure a doctor would say it's the start of this migraine." But I don't want to go over to the spot to show her. She runs the EMF meter near the sink. Three of the four red lights come on.

"Turn out the ceiling light," she says. "And tell me what you see."

I'm in this far, so I keep going. We stand in the dim glow from the stove. "Nothing," I say.

She runs her monitor around the kitchen. When she gets to the pantry, all four red lights turn on again.

"Well, yeah. There's a refrigerator, a freezer—" I begin.

Something inside shatters. We jump back. A can hits the linoleum floor, and a jar breaks. I consider that Salish is in the pantry, in a complete state.

"Find your dad," I say.

"I'm not moving," she whispers.

"Then I'll get Paul."

"Don't leave me."

"All right, I'll stand in the doorjamb with my eyes on the pantry, and you go to the bottom of the stairs and call Leon. I saw his light on."

She hesitates.

"Go," I say.

The pantry sounds stop when Leon appears, as if a timer had been set. He thinks this is all pretty funny. He's in a pair of shorts, bare chested, large flashlight weighing down one hand, hair bent upward as if it's a flame lit by sleep. Yet he seems happy to show off for Jones. The handle is unlocked, but the safety locks are tight. He goes down to the toolshed and comes back with a single rechargeable screwdriver.

"I'll do it." I stand on the stool to reach the latches that hold the locks. When I have them off and I've stepped down from the stool, Leon opens the door swiftly. Inside, bags and boxes have spilled and split open. Peanut butter starts to pool from a giant broken jar. Flour still falls through the air, a couple of jars of jam and mayo broken, cans of stewed tomatoes on their sides, a large bottle of vinegar busted, and a bag of cookies torn open, all on the floor of the pantry. I turn away from the smell.

"Fuck," Jones says.

"Fuck," Leon agrees.

Flashlight blazing, Salish appears in the dining room entry. She comes over to the pantry and screams as if a director has pointed to her, saying, *This is your moment.* Rushing outside to her burial ground, she starts to dig the packed soil with her hands, clawing at the earth.

"I'm getting my camera," I say and rush upstairs.

I find Paul buttoning his shirt. Ignoring his call to fill him in, I grab a camera and hurry down, into the night air.

Turning my lens on Salish, I capture her pulling the other two tackle boxes from the ground. Jones and Leon join me. All of us wait. Salish pries the first one open and finds it empty.

"What was in there?" Jones says.

Her mother is on the ground rocking back and forth, trying not to cry and not doing a very good job of it. "My favorite ones."

It doesn't take much to see myself in this moving image. The way my body shook and swayed after I lost Takeo. Only this is about *stuff.*

I get some footage when I suddenly think of Lily. I run upstairs to make sure she's all right. I find her sound asleep, nestled in her bed. I place one arm under her neck, one under her knees, lift her up, and hold her close. She rests heavily in my arms as I rock her back and forth.

Gabe comes out of the boys' room and enters Lily's. "Have you seen Jones?" he asks.

I nod and tell him she's fine. I fill him in on why his wife let out such a scream.

He reaches over and pulls the covers back. "It's okay," he says. "We'll put Lily back in her bed." With reluctance, I allow him to get her settled again.

"Could you check on the folks?" he asks, touching my face.

"Yes. I'm sorry," I say, without knowing what I'm sorry for. I go down the hall, up the three stairs, and peek inside. The hall light beams into Elizabeth's eyes. Stepping inside, I close the door partway.

"Are you all right?" I ask and click on a small light sitting on a dresser.

She's unnerved in a way I've not seen her look before. Pupils dilated, face drained of color, one hand clutching the other.

"Catherine?" she says.

"No, I'm Nora. Here to help. What did…?"

Then I see what she's seen.

———

Jones and Leon help Elizabeth downstairs. They sit with her in the dining room without being asked to. Salish, who tries to compose herself by cooking, has already burned a batch of French toast and scalded the coffee. My husband isn't speaking to me now that I've brought a camera into the room with his father's corpse.

The little ones are still asleep despite everything. If they weren't all such sturdy sleepers, I would worry more.

The windows are fully open, and I imagine it will be a hotter day than yesterday, that the trees will invite the children into the woods, the cabins will be quiet and mournful, the dogs confused as they follow one and the other of us about. I steady myself to document the way the brothers tend to their father's body. Paul is particularly angry with me because, he says, I feel too much about some things yet stand too far back from others.

When Gabe takes scissors and cuts the soiled pajamas, they peel away like an old pelt. His brother looks as if he's about to say something. I don't know why he doesn't. It's hard to know if he's guarding me or himself. Finally Paul spits it out. "You want to document *this*?"

It's true that some documentarians want distance from their subjects—to the point where most things, most people become observation and detail. Others throw themselves in, almost recklessly at first. We can lose boundaries by intention, appear in the work, live with families, upset the balance. The people who document war, that's the toughest. I have a friend who's done this for years—Afghanistan, Iraq, Gaza—where I've always been interested in the small wars. I worked on one film about an abused wife; one on two runaways—a young couple; another about a refugee family trying to reunite while a country wanted to expel them. Though I don't begin with this in mind, I sometimes become an advocate. Regardless, the question of how I might harm or protect by recording difficult things never goes away. I get through by holding the camera as still as I can until I reach that point where I know I have enough footage and the story will tell itself in the editing. That's typically when the full weight of the thing hits me.

I have an almost overwhelming need to record this moment with the two brothers as they attempt to put their terrible father to rest.

I can't even start to respond to Paul's question.

"How long will it take the doctor to get here?" Gabe asks.

"I'll call him if you finish up," Paul says to his brother.

"There it is," Gabe says.

"What?"

"Leaving me to clean up. Why does that seem familiar?"

"If you two have nothing more to work yourselves up about," Paul says. "I'd like to get this wretch into the ground."

"Fuck you," Gabe says. He goes into the bathroom. He lathers the soap. Maybe this is his effort to wash off the sins of the father and the brother. He yanks the towel off its bar, throws it on the floor, and storms off.

The minute Gabe is gone, Paul washes his own hands of everything, and he disappears.

I turn off the camera and set it down on Elizabeth's chair. With a fresh bedsheet from the stack on the dresser, I cover Emmett's blue form entirely, but I won't be able to hide his grimace from my mind. Maybe his sons will return to finish cleaning him up before the doctor arrives, maybe not. I wish I could go back to my room for a cry, but it becomes harder, not easier, to do.

Turning to leave, I stop when I see Lily standing there with Mason. Lily holds her nose. He's got a goofy rubber mask over his head. It's clown-like and looks rather old. Being a big fan of the photographer Ralph Eugene Meatyard, I've come to realize that Mason isn't simply a child cosplayer, he's making sure all of us stop and pay attention to a form of art. Without Timothy's ability to rattle nerves or Lily's cuddliness or Jones's cool, this is his way of marking out his territory. I think this small boy who tends to get lost in the shuffle but observes the world through many masks may someday be a sculptor or actor or painter.

Rushing over, I try to scoot them out of the doorway, but Mason resists as if his feet are glued in place. "What's that?" he says in a voice that bounces off his mask.

Again, I am met with a moment when I can't imagine how a parent talks about the large matters of life and death. Lily wriggles herself backward to the edge of the top step. I scoop her up in my arms and take Mason's hand.

"That's the ghost," Lily says.

"She's been stealing Mom's knives," Mason says. "Look."

I don't know what he's talking about, so I try to see things from his height. That's when I find the glint of metal beneath the bed. I set Lily down.

"You're looking at part of the bed frame," I say, blocking his view.

"I can't see," Mason says.

Raising my voice, I say, "Go downstairs. Both of you. Now. Or I'm counting to three." Mason stares at me through his eyeholes. Lily looks stung. I have no idea what I'm doing, but know I better change tack. "I'll give each of you a chocolate bar in a while if you go downstairs and get your breakfast."

After they run off, I shut the door. Getting on a pair of latex gloves, I go over to Emmett's bed and crouch down. My horror reflex kicks in, and I imagine him reaching out from beneath the sheet to grab me. I remove Salish's cleaver by the handle, slip it into a plastic garbage bag, lock the door, and go back to the Quarter Room.

I enter Catherine's room. Despite not having a whole door, I feel safer here. I stand on the lower edge of the open wardrobe and stretch to hide the cleaver on top. I look at the dresses again, the blue uniforms, the coat that would never get anyone through a winter here, then I try it on to understand her size. It's only slightly larger than my coats, the sleeves a little long. I imagine Catherine standing here, ready to explain what happened.

There are no names stitched on the pockets of the uniforms ironed without starch, an old scent of hard work and deodorant still under the arms, as if she planned to get one more wear out of them before doing her wash. The shoes are a size or two larger than my shoes. I go through each item again looking for anything she might have hidden before she left to be with her family.

In the other half of the wardrobe, there are five drawers. A small collection of practical underthings includes white panties that would pull up to the waist and white bras stitched into soft points. Socks rolled up with one missing its match. A few T-shirts, some with long and short sleeves. Three cardigan sweaters, one from Denmark embroidered with flowers on the collar, wrapped in tissue paper as if it had never been worn. In the bottom drawer along with the pajamas, I find a small photo album, some of the pictures stuck to their plastic sleeves.

I pore over a series of family pictures, one in a hilly region, maybe homeland for the girl who grows up successively in the images. The early prints are scalloped at the edges and fade into orange impressions of the late 1950s. Now I see it's Denmark as I consider the town, the signs over the doors. The photos stop abruptly, and more than half the album was emptied out or had yet to be filled. I find a small flat pocket inside the back cover and slip my fingers in, shifting a photograph back and forth with care until I'm able to draw it out. The girl with the long blond hair has become a woman in her late twenties or early thirties. She's with a man of roughly the same age. He has an arm around her shoulders, and she leans her head against his chest. Surely, they were in love. This was taken by the boulder where we spotted the marker. There's nothing written on the back. I believe I've found Catherine and Walter. It feels as if I've discovered lost family members. I put them in my pocket for safekeeping.

Before I close the drawer, I notice the tip of a small box at the back. Inside is a pair of gold earrings, quite old, perhaps her mother's or grandmother's. I put them back. It makes me mad that no one took the time to send them to her along with her other things.

The side table by the bed has a box of Kleenex on top, and a tweezers, hair clips, scissors and so on in its one drawer. As I turn back toward the opening, I'm badly startled by Jones on all fours.

"Jesus Christ."

"Shhh," she says.

I'd forgotten to brace the chair against the door of the Quarter Room.

We return through the opening, and she takes a seat on my

bed. She grabs one of my hair ties off the bookshelf and draws her hair into a loose ponytail. I show her the photograph. Then I fish around in the file where I placed the other photo—the one I had stolen from the Wedding Room. "Catherine," I say. I explain who she was in relationship to Walter.

"Oh my god," Jones says. "Wait here." She leaves, and I can hear her in Leon's room. She returns a few moments later.

"Leon found a suitcase in a crawl space at the back of his closet. There was a tuxedo inside and a fancy shirt and one of those things that goes around your waist..." She gestures with her hands.

"A cummerbund."

"And dress shoes. And this." From her shorts she pulls a packet of photos and negatives. The photo she removes and places on the bed is identical to the one I've removed from the inner room.

All the rest are images of Catherine around the campground. I assume Walter took them.

"Have you ever seen a really great magician?" I ask.

"I saw David Metalfarm make a bus disappear on TV."

"It's possible someone is making everything *appear* like a haunting."

"Explain the pantry," she says.

"The food is thrown around when we're out of the house. A recording of the sounds is made. Or pulled up from the internet."

"Then we'd find sound equipment."

"Were you the first to clean up in there? I wasn't," I say.

"What about the flour in the air?"

"It might have been the draft from opening the door

suddenly. The thing is, if we're being manipulated, who would do that?" I ask.

"Cuts? EMF readings?" Clearly agitated, she gets up from the bed.

To this I could add the way in which Walter's name was cut so quickly into the closet of the cabin. "I'm still trying to piece things together."

"I heard you found something under Emmett's bed."

"News travels."

"Mason was pretty hopped up about it."

When she gets to the door, I say, "Before you take off, can I talk with you about something else?" I know my voice strains. She comes over and sits at the desk. "I want to say there are reasons to use protection. I picked up a box of condoms, and I've tucked it into the linen closet. It will be there. Just saying."

"What?"

"You know, with Leon."

She laughs and says, "You can't be serious. He's my cousin."

———

The doctor arrives in the late afternoon in his small gray sedan. He's short and trim, and despite a heat wave that kicked up yesterday, he wears a suit and tie. Dr. Liebold appears to be in his late fifties or sixties, and his hands redden when he washes them, even under cold water. I don't know if the illness or death of one of his patients makes him cheerless or if this is his usual self. Maybe it's the way the washboard section of road works on his kidneys.

Salish offers him a cup of coffee.

"I'll see to Emmett first," he says, waving her off.

Paul, who eventually returned to the house to clean his father's body, goes upstairs with the doctor. There hasn't been any construction noise over the course of the afternoon. Gabe is down at the dock with the younger kids, fishing. I've not seen Jones or Leon for a while. I sit in the game room with Elizabeth, reading to her from the Bible and watching her nod off.

After a time, Dr. Liebold comes downstairs by himself with his medical bag. He washes his hands again and comes over to take Elizabeth's pulse.

"Should I wake her?" I whisper.

"Let's let her sleep. Has she been eating right?" he asks.

"A little less the last couple of weeks. I worry she's not getting much in the way of physical activity."

"It would be good to get her moving," he says. "Either way, you might see a further decline now that Emmett is gone. Will you check in with me next week?"

"Absolutely." Then I ask if he'd take a quick look at a condition I have. He wrinkles his brow. Perhaps he's had a long day.

"Yes, if it's quick," he says and follows me over to the back stairs.

Salish steps into the hallway just then with a cup of coffee and a bit of pastry she made that morning.

"Dr. Liebold is going to look at a small injury I have. We'll be down shortly."

"I'm happy to look at it," she says, "so he can get back on the road. He has a drive ahead."

"We'll be right down," I say.

"Is it a cut?" she asks.

"This won't take long," the doctor says, ending the discussion.

Upstairs, I ask if he could wait one second. I understand his lack of patience, but I retrieve the cleaver, seal the small door, and invite him into the room. I sit on the edge of the bed, and he takes the desk chair.

"I assume anything I say will be kept in strict confidence."

"There are certain reporting obligations," he says, opening his bag.

"I understand. That's what I'm hoping, actually. That you can report something to the authorities. I found this underneath Emmett's bed. There's a trace of blood on the blade." I set the plastic bag with the cleaver down on the desk.

He peers at the contents without touching it. Giving me a frustrated look, he says, "I was about to let his sons know that Emmett died of natural causes. Honestly, I'm surprised he lasted this long. There were no signs of harm. No lacerations."

"I'm not questioning that, just the reason the cleaver was under his bed and whose blood this might be. There have been unsettling things going on."

"I realize you've been through an ordeal. I'm happy to prescribe a tranquillizer or something to help you sleep."

He might as well have used the word *hysteria*.

"I don't need to be subdued, but I am mostly stuck here without a car, and I'm asking for your help. Would you give this to the deputy?" I push the blade along the desk in his direction but he doesn't pick it up.

"I rarely get over that way," he says.

"I've talked with her, and she can't really help with anything unless she has evidence. And you'll get there sooner than I will and…"

"Evidence of what?" he asks. There's a particular look, the one certain men reserve for women who have something important to say.

"I've explained everything to her. I'll get her on the line if you stay one more minute."

"I'd suggest you give her a call after I'm gone." He stands and leaves the cleaver on the desk. "If there's nothing I can do *medically* to make you more comfortable in the coming days, I'll say goodbye."

———

If I were to post my current life into a diary entry on social media, to get a reaction from *friends*—including the volume of people I have never met—I might get information on anything from how to behave around ghosts to what to do when the knives go missing. A string of jokes would follow. A couple of GIFs. A long, dopey meme. The people I love would tell me to protect myself and the children. Then I would be reminded by other, more distant connections, that Lily's not mine and I have no legal standing if I whisk her away, as if I'm about to do this. I can hear the one guy who would say, *Certain circumstances should defy the law.* There's always a troublemaker, but maybe that makes him a little smarter than the rest. I just don't know.

I've seen enough to understand that Gabe loves his children. He sees to them the way he sees to his birds, at least when he's about. But he can't tend to his mother, the meals, the house, his research, and the little ones, along with the material culture of the property, as his brother concentrates solely on buildings and his wife weeps into a bucket out back because she can no longer cope, if I take off.

My mother once said if a parent has done a decent enough job of things, we hear their voices in our heads in a healthy way. Dad's voice tells me to pack a bag, have a plan, and be brave. Mom's voice defies all her own advice about autonomy and tells me to come home, *now*.

But I can't leave my girl, Lily. Or Jones. Or the boys. I want to call child protective services, but I'm sure I would end up with the kinds of reactions I got from the deputy and the doctor. *Have any of the children been hurt? Do they have shelter and nourishment? Are they in imminent danger?* And so on.

———

I'm surprised they bothered to put Emmett in a decent suit. And then I realize it's the one Paul brought for himself, just in case he had a need for one. It's his wedding suit. Emmett drowns in it, and the whole idea unnerves me. Paul stays up to make a simple casket. It is rough-edged, absolutely rectangular, and goes into the grave they dig away from the house and the lake yet still on the property. Their father is lowered by ropes that the brothers wrestle into the ground.

Gabe assures me it's better that Elizabeth remain in the house during the burial and imagines her husband is away. Paul, who has a different opinion, thinks Elizabeth should be graveside for the burial. This leads to another argument I stay out of entirely. I'm surprised to see Salish side with Gabe on this. I imagine it has to do with the extra work she might go through if Elizabeth becomes too upset. For now, Elizabeth stays put in her room.

No words are said over Emmett. At least none that will help. No hymns sung.

The children are asleep, and Salish and Gabe will talk with them.

"They hardly knew him," she says.

It's true Salish was always shooing them away. I can't imagine a colder way to return to the earth.

The rest of the morning is quiet, and I begin to weed through my things to consider what I will take if I have to leave in a hurry and what Lily will need.

CHAPTER ELEVEN

Better Run

Jones is paid to take her sister and brothers to Brenners today. Near the stream there's a badminton net on almost level ground, and the store is newly outfitted with cheap toys. But it's the smelly freezer full of ice cream they're after. Paul will drop them off along with an emergency food list so we can restock our pantry. Jones will fill a cart with any items in stock that aren't too old. Then she'll give an amended list to Mr. and Mrs. Brenner to call into the distributor that covers our rural route, which means we'll probably end up with some of those post-sell-by items anyway. Gabe will pick the kids up in the early afternoon.

Jones is eager to get another package that should have arrived at the store by now, and all are given spending money. They will return with bags of candy, too many of the dollar toys and god knows what all. Last time, Timothy brought a cable cutter back with him that Gabe took away and locked in the toolshed. Keys are no longer left over doorframes.

As Salish packs their lunches, Lily sits on my lap at the kitchen table. The boys are out in the yard, and Jones has started the clock on her time card. Lily takes my face in her hands and tilts my head so she can whisper to me. Her fingers are sticky from ketchup, something she likes with her morning eggs. "You should come with us," she says.

"Wish I could."

Salish takes the lunches and separates them into four backpacks. "Keep a good eye on them today," she says, "especially near the stream."

"And I wouldn't because?" Jones says.

"Sorry."

Lily is like a small radiator. A bead of sweat rolls from my right temple, down the side of my face.

"Why are you crying?"

"Just warm, sweetheart."

She buzzes in my ear. "The woman does that."

I'm not sure if *that* means crying or sweating.

"What woman?" I whisper back.

She might be thinking of her grandmother, or maybe this is something from one of her books or a recurring dream. I've often wondered what Lily sees when she sleepwalks. Jones begins to pay attention to our conversation.

"The one who smells like oranges." Lily's favorite bubble bath is orange scented. "She likes your room the best."

Jones gives her a look with a little scold, and Lily pulls her lips together into a straight line. Salish seems too busy to notice. Jones did tell me that small children can see ghosts.

Later I'll add Lily's observation to the computer file I keep with known events in one column, along with impressions and speculations in another. I have been keeping a tally of the knives, and I've made simple renderings along with taking photos and hours of video.

"I hope you didn't put brownies in. They get wired enough," Jones says. I'm surprised she hasn't bothered with eye makeup today, but she does look half-asleep.

Salish removes the brownies.

"Coffee?" Jones asks.

"You don't want coffee?" her mother asks, tugging a thermos out of the biggest pack.

"I'll die without coffee," Jones says, getting more annoyed. "But I'd like it iced and sweetened."

Salish pours out some of the coffee, slips in ice cubes and scoops in sugar, shakes it vigorously, and puts the thermos back in place.

"I was dreaming about egg salad sandwiches last night," Jones says, looking out toward the lake.

"Oh, I made chicken salad sandwiches. Do you want egg salad instead?"

It's curious to see these moments when Salish is little more than a short order cook and Jones takes full advantage. "That's okay." Jones yawns, goes over to her mother and puts her arms around her shoulders, embracing her in a funny sag. Salish welcomes Jones's slack affection and tucks a strand of her daughter's hair behind one ear.

The boys wrestle outside.

Going over to fill a glass of water at the sink, Jones watches them for a while. When she turns back, she says, "What are you guys up to?"

"The adults are meeting about the…you know," I say.

Jones looks toward the knife drawer and shakes her head.

"I know the you-know," Lily says. She never likes to be left out of anything.

"What?" I ask.

"You know," she says.

"Ah, I thought you knew," I say.

"You're wasting everyone's goddamn time," Jones says to her mother.

Lily's eyes go giant.

"Lang..." Salish stops herself. Clearly, she doesn't want the day to unhinge over a swear.

Jones grabs the backpacks. Lily jumps down and scoots in front of her. The screen door slams behind them. "Let's go," Jones shouts to the boys. They walk over to the van, and her sister hoists Lily into her booster seat. Thankfully Jones tends to favor her. Mason sticks his tongue out at Jones's back. He wanted to spend his day diving from the dock in his scuba man outfit. Timothy drags his feet, though he usually likes to go into town.

"Jones will be all right," I say to Salish when the van disappears down the road kicking up a plume of dust.

"She wasn't like this before we moved here." Salish reddens.

"It's a lot of isolation for someone her age, with a mind that quick."

"I can't say Leon is a good influence."

"I wouldn't worry too much about him."

But Salish doesn't want to not worry about Leon. "We better get started," she says.

I shrug. "Every minute counts?"

Salish inspects all the drawers and cabinets in the kitchen. She rifles through the dining hall. I upturn the children's rooms—extra careful to put things back in place in Jones's room where I find a small blown-glass pipe that appears to be recently used, a bag of weed, and the box of condoms I left in the linen closet, that I quickly tuck away in case Salish appears.

When Paul gets back from dropping the kids off, he hits the office and the game room. Together we check the bathrooms. Leon goes through the cabins, starting with the unrenovated ones, and eventually goes through the showers. When we're done, we meet at the boathouse.

Along with the rowboats, there are rafts and floats, umbrellas and towels, snorkels and water toys stored in one shed alongside the washers and dryers. I ask Paul about an item, thinking it might be a knife thrower's wheel. But he tells me it was spun to give prizes away when there were camp competitions.

"So no wives strapped to the wheel?" I ask. He gives me his impatience where once he seemed to like my humor.

In a nearby shed are pickaxes, low chairs, collapsible huts, and fishing poles for the cold months. Paul had moved his tools into a third shed but eventually changed course and set up shop where Walter used to work. I wonder which shed had been used to skin animals. Regardless, Paul is the keeper of keys to all these things.

When we're done, we split up and go through each other's rooms. No one says out loud that this is as futile as the locks and keys on the pantry door—someone could shift the knives around as they search. Anyone could make an arrangement with anyone else if they were so inclined. And did we look through every last thing?

We turn up little more than frayed nerves and a barely placated Salish, who pled with us to do this search. There isn't a single blade or object of deeper curiosity that surfaces, but Paul finds the USGS maps, saying we can fan out another day and look for a squatter, despite the fact that some of us have pretty much scoured the area on our hikes. We finish the search in Elizabeth's room, though it's not as if she would take the knives. I go up with Gabe. We find her conversation more disjointed than before, as if all of time exists in the present moment. Something from the 1960s happens along with something from the 1990s and 2019. She asks where Emmett is, and I say he's out of town for the day and should return soon. This does seem kinder now than making her live through his death repeatedly.

———

Salish tucks her hair into a rubber swim cap and adjusts the bottom of her one-piece. Power tools sound in the distance. Once her flip-flops have started to smack against the dock, I go outside and ask Gabe for a ride. He's fired up the minivan to pick up the kids.

"Hop in," he says.

We seal the windows and blast the air-conditioning. But when we're out on the road, the sun hits my eyes at a direct angle just as the washboard begins. We rise and fall until I ask him to stop. He turns the engine off in the middle of the road, confident no one will be coming or going. I get out and throw up by the grassy edge. It's as if an entire lake full of fish and algae spills from my mouth. This has been going on all week, and I'm aware this happened the first time I was pregnant, in the first trimester—the daily purge. If it hadn't gone away, I would have been checked into the hospital.

He's out of the van, asking if I'm all right.

I wipe my mouth on the back of my hand. "I should make

a film compilation where people are asked if they're all right while throwing up."

He comes up with a bottle of water overwarm from sitting in the van, and says, "As long as I don't have to hear the soundtrack."

I rinse and spit, and wash my hands. "Did the food make you sick last night?" I ask, hoping to pin this on Salish.

"You've got food poisoning?"

"Possibly."

We get back in the van, and this time Gabe slows down over the bumps. I'm not sure what's worse, the fast or the slow approach.

"I'll feel better when I get a cold Coke." I move the visor around. "Tell me how you're coping."

"As long as I'm working, I'm good. And it lifts my spirits to be around you, to be honest."

I ignore this and say, "The kids seem extra restless."

"They're worried about their mother, and they need their friends, and they need to get back into school this fall."

This is the thing about Gabe. He will simply answer me. Nothing held in reserve, nothing that seems buried.

"If you have one too many, I'd be happy to take Lily off your hands."

"Not a chance."

The road evens out, but the lake still churns in my stomach. I grip the dash. We approach the store, and Lily rushes from Brenners into the road to greet us. Jones runs after her, and as I brace myself, Gabe stomps on the brake.

I jump out of the van. "You can't run out into the road, Lily," I say. "It's too dangerous."

"I saved a Dreamsicle for you," she says, looking weepy.

"Listen to Nora," Jones says, pulling her sister in close. "We don't want you to get hurt. We love you way too much."

Gabe seems to understand that Lily doesn't need a third scolding. She comes over and tugs me across the road into the store, where I hand her back to Jones, with an assurance that I'll be there in a minute. It has to be ninety-five degrees out. I have the dry heaves in a patch of shade on the other side of the road. The dresses in the abandoned store seem to move when I look up.

Gabe hands me an icy Coke as I return to Brenners, then he challenges the little ones to a game of badminton. Mrs. Brenner distributes rackets and birdies, and they head outside to the net. Lily has forgotten the Dreamsicle but turns and says, "You have to watch me."

"I can't wait. I have a couple of things I absolutely have to do first, and then I'll be right there. I promise."

Mrs. Brenner picks up ice cream wrappers and starts to wipe down the counter. Jones looks through the magazines, pretending a celebrity rag from five years ago is of interest. I know she lingers to hear what we have to say.

I write on a piece of paper and hand it to Mrs. Brenner. *Two more kits please.*

She smiles just a little and opens a brown paper bag. Dipping under the counter, she places two pregnancy tests inside. Mrs. Brenner straightens and folds the excess bag, sealing the whole thing with a rubber band. I don't turn to see what Jones is making out of this.

"Are there any letters for me?"

"Nothing from Japan," she says.

This isn't like Satchiko. I wonder if I should write a second letter. Or send a note to Akiro, my brother-in-law.

"You know the scrapbook I'm putting together on the camp? Is there a chance you have a card or letter from the great cook you told me about? Catherine?"

Mrs. Brenner glances at a bulletin board filled with postcards from former camp people. "She's up there somewhere."

I look over at Jones, who has flipped quickly through the stale list of Hollywood breakups. One of her eyebrows is raised. Mrs. Brenner studies the board with me, drawing out pushpins and flipping cards over. She pulls one down with no address, a clear postmark, and foreign stamps. A winter scene of a quaint village is depicted. It's written to Mrs. Brenner, whose first name is Clarice.

We've had beautiful holidays. I hope everyone is well and enjoying the break. I'll see you at the end of the month.
~Catherine

I note the date stamp is from the year Walter died. "May I take this? For the albums?" I ask.

"I don't see why not. Now, what else can I get you?"

"I'd like two six-packs of Coke. I can grab them on my way out. And I need some rope."

Mrs. Brenner sends me over to the spools of rope, cord, and lanyard material so I can cut what I need.

Her husband comes out from the back just then. "We won't be ordering more rope, so you'll want to use it sparingly," he says. There is nothing but rope on giant spools in various thicknesses and materials. Miles of rope tightly coiled. To his wife he adds, "Your soap opera's on."

I cut what I need, and Mrs. Brenner adds the total to our account. She reminds us to return all the rackets and birdies before we go, and excuses herself. Jones puts the magazine up, and we go outside and watch the game for a while. As I nurse my Coke, I see she has a box with some type of equipment tucked into her pack.

Timothy is almost as proficient at badminton as he is with archery. Lily calls to me when she finally hits a birdie, but she and Mason drop away before too long out of frustration. Gabe and Timothy play a fierce round, and I suggest we go back to camp when another match is proposed. I want to lie down, and Lily is getting grumpy and mulish. Jones has already gone through the wooden lost-and-found box out front, something she does each time she comes to Brenners, as if a treasure might surface. A sullen Mason is just wading into the stream in his rubber fins, snorkel, and Godzilla T-shirt, looking like a creature from the deep. I've not driven into town with all the kids before and realize anew what a lot of work they can be.

On the way back, the little ones make the sound of *whoa* in chorus each time the van sinks over a line of washboard. Gabe directs the AC into my face to soothe me. I put my head between my knees as if I'm on a flight going down.

"Nora isn't feeling well. Can we have a little quiet?" he says.

"Is she going to die?" Timothy asks without a cynical note.

"No!" Lily says.

"She's fine," Gabe says. "Everything's fine. It's just her tummy."

"I'm okay, Lily," I say.

"A blue jay!" Mason shouts.

"He was *like* a blue jay," Gabe says. "I'll show you later in one of my books."

"I don't feel good," Lily says.

"Copycat," Timothy says.

"It's 'cause she ate four ice cream bars," Mason says.

"Did not," she says without convincing any of us.

"Did too," Mason says.

"Everyone shut up," Jones says. "You're giving me a headache, and Nora doesn't feel well."

Then it's settled. Except for the occasional small groan from Lily, it's just the tires and shocks rising and falling and dropping through our stomachs, the engine trying to keep up with the AC.

———

Salish strikes the dinner bell in a manner that says, *You better run if you hope to get a scrap of food.*

I take one of the six-packs of Coke down to the water and thread the rope through the plastic yoke, lowering it into a cold spot. I know in cooling them this way, they become vulnerable to seizure. Mason in particular likes his Cokes. But I'd rather not depend on Salish for opening the pantry and meting out one ice cube at a time. I tie the other end to the dock.

The small black dog comes along and sits next to me. When a good breeze picks up, I think of the couple of days

I had with Takeo in Salzburg up in the high country. I had almost made it to the second trimester. I had no interest in learning to sail or pedal about in the water, so we decided on a slow-moving tourist boat that stopped at various docks. At one of the landings, a caregiver wheeled a teenage boy onto the boat in an adult stroller seat. The man lifted him out of the chair and carried him up to where we sat drinking tea. This boy had no control of his body. His head repeatedly jerked to one side at a painful angle. You could count the seconds by the way he called out in yelps. He had no words, but the earth and the sky knew his agony. Several people got up and moved away from him. Takeo was the one who moved closer.

We drank our tea and took in the mountain peaks and heard this boy's voice echo against the homes along the shore. Halfway through the ride, the boy began to laugh using the same energy he had given to his cries. I wondered if the water or the motion of the boat had finally soothed him. I looked at Takeo. I prayed our child would never know this kind of suffering, but if she did, I understood Takeo would be there to try to alleviate it.

The black dog follows me when I get up. I find a cluster of trees far enough from the campground to hide behind, and I tell her to sit. Removing the rubber band, I take one of the kits out of the paper bag. I check the use by dates; good for another year. I piss on the stick and pull my shorts up. We wait with limited patience, both of us pacing about. She sniffs the spot where my pee soaks the ground.

A plus sign swims across my vision. I wonder if this could be right. The dog decides she is bored with my company and takes off for the cabins.

———

In the middle of the night, with a half-moon hanging over the treetops, I hear our coyotes. They've moved closer to the camp. But it's the sound of the lake hitting the shore that makes me think something is trying to reach the house.

I stretch one arm deep into the linen cabinet and find the paper bag with the second test. In the bathroom, I pee and pee over the stick, as if I will never have enough pee to know for certain. With my penlight, I read up on false positives and take this plastic stick with its plus symbol, its sincere possibility, and put it back in the box like tucking a child in for a nap. I'm aware of tiptoeing around my emotions, afraid to startle them.

Wrapping the box in its brown paper bag again, I fit this into its hiding place. This seems safer than the garbage. I feel certain Salish examines the waste with her thick rubber gloves and a medical mask, as if her thief can be exhumed from our coffee grounds, used Kleenex, and empty bottles of bug spray.

———

Into the early afternoon, I've kept company with the spirits in a favorite novel, *Eva Moves the Furniture*. Finally putting down my book, I get up and reach toward the ceiling, bend to touch my fingertips to the floor, stand with arms out and twist at the waist like the slow movement of an oscillating fan. Once I'm done with a full routine of stretches, I get into my robe for a shower, and that's when I hear two people talking. They sound as if they're in the room with me, but I can't make out their words. I'm convinced it's a man and a woman. I don't think they're arguing, just engaged in intense conversation.

Looking down into the courtyard, I see no one is about, just the rutted ground, a Hula-Hoop, small trucks, and the empty henhouse. Sounds can certainly bounce around in this U-shaped house, but all the rooms are dark and quiet, only the voile curtains tugged by the breeze until they're drawn back again. I go out into the hall, where everything is still except for the sound of a whisk scraping against a metal bowl in the kitchen.

The farther I move from the Quarter Room, the more the voices notch down to soft whispers. The closer I get, the louder. I go out and come back in to convince myself. Standing near the window, I press one ear to the wall Catherine and I share. They sound louder still. I take a glass off the desk, swallow the water inside, and hold the glass up to the wall, my ear against the bottom. The voices amplify, but meaning remains a decibel out of reach.

Securing the bedroom door, I go over to the bookshelf. I press against it three times until it pops open. The voices stop. I'm too scared to look inside. I can't run because I suddenly can't move. I am, however, able to break into a sweat. I feel light-headed and start thinking about orange things: floats and sticky orange pastries and a mixed drink I tasted once called a Warhol Orange. Something eclipses my vision as I drop.

Splayed out on the bed when I wake, I note the passage to Catherine's room is closed, nothing out of place. There are no unusual sounds, the temperature is constant, and whatever orange thing Salish has cooked—or Jones would say the spirits have cooked—no longer fills the summer air. It must have been someone talking in some part of the house.

———

We get a hard rain the next day that exposes the tops of a few straggler carrots in the garden and keeps the dogs inside. When Takeo was alive, he was the only one I considered when I needed to be alone. I went off to the loft where I had my equipment and desk, and he understood this impulse. Of course, we ate most of our meals together, slept together all of our nights, worked on the house on weekends, had dinner parties. But it was easy to go off and think or brood when I needed to. Now there are people everywhere, yelling to one another as the lightning strikes.

Looking out the dining hall windows, I wait for the next bout of thunder.

Timothy says he wants to play Guillotine. Lily and Mason insist on Candyland. After a while they settle on Clue. Leon and Jones are willing to sit at the table with the lazy Susan to help the little ones understand the mysteries of life and death, Professor Plum, and candlesticks. But even the knife that's supposed to be in the game isn't in the box. They use a dime in its place, and none of us says a word to Salish.

Paul decided today was the day to finally get around to removing Walter's name from Violet. I hope he stays put until the lightning stops. It's right there, striking the lake. I knew someone struck by lightning as he sat on a beach—ignoring all the warnings—as if the only dangers were in the water.

Gabe is upstairs logging in swallow data. Salish is trying out new coleslaw and fried chicken recipes. As I head up to my room, I hear Leon on his guitar. Putting my hands in my pockets, I feel the edge of Catherine's postcard. Her full name is on the card, so I search online until I come up with a phone number.

When a man picks up, I ask if he speaks English.

"Little."

"May I speak to Catherine?"

"No Catherine."

"May I ask how long you've had this number?"

The line goes dead.

I get the international operator and find out the number of the post office for the town where Catherine lived or the town where she dropped the card in the mail. The official who answers at the postal station speaks fluent English but is busy and doesn't give out private information. When the clerk hangs up, I slump back in my desk chair. Spending another hour roaming the internet for Catherine, I watch as the worst of the storm passes over.

Returning to my list again, I add more. *W. Walter. Animals. Bonfires. 1-inch cuts like ladders. Bowie, paring, slicer, cleaver, butcher's, boning, fluting. Marriage. Ghost marriage. Coyotes. Broken doors, locks. Sleep, no sleep. Woods, lake, cabin fever. Pregnant. Lily. Ghost movies. Ghost stories. Campground. Tropes. Hot and cold, life and death. Documentary. Truth. Lies. Keep batteries charged. Something is terribly wrong. Maintenance man. Dead man. Apnea. A room within a room. Voices. Slaughter. Blue light. Slap in the face. A coil of rope. A letter in Danish.*

Try as I might, I don't know how to crack a code in which some things at Hidden Lake can be so easily explained and others fly off in the face of time, space, and reason.

———

I would never say Takeo had an interest in death. But he did love history where death is a close partner. When he first mentioned the catacombs in Vienna, I wasn't so sure. We had already taken three ghost tours in Prague, and we had driven out to the Sedlec Ossuary—the most bizarre skull-and-bones chapel I have ever seen. But he asked sweetly, and there we were, descending below the Church of Saint Nicholas on our honeymoon. "We might not be back in this region again," he said, and he was so happy on these tours. Takeo was the one who asked the tour guides extra questions, tipped them more than our tickets cost, referenced these experiences in dinner conversations.

In the rooms of the catacomb, peering through small internal windows, we viewed bones heaped like mounds of broken china. I couldn't imagine how long it might take to dig to the bottom of one of these piles if anyone had to. Skulls, tibias, collarbones. Some had died from illness, some from war, starvation, childbirth, strife. Most of the living taking the tour wanted to get a look, or couldn't resist a glance, but Takeo stood transfixed. And once the tour was complete, he promised to take a selfie with me in front of Klimt's *Kiss*. Like adding a love lock to a bridge, I didn't need to be unique in the way I loved, just his. I liked the small rituals he teased me about. A couple of nights after that tour, I saw a child standing by my bed in the middle of the night, a small girl. Gradually, I realized I was dreaming, and this child dissolved. This was the first time I saw someone, or my imagination of someone, appear that way. Later I would wonder if this was the girl I lost.

———

I wait until lunch when Paul comes up to the house with Leon, both of them sweaty and dirt-streaked, ready for a large meal. Each gets a cold glass of lemonade with ice cubes that Salish sets out for them.

She tends to push the rest of us away, directing us to the small bathroom near the office to wash up. I stand by the coffee machine and watch my husband work the soap into a fierce lather. Reaching for the nailbrush she allows him to keep by the soap dish, he tears at his skin not just around the nails but over his knuckles. He goes at his palms as if he's trying to eliminate his own lines, fortune and life, certainly heart washing down the drain.

He hasn't spoken to me since I filmed Emmett in his death state. I've reached a limit with the rasp of silence. "That's gross," I say.

He doesn't respond. He doesn't turn around.

I repeat this louder, and Salish drops one of the hamburgers she was about to place on a serving platter. She's so angry, she opens the screen door and pitches it to the dogs. Paul turns all the way around, soapy water dripping off his hands. Leon watches.

"That's where we wash vegetables and dishes. Can't you clean up in the bathroom like the rest of us?" I say this though I don't give a rat's ass where he washes up, and he knows it.

"I don't see what you're worried about," Salish says. "*I* wash all the vegetables *and* the dishes."

"Because you're a control freak," I say.

"*Now* what's going on?" Paul asks.

Leon laughs.

"Why don't you hand him a nice fluffy towel," I say to Salish, "so he can get ready for another one of your gluttonous meals."

Her eyelashes flutter wildly.

"You have to have something better to do than pick on her," Paul says. "She's working pretty hard around here."

Gabe steps into the doorway from the dining room. "Everyone okay?"

"Don't you start," Paul says.

Gabe looks to me for an answer.

"Paul and your wife here think we want to run a campground instead of selling this hellhole," I say.

"What?" Salish says.

"Hellhole?" Paul says.

"It'll be Christmas by the time you start on the house," I say.

Just then, Mason sneaks up behind Gabe, wielding his plastic knight's sword. Paul sees him standing there with his helmet slumped over one brow, but none of us seems capable of checking ourselves.

"I refuse to talk to you if you act this way," Paul tells me.

"You won't miss much," Leon assures me. I didn't realize they're coming unglued as well.

"Ha. And I refuse to sleep in the same bed with you until you get this f'ing place sold." My dilute swear in honor of Mason.

"I'm happy to sleep in one of the cabins," Paul says, turning back to rinse his hands.

"He's finally happy, folks. Thank god for small blessings." I feel a miserable satisfaction in reaching for this last foothold but I know he's not about to move out into one of the raw cabins.

Timothy smiles. "She said *fucking*."

Gabe says, "Almost. And she's an adult and—"

"I wouldn't say that," Salish says.

Gabe tells Timothy to go call his siblings to the long dining room table. As soon as he runs outside, I move so I'm standing in front of my sister-in-law. "Enough!" I say and slap her across the face. Leaping at me, she hits me on the head. Paul, who's closest to her, grabs her around the middle and pulls her away.

"Go for a walk," he tells me.

"Fine," I say. "But when I come back, I'm going to make a sandwich and have a Coke with real ice cubes, and if any of those fucking locks go back in place before I get a fucking chance to fucking do that, I'm going to take a fucking sledge-hammer to this fucking kitchen."

"I think you can let my wife go now," Gabe says to Paul and walks outside.

I go down to the lake and look out at that roiling view where they can't see my absolute relief.

CHAPTER TWELVE

Voices in the Next Room

Gathering wildflowers for Elizabeth, I hope they will entice her to take a stroll. Or that the colors, at least, will call up a pleasant memory. Arranging the purple flowers in a mason jar, I tell Salish that Elizabeth needs extra jam for her morning tray. She dishes it up aggressively.

The yoga instructor I work with back home is a big believer in visualizing good outcomes. I'd like to imagine Elizabeth might do well in a comfortable nursing home once she settles in. There's the one my grandmother lived in for a time. I believe it was run by the Presbyterians. I write to Mom to get the name and ask if she recalls what they paid each month.

Humming to myself, I go upstairs, where I tap lightly on Elizabeth's door. "Good morning," I call. Going in, I don't see her. There's a mound of Emmett's clothes on her bed, some on the floor surrounding it, as if she was searching for something—maybe him. The bathroom door is open with no one inside. I set the tray on the table. The closet is half-empty. Only her dresses and coats remain. All the hangers on his side are bare, and his dresser drawers are open and mostly cleared out.

Hearing a muffled sound from the bed, I quickly yank the clothes off, and she takes a gasping breath.

"Are you all right?"

Her mouth is open, and her eyes are wide as silver dollars. "I think I'm dead," she says matter-of-factly and starts to pull herself up to a sitting position.

"You're okay. Fully alive," I say.

"But I haven't gone to confession. He might not let me into heaven."

I push the last of the clothes onto the floor. "Of course he will. We'll just have some breakfast, and then we'll get you fresh bedding and a new outfit so you'll be ready when he comes." I have begun to speak in plural.

Elizabeth nods but is still shaken.

"Who did this to you?" I ask.

"I didn't see her."

"So a woman?"

"Yes."

"Have you been awake long?"

"I don't know."

Once I get her sorted, I look at the heap of Emmett's clothes. "I'm going to get the maid to wash these," I say.

"I like it when they hang on the line."

"I do too." Looking down into the empty courtyard, I start to feed Emmett's T-shirts and pants, work shirts and underwear, nightclothes and socks out one of the windows, my anger aloft for the way he treated her.

I hear the kitchen screen door smack against the side of the house. "Stop that!" Salish yells from down below. "Stop it right now!"

Elizabeth gets up and steps over to the windows. She takes

the last few shirts out of my hands, and one by one, we watch as they flutter in the breeze. When we're done, I look back at her.

"The color has returned to your cheeks. I was thinking you might want to take a walk with me today."

"Maybe tomorrow," she says.

As I pick up the room, Salish appears in the doorframe, out of breath. Taking a quick look around—at a space freer of Emmett—she glowers.

"Tomorrow it is," I say.

Elizabeth waves goodbye as if she's about to set sail.

———

I find Paul throwing *his* clothes into a suitcase on our bed. He stops as I sit down next to it. "You don't have to sleep in one of the cabins," I say.

"You'll be better off." He grabs a stack of his T-shirts and crams them into his duffel on my desk chair.

"What's this about?" I say.

He pulls a handful of balled socks from his drawer, and they shoot from his hands. Finally, he looks at me. "I can't compete anymore."

"With your brother?"

"What about my brother?" he says.

My face heats up as if I've done something wrong. I've never welcomed Gabe's attentions. "Okay, I'm lost."

"You're living with someone else, not me."

The blue light is back. It fills my vision like a sheet of wavering glass. I close my eyes for a moment. "If this is about Lily…"

"I understand. Takeo was a great man, god knows. But you haven't even tried to let him go. When I ask if you'd even consider keeping this place with me and building the life I want instead of the one you had with him, you have nothing to say. You're living with a dead man."

My heart arrests and then beats too fast. I've never compared him to Takeo. Not out loud. Not once. And this idea, that Hidden Lake is what he wants so badly, sounds like a holy grail. What on earth does he churn over as he works on those cabins? "That's the cruelest thing anyone has ever said to me."

"I'll apologize if I'm wrong." He zips the duffel and pushes it onto the floor. "I'll get this shit later. If you don't throw it out the window."

I reach out and grab his arm. "He was my best friend too, you know. And I never lied to you about anything. And I'm here, aren't I? I've seen to your parents. I've put my house in jeopardy. I've—"

"Jeopardy," he says, pulling away. "If you thought my work would put you in jeopardy, why the fuck did you agree to a second mortgage?"

I am struck by the way marriage and mortgage seem so interchangeable now. I try to imagine a world in which I'm able to forgive him in time. But all I want now is safe passage for the kids. I soften and say, "Maybe once we leave here and get some perspective..."

"That's why I told you to go home," he says as if I've disobeyed him.

I could tell him I'm pregnant with his child, of course. I could tell him I love him. But I can't.

I follow him out to the hall and watch him descend the stairs, through the icy landing, and deeper into the pain Hidden Lake cuts into us.

Repacking his clothes, as if this will help anything, I zip both bags and place them in the hall by the door. I make a strong tea and send a note to Lauren. This is the middle of the night for her, so she won't get it for several hours. I ask her to think of the Hidden Lake children next time she meditates in the temple she visits. I ask her to pray.

As soon as I hear a hammer strike wood again, I walk down to the lake. The small black dog follows. Going to the end of the dock, I feel the binding of this place tighten. I strip down to nothing and dive in.

Surfacing, I turn to face the property as Leon steps out of a cabin, his tool belt sagging on his hips. He just stands there. Gabe is in the water near one of the coves. He swims my way. Moving in the opposite direction, I head to the far shore.

Despite my hard strokes, Gabe catches up and we stand neck-deep in the lake breathing to exhaustion. Leon looks tiny, the dock almost invisible. In the bright sun and water, Gabe's head appears to be separated, almost floating away from his body, and his expression is apologetic. When he shifts into a shady spot, his full torso reconnects to his head, and maybe he looks sly.

This will be the hottest day yet. Ninety-eight, I read this morning. I fear we're going into a dry spell.

Gabe's responsible for more people than I am and has differ-ent types of loss to address. I tell him about the way I found

Elizabeth this morning, that it's time to take the children and leave. All of us have to leave. The worry I see in him creates its own current in the water.

"Salish would never let me take the kids. Not in her current state of mind."

"Just take them. You have rights. Or let me go on a trip with them until this is over? Sign something—like temporary travel permission. My parents would help."

He looks at me as if I'm taking on water. "I told Paul this morning I'm going to grab a tool belt and get to work each afternoon, get up earlier every day. I've got the files we need out of the office. We'll make this happen as fast as possible."

They imagine they can stop time before the past buries them.

I swim back to the dock and pull myself out of the lake. I find a towel in the boathouse and head back to my room to rest. I'm no longer throwing up every morning, but I do get caught in waves of nausea.

———

In the overly hot air, I think about my afternoon with Lily. Everything is better when I'm with her. She recognizes some of her letters now, many colors and animals, and is learning how to swim without water wings.

I start to tell her sister this, but she shushes me. Jones has set up a new recorder and microphone in Catherine's room. All of this because I said something about the way sounds can travel in an old house—barely touching on the muddled conversation from the hidden room. We wait until the house is fast asleep, and we're sitting on the Quarter Room floor in the computer's faint glow. I have a camera ready.

Usually, I make out moths at night against the window screens but not this evening. The moon is a sliver.

"Shit," she whispers. "Hear that?"

"Just the pipes."

"Okay, don't say anything."

We wait and listen so long, I nod off. I wake to that baleful animal sound. Jones pokes me in the arm. "Ask him if he's here."

"What? Ask who?"

"Your dead husband."

"Oh, no. No, that's a bad idea," I say, sitting straight up. Much as he loved pop culture, if he were alive, Takeo would be embarrassed by this display. I am. But I'm also a little curious.

"Are you Nora's husband?" Jones asks.

My ears drum.

"Can you talk with us?" She jabs me in the arm again, and I open my mouth as if she's trying to turn a rusty key. "We're here to understand."

"I can't," I say.

"We want to know how you're doing," Jones says.

A sad temper moves through, and a high-pitched sound begins, similar to my tinnitus but different. More of a pulse.

"Are you moving the knives around?" Jones asks.

The sound picks up. It's almost a chirping now.

"Okay, that's ridiculous," I say.

"Don't you want to know?"

I push the red button on the surge protector. The equipment goes cold. "I really can't. I'm sorry."

"No worries," she says. "I'll run what we have through the program. You don't have to listen. If you'd rather not."

"I guess I'll listen," I say and direct my camera on this operation. "But then I'll try to get some sleep."

She flips on the surge protector. When things are up and running again, she downloads the recording to Audacity to boost the faintest sounds.

Are you Nora's husband? There's a sound with a high lilt, nothing like my husband's tenor. "Did you hear that?" Jones asks.

"Maybe...a female voice?"

"We'll keep going," she says. *Can you talk with us?* Another indistinct cluster of sounds follows. "Jesus. There it is. *Knives talk.*"

"I might have heard the word *nerves*," I say.

We're here to understand. The next string of sounds is the most garbled yet.

"That one. That was clear as a bell," Jones says. "*Listen to them.*"

"I think I heard *lustibum.*"

"What does *lustibum* mean?"

"Hell if I know."

We want to know how you're doing. There's a long pause and then a low, guttural sound. *Are you moving the knives around?*

The recording cuts out.

I crawl into bed and shut my eyes. My whole body feels scratchy.

Jones turns a light on, and I open one eye long enough to see her tug the recorder and microphone back into the Quarter Room by the cords so she doesn't have to go into Catherine's room. She seals the bookcase shut. Now that it's quiet, I'm glad for her company.

"I definitely heard *knives talk* and *listen to them*," she says.

I shift about until I find my usual hollow in the mattress.

"What do you think the knives are saying?" She seems younger in this moment. Her voice a little scared. Reaching for her water bottle, Jones nudges me to move over.

It's a decent psychological question if nothing else. "Let me think."

"The chicken thing really freaked me," Jones says.

"When we went to Walter's stone, the swallow was pinned to a house. And the knife in the mantelpiece pointed to the photos," I say. "And the name Walter in the cabin was clear."

"The cleaver under the bed, that's like a curse. It has to be Catherine."

"...who's angry and brokenhearted because Walter was killed at the campground?" I say.

"Fuck, you didn't tell me that."

I do my best to fill her in on things held back. But I return to this thought: if there were spirits, I would hear Takeo. He would do anything to help me.

When I'm back in California, my mother will come up with real-world explanations for each peculiar event I'm willing to divulge. My father will consider the lighting I describe in detail. And then, after a while, he will say I should think of this seed inside me as Takeo's and mine and never tell Paul. Mom will agree.

It's 2:00 a.m. when Jones slips away to Leon's room. I remain awake until morning.

—

I get a hard-boiled egg to swim in the bottom of my stomach. This must be my first craving. I shake plenty of salt over the next one, suddenly in need of saline. I don't want to see the yellow, or a fleck of red, but I need to taste the yolk intensely. Shutting my eyes, I gobble it down and start to peel another. Salish watches with interest but turns away the minute I stare back. We've barely talked since the kitchen brawl. The family continues to seal its doors.

With the start of a headache, I've made the decision to not use anything, even Tylenol or Motrin, until I see my OB at home. Grabbing two more eggs and one of the saltshakers, I go into the office and dump out a box of old receipts. Upstairs. I make a nest in the box for the camera that has a way of sitting in my hand with familiar ease. This is the one that produces the most crystalline images—the irreplaceable one. After this I make sure I get the latest backups of my files to the laptop. I send what I can to Dad online. Shoving the box into the far reaches of my closet, I cover it with the dirty laundry I have little interest in doing. When I flee, I'll make it seem like I'm simply going to the store. I'll be ready the second I can take the kids.

Standing by the window, I listen for noises: ticks, whirs, chirps, as if the code has been broken on random sound and words are built in, waiting to be found. The power saw starts up.

It's odd for Salish to go for a swim this time of day, especially the way the wind roughs up the surface in patches and tugs at the trees. I go down to an empty kitchen to see if there's anything to eat and realize it isn't Salish. Elizabeth is the one heading toward the lake in a housedress.

When I see her call to the little ones—Lily and Mason taking hold of her hands one on each side—I fly through the door and ring the bell as hard as I can as they get their toes into the water.

Running down the hill, I scream, *"Help! The kids!"*

Time sputters and brakes while my muscles strain their limits to reach them. No one comes. Lily is trying to dog-paddle the way I showed her. Mason is trying to keep up. Panic is swift, almost moving me backward as I call out again for someone to help. I get to them just as Lily dips below the surface.

Diving into the water, I sweep my arms around until I touch one of her legs. With both hands, I pull her up from the bottom. Mason is still above the surface. I tell him to keep paddling as I hold Lily to my bosom, carrying her onto the shore. I check her breathing and pulse and begin CPR. When I turn back, I can't see Elizabeth. Water leaks out of Lily's mouth. She begins to cough. Mason has started to flap wildly. "Use your arms and legs," I shout. "Kick, Kick!"

I get up to run into the water, but Leon is ahead of me. He reaches Mason just as he slips under the surface. Leon cradles his cousin and brings him to shore, turning him on his side. I think Mason has taken on more water, more of the muck than Lily. In my sorrow, I see small vessels, floats, and underwater toys pour from him. Blades of light flash in the shape of fish.

For a moment Takeo is on the ground unable to breathe, life going out of him.

Mason's water runs like blood. I can't help think, if he had dressed as one of his superheroes today, he might be in better shape.

Paul rushes by and hauls a boat into the lake. He rows out and out, circling, caught in the same rings made from the tips of his oars.

With Leon seeing to Mason, I hold Lily close as she cries. My husband stops and puts up his oars. He hauls his mother's lifeless body into the boat by her arms. My brother and sister-in-law appear in too many stages of dread, Salish pulling Mason from the ground, Gabe tugging Lily from me. They carry the little ones up to the house.

Jones stands on the shore with me as Paul and Leon get Elizabeth's body from the boat. Her long white hair, broken free from its tie, is laced with algae. Water streams off her dress and body.

"She's already a ghost," Jones says. Leaning against me, she breaks down.

———

When Jones returns to the house, I sit by the water and think of the day we buried Takeo. His family has one of the older burial sites in Kyoto. Up a low hill, surrounded by maple and cypress. Each leaf green and healthy as if life would go on. There will be room for me one day, his mother assured me with delicacy, when she asked if she could lay her son to rest in Japan. I had never heard Satchiko sound that frail.

I couldn't recall where I had read that there's a shortage of burial sites in Japan. That's why developers put up buildings sometimes mistaken for offices or condos until the signage goes up. Inside, each floor is lined with tiny vaults that gradually fill with urns. In one building, with a personal code punched in, panels light up in a variety of colors, and an image of Buddha retrieves the family remains. I was glad Takeo wouldn't be kept in a vending machine. I hope I didn't say that to Satchiko. She's too dear to me, but I was having trouble knowing when I said things inside or outside my body. I agreed he should be set to rest in Kyoto, and someday, I would join him.

As the ceremony began, my mother squeezed one of my hands. A Shinto priest officiated. I recognized distant family members from the small trips Takeo and I had taken around Japan, though names slid in and out. Once a year we went to Kyoto, where Satchiko, her other son, Akiro, and his family live. The sons grew up in that city of temples. We always stole away to new regions during our three- or four-week visits. We went to Karuizawa, Nagoya, Sapporo, Osaka, to name a few, and often to Tokyo, where he indulged my curiosities. We had lunch with giant stuffed animals, went to the top of Skytree, walked inside Buddha's head in Kamakura, ate at conveyor-belt sushi bars. We stood in the middle of Shinjuku bathed in neon light and checked out the best yakitori restaurants tucked away in narrow alleys. Our favorite was back in Kyoto, and we saved this for the last day of each trip along with Sanjusangen-do, the temple with 1,001 statues of Kannon, goddess of mercy, each statue carved of cypress and covered in gold leaf, where I had prayed for a child many times.

As the priest recited his prayers, I wanted to run away to Tokyo with my husband, riding the train through the rice fields to see a view of Mount Fuji, though it's typically shrouded in fog. But I was there at Takeo's burial studying my brother-in-law's face. He was the one who had to sift through the ashes to pull out fragments of bone at the mortuary. I knew at the time that this wasn't occurring. I know none of this ever occurred.

My dress fluttered against my legs in a sudden gust as if I were fully present. I looked at each face like this was a casting call for a documentary no one wanted to be in. The robes of the Shinto priest billowed as he went through songs of death. His hat was kept in place with a chin tie so it wouldn't sail off and become a silk boat. Incense coiled against shafts of sunlight, and a tall white birch ached.

I didn't want to think about the air that day and how turbulent it was. But I wouldn't have wanted Takeo to be buried on an ugly, calm day. Down the hill, a few hundred feet from the grave, is a temple. As I looked at it, I realized I'd been there with my husband once. It's dedicated to Marichiko, the boar god. Paper prayers danced on wooden racks, and the longer I gazed at them, I found myself there, writing out wishes and tying them with red ribbon along with everyone else at the temple. And, just as quick, I was looking up at myself at the gravesite, at the woman who had lost her husband. For a moment, I was in both places at once. Maybe this is the one thing I know about death now—that we leave our bodies as the dead leave theirs.

The prayers stopped, and my father steadied me. Some of the elderly relatives started to disperse. I had been unable to cry from the moment of my husband's death, and I had cried so hard, I had turned to salt. A monk at the temple pulled a heavy beam suspended on ropes and struck the giant bell. I heard the sound *widow* travel up the hill to meet me. When I looked back, I saw Takeo.

The air was knocked from my lungs. He stood next to Satchiko. I knew he wasn't there, and I knew he was. I mouthed the word *wait* to him. Quickly, I told my father I needed some time by myself. While Satchiko and Mom negotiated my aloneness through a series of looks, I worried that Takeo would grow impatient and leave before this was settled. I said to them, quite firmly, "I'll join you in a little while."

Drawing a small thermos of tea from her bag, my mother-in-law placed this in my hands. Then she started down the hill with my parents. Taking a seat on the bench, I finally turned away from them. There was no one visiting the other plots at that moment. Takeo's eyes were glassy and sleep-deprived, his hair mussed by the wind. I had wondered, if he came back to me, how he would look. He loved Japanese ghost movies, but he would never want to scare me. The slashed-mouth figures are the worst. But his mouth was his mouth, and he wasn't blue or ashen or thin as film. He was just Takeo in a pair of black pants, the charcoal jacket I bought him last year, and a white shirt with no tie, as if to say he understood the occasion but wasn't taking it too seriously.

I touched the bench. "Sit with me."

This drew a smile, but he stayed where he was, and I realized I couldn't move, as if fatigue had fastened me in place. The tree made that sound again, and I understood it could collapse on us. Wiping my face with my sleeve, I said, "The thing is, if you stay here, in Kyoto…"

The sky was full of alarm at my words, and I couldn't finish my sentence. It was essential that he follow me home. I wanted him to hold me tight as binding and pour everything back inside me, but he lingered in that one spot, listening. Or what I imagined was listening. I have plenty of footage of him that I can watch on an infinite loop. But this will never fill in all the gaps. In time, I will forget his speech patterns when he was surprised by something; how he looked at me when he wanted to make love in the afternoon; the way he sometimes raised an eyebrow as he glazed his pots. I'll be left with a facsimile in fixed scraps of time.

"I wouldn't do that," he said, his voice animated.

"Promise."

"Yes," he said. "I promise." This was his most serious tone. I waited until it stopped echoing against my inner ear. With his assurance, the days of little sleep began to tug at me.

"Rest," he said.

"If you stay with me."

"I'm here," he said.

I shifted around on the bench. I removed and folded my coat, and nestled it under my head. Tucking my legs up, I lay down near my husband's grave and tried to keep my eyes open.

When I woke up, I was at my mother-in-law's, in Takeo's old bedroom, on his futon. They said I slept for two days and nights and was halfway into a third. I don't recall anyone carrying me, the ride back to her home, the business of getting undressed and putting on a nightgown before I dropped off.

After I bathed and ate something and had a night with his family, I flew home with my parents. I held the secret of Takeo's appearance close. If I told anyone, they would say it was a dream. And my mother would remind me again of the things shock can do.

CHAPTER THIRTEEN

Graveside Tales

D r. Liebold comes out to the house again, and I do my best to explain what happened, though I'm guarded with him. I don't mention anything other than the way Elizabeth walked into the water, holding the little ones' hands, as I ran after them. Leon adds what he can, followed by his father.

That night, I see the glow of lantern light through the trees from Paul's cabin. He sits at a separate dining table at lunch the next day. We don't talk as we pass each other. It's when he gets a shovel out of the shed and I'm heading down to the lake that he confronts me. Driving the sharp tip of the blade into the earth a couple of feet from me, he says, "When did you see her enter the water?"

"I ran the second I saw her going toward the lake. You were there when the doctor said it was probably related to heartbreak syndrome."

"You should have kept a better eye out."

I hold back from telling him this is irrational, but I do say, "I was the one who kept insisting she be in a nursing home."

He pries up the shovel and heads toward the burial site.

I call after him, "And I'm not the one you're angry at. You

realize that, don't you?" But it's possible my voice echoes around the lake and just misses him.

———

Maybe Catherine's ghost swept in and killed Emmett like pulling a giant statue of a dictator from their pedestal. But all Elizabeth seemed to want was to sit by her windows near her husband and listen to Bible passages and wavering music. If I had to diagnose her underlying illness, the thing she couldn't rid herself of before Alzheimer's took over, I imagine it was fear.

Gabe tells me Lily has made a full recovery, and I should see her running about today. She doesn't want to go back in the water, however. Mason has developed a heavy cough. I've heard it in the courtyard echoing out of the Wedding Room where he rests today, and I worry about the way Salish will try to treat this condition.

As I sip my coffee and mull this over, Paul steps into the Quarter Room without knocking. Dirt covers him from head to toe. He drops a packet of mail on the bed. "Grave is dug if you want to come and say something. Or just be there." He looks contrite, at a loss.

"What about a casket for her?" I see the top envelope is from Japan. Paul's dirty fingerprints are impressed there.

"She never wanted one."

"She told you that?"

"More than once. I'm… Maybe you want to read something from her Bible?"

"I'll be there shortly."

"Look, I'm sorry. About things."

"What things?" I say. Because I honestly don't know at this point how short or long the list is in his head. I knew a woman who went back to her husband each time he apologized. I saw the bruises.

"Never mind," he says his voice pulled taut. "They came a few days ago," he says, indicating the letters. Then he just stands there, waiting.

I'm not sure what I'm supposed to say or, if I say it, how he'll react. But I can ask this: "Why didn't you give them to me a few days ago?"

"A half hour, and then I'm covering her." He says this as if he's putting a car cover on for the night.

I shut the door behind him. Taking the rubber band off the stack, I try to brush the fingerprints away. I open the letter from Satchiko.

She tells me about her garden and a theater performance she went to. She is reading the new Murakami book and wants to know if I've started it and, if so, what I think. We've read all of his earlier ones at the same time, starting with the first. She reads him in Japanese. I read him in English. My mother joined us after a while so the three of us could discuss the books by mail. I've kept all the letters.

There's a broth-less ramen recipe she's written out in her small handwriting that forces me to read her words slowly. But I am also savoring, anticipating. I get to the paragraph that reminds me of the lanterns we set along the Kamo River in Kyoto. As we watched them move into the current, Takeo wrapped his arms around me, all of us sending out prayers for continued happiness. We felt profoundly lucky.

I would give anything to know you and Takeo were coming here this fall. My life was full of joy when my sons and their wives were in Kyoto. I know that neither of us will fully recover from his loss. I see him standing in his old room. I see him in the garden. He takes my hand when I cross a busy street. He opens the umbrella for me when the rain strikes at a hard slant. I hear his voice in the morning before I call up to him to see if he wants eggs or fish.

I worry that you are too lonely at this camp and that this man is making you lonelier still. Have you considered going back to your own home where you can be near your parents? You must know you are always welcome here. You could stay in Takeo's old room for as long as you like and we could go to temples and pray for him together. There is a small one that is close to the grave site. It was built in honor of the boar god, Marichiko. I sat inside and asked that things go well for you. As soon as Matsu shows me how to download the photographs, I will send you some pictures.

Before I close, I want to say, don't ever hesitate to do what Takeo would wish for you. He wanted you to be happy, more than anything in the world.

There are something like sixteen hundred temples in Kyoto. We could visit them all.

I am full of tears I can't express. It worries me knowing Paul could find this letter. He could rip it from my hands. Maybe he's already read it and resealed it.

This is not written on the kind of paper I could hide in plain sight. In thinking over how to protect it, I open the bookshelf.

This is the first time I've approached Catherine's room since the recording. As I peer inside, I listen intently but find no chirps or ticks. I see where the recording equipment made a trail through the dust when Jones pulled it back into the Quarter Room. Going inside, I feel calm in the unbroken air.

Looking in the wardrobe again, I find the same dresses, blue uniforms, and coat hanging there. I examine the drawers as if she could fold herself into a sweater. She's not under the bed. When I step to the window, I place my hands against the glass and push it to the top. Mason's cough is rougher now, almost untethered. It sounds like asthma might be contributing to his problems.

I hurry back through the opening, and take a moment to stop in the bathroom to wash my face and brush my hair. I slip Satchiko's letter into my bra and go after the Bible.

———

Standing inside the grave, Paul pitches the shovel up. It slams into the tree under which his mother will rest. With Gabe's attention on Mason's illness, Paul has been the only one to dig into the soil laced with clay. This hard-sliced earth is packed with an abundance of roots, far more than his father's grave an eighth of a mile from here. I feel certain Elizabeth would want to be right up against his casket, right in the heaven and hell of her husband, assuming there was some fragment of heaven I missed. But Paul has centered her in the shade of this oak tree—unlike his father's balding patch of grass—and dug himself in. Elizabeth's body is wrapped in a quilt in the back of his truck, waiting.

Gabe appears, and Paul tells him to hand her down.

His brother has received three children into the world, held them and rocked them and lifted them into beds, cars, and houses, no doubt whispering to them in their sleep. I could imagine him scooping his mother up this way, until she's cradled nicely against his body. But Gabe shakes his head. There are a number of signals he conveys with this gesture, and I can't interpret all of them.

As the winds hit, I see the quilt lift off her face. Her long white hair is unbraided, her eyes skyward. No one has bothered to shut them, to let her rest. I wonder what they want her to see.

Paul pulls a handkerchief out of his back pocket to clean his face, but this only smears the dirt and sweat around. He looks down at the cloth as if it contains his image and he isn't sure what to do with the way it looks back at him. Shoving this into his back pocket, Paul holds on to the lip of the grave and pulls himself up and out.

My husband gets off the first blow and a series of smaller jabs. This is the same hatred that has worked its way through each board he's replaced in the cabins, each tar patch he's fixed to the roofs. It rips through the air when the power tools kick in. It levels its judgments on all of us. But Gabe has buried his hatred deeper. He strikes Paul's jaw hard, and Paul goes for his brother's gut again.

When Leon approaches, I'm surprised the brothers care what he thinks, but they stop and back away from each other. Everyone is exhausted. Gabe gets Elizabeth covered again.

The scent of marijuana travels with my stepson all the time now. He looks at his father and uncle and says, "You're disgusting."

I emphasize to the brothers that the little ones will be here soon.

Leon drifts down to the dock, and Paul and Gabe get their mother in the ground, securing the quilt around her. When the family is assembled, I look at the brothers to see if they have anything to say over her. There's a gap in time as if they can't see the opportunity as it rushes past. Gabe bows his head. Paul looks away. Jones signals to me that I should proceed. Leon comes over and stands next to me. I can tell he wants to get this over with as he shifts about.

It seems Timothy has a collection of found objects in his pocket. He pitches a pebble at my ankles, and then another, both shots hitting their target.

"Stop that," Gabe whispers loudly.

Jones picks Lily up and holds her on one hip.

I reach down and rub my ankles where the rocks stung. "Elizabeth liked this passage," I say, straightening. "So that's what I'll read."

Timothy sneaks into his pocket again and hits my right shin. Coming around behind him, Gabe clutches his shoulders in a firm grip to make him stop.

I open the book, and the piece of paper I used to mark the spot flies out. I try to catch it, but it lands facedown in the grave. My mind jams. Timothy laughs openly, and Gabe appears to grip tighter. I know it was in the Book of Revelation, but I blank over the passage. I pull Elizabeth's Bible open at random and start to read. "And their widows will not weep for them. Though he heap up silver as dust and prepare raiment as the clay…" I have landed on Job, and we are all a little confused. I stop and suggest each person drop a flower or feather or *pebble* in the grave.

Lily whimpers, "I don't have a flower."

"Hold on," I say and find a wildflower for her. "I think this tired girl needs a snack."

"I need lots of snacks," Lily says.

Jones leads the way. The grandsons and granddaughters head back along the path. The orphans remain.

Paul picks up the shovel.

"I'll do it," Gabe says.

"I'm going to do some editing," I say.

"When there's real work to do?" Paul says. This is from Salish's list of complaints. It echoes with all the people who think art is a way of pushing off responsibility instead of taking on more. His voice has even picked up her inflections.

"Give her a break," Gabe says, grabbing the shovel and starting the first rain of earth over their mother's wrapped corpse.

"Stop fucking with me," Paul says.

"That's funny. Are you fucking with him?" I ask Gabe, who laughs and continues to pitch the earth.

"I don't think so," he says.

Paul goes over to his brother, gets up in his face. "*You* were supposed to stay."

"What the hell does that mean?" Gabe says.

"I would have killed Emmett if I'd stayed." And there it is. Paul has untied one of his masks, his sorry head weighted down with masks.

"You left, I get it," Gabe says, trying to express something close to understanding.

"But you left *her*," Paul says.

"I was supposed to be sacrificed to him since you couldn't be? Do you have any idea how twisted that sounds?"

"You'll never get it, will you?" Paul says.

"Not unless you explain it to me better than that."

Paul walks off, maybe to shower, maybe to swim or just to sit on a cabin bunk clinging to his picture of things. Gabe continues to fill in the grave. I go up to the house, throw a few items into my pack, circumnavigate the cabins, and head into the woods.

CHAPTER FOURTEEN

Starting Fires

My plan is to walk for a couple of hours before dinner and know anything other than the fevers and chills this camp produces. Takeo and I hiked for miles on end after we first met in Prague. When we moved to Berkeley, I showed him my favorite trails in the Bay Area, and we backpacked in the Sierra. Each fall we found a way to travel, stretching our legs out by rivers, and working our way up steep approaches, down narrow streets, and along wide boulevards. We considered pet rescue sites once it became an essential idea to find a good hiking dog who would circle and protect. After a search for breeds, we talked about getting a border collie or an Australian shepherd. But then I became pregnant and we decided we'd wait until after the baby was here so we wouldn't take on too much all at once.

At Hidden Lake I've mostly circled through the woods in a loop that's five miles round, or gone down along the cabins and the lake, then up the hill where there's a giant rock outcropping with orange lichen that looks as if the rocks are set on fire. Both of those trails would be too hot today. I head straight to one of the older, somewhat overgrown paths I haven't tried yet. It's well shaded and cool, and foraging might clear my head. A raptor calls above the canopy, most likely an eagle.

I begin to think about life after this camp. Maybe Gabe and

Salish will calm down once they're in their own home. The kids will return to friends and school, of course. I wonder if there's a way I could go through an entire divorce without Paul finding out about this pregnancy, if the lawyers could simply do battle over assets.

Sitting on a downed tree, I bite into an apple, working through the moment when I will tell my parents. I imagine we'll cluster in their living room or on their patio chairs if the weather is nice. It's always hard to catch whole conversations near the koi pond—the hum of the old motor, Dad and Mom joking about the rock concerts that did their hearing in.

A trail of large black ants moves along the log where I sit as I get out Satchiko's letter again. Standing up, I'm aware of the closed-in nature of the woods and the way the light has started to recede. I don't have my small flashlight or the kinds of items I would take on a longer hike or overnight. I've actually lost the direction to the camp.

A metal feeling hits my chest despite years of packing and knowing how to get to work. I sip some water and take stock, coming up with a thin plastic rain poncho, mosquito repellent, a snack bar, a couple of ounces of walnuts, and a banana that's brown from the heat inside my pack. Headband, phone, Kleenex. I wouldn't mind having some of that rope I bought or a box of matches or my Swiss Army knife. I check the outer pockets. Seeing the snakebite kit, I realize it includes a small scalpel. There's Takeo's compass with its stuck needle that I keep for good luck. I have a half bottle of water.

My choices are to keep hiking while there's some light, and risk going off in the wrong direction or settle in for the night and make a fresh start in the morning. I read about a woman in Hawaii who planned to take a short walk on a trail and left her water bottle in her car. She pressed on and took a wrong turn. Seventeen days later they found her caked in mud and eating the large moths that landed on her.

I clear some ground. Using the scalpel, I carefully whittle one end of a stick into a point, hoping the blade won't snap. I take a bigger piece of wood and make a crosscut in that the way my mother taught me years ago when we took family camping trips. With the sharp tip set into the crosscut, I get some friction going. My hands tire as I rub the narrow stick back and forth in my palms. Tiny sparks flare, and I add a bit of dry moss and leaves. They catch fire but go out just as quick.

I refocus and gather more dry material and more downed branches. Before the last of the red light draws out of the treetops, I have a good fire in place and dig a cat hole for a toilet.

I work on a basic lean-to, cover those branches with my raincoat, and fill in the floor with any materials that are close to soft. I have to eat the whole banana since there's no way to preserve it. I do this slowly, relishing each bite. Then I bury the peel. I know I'll have a headache by morning without any tea to drink.

There's still no signal on my phone, not that I expect one. Just the habit of phone. I could pull up the book I downloaded, the music, or turn on its flashlight, but the battery is low. The fruit in my stomach feels overripe.

I take a piss, cover this, and sit by the fire until I'm drowsy. Before I get into the lean-to, I knock the fire down. Using my backpack for a pillow, I try to rest. Despite these efforts, the entire earth pokes into my back, and each time I shift, the leaves chatter.

Coyotes begin to sound. They must be close. I've read that only two people have been killed by coyotes in North America, so I'm not too worried. I turn on my side trying to get comfortable, and then I let go of the idea of comfort and think of Takeo, his mother, my parents, and Lily.

When I wake, it's pitch-dark. There's a noise. That huffing animal sound is close to me. I want to pull my feet in tight to my body, but rustling leaves would announce my location. With some animals, any movement is a bad idea. I lie still, pretending to be dead.

Breath chuffs against my ankles. It slowly moves over my legs, takes hold of my arms.

Pain cuts into my chest, and I feel blood ooze down my torso. I try to stop shaking. Covered in sweat like a second skin, I press my hands against the wound and wait out the terror. A high, fleeting voice says, "It wasn't Emmett."

It's beyond reason, but that's what I hear. Precisely. Loudly. It's something like the voice we recorded and filtered in the Quarter Room. It has that same lilt and insistence. I don't believe for a second that I'm hearing voices, and I can't not believe what I hear. As I turn this over, I see her standing by the cold fire. She has the short-cropped, blond hair and the swimmer's body—the woman who, like me, has lost her great love.

Like a fairy-tale moment of being granted three wishes—or that instance in the Prague underground passages of the Astronomical Clock where Victoria lit up the EMF meter—I know I should ask something. But if I do, am I asking about

Takeo as if all spirits are linked by some means and she will get a message to him? Do I press to get her to name Walter's killer? Do I trouble this glimmer in the woods about the god-blessed knives? As I quickly run through my choices, I direct my phone's camera in her direction, shoot, and she's gone.

The pain and blood start to subside, but now I can't sleep.

For months I've hoped to hear Takeo's voice again, to see him appear, even a shadow moving from one room to another in the house. Any little sign or foolishness to let me know he's still with me.

Maybe he could only be with one of us and Satchiko called to him with greater urgency. As I think this over, whether he is close or far, I doubt he has the same sense of time that I do, otherwise he wouldn't make me wait like this. I begin to wonder if all this calling out to him, this deep summoning, unearthed Catherine instead. I try to find some logic in the illogical, sleep in the sleeplessness. I know what my mother would say about all of this.

———

There's the fresh cut down my chest at first light, my T-shirt stained with blood. When I check, the scalpel is in the side pocket, back where I put it. Trying to steady my nerves, I fold the raincoat and stuff it in my pack. I sip some water and eat a couple of walnuts. Remembering the picture I took before I fell asleep, I turn on my phone and pull up an image of the woods made stark by the flash. Nothing out of the ordinary, except, perhaps, the thinnest band of light, like the edge of a one-foot ruler in the distance. I'm trying to account for this when I remind myself I will have plenty of time to study it later. I better keep as much battery as I can.

I don't know how far off track I've gotten. I eat sparingly.

Slipping Takeo's stuck compass out of my pack, I place it on a boulder. Taking a small rock, I smash the glass face. I pick the stuck pieces out, wedge the scalpel under the needle, and free it right before the blade snaps in two. I'm facing north. This doesn't provide a direction since I don't have a current location, but I did a good deal of uphill yesterday, mostly it seemed, in a northerly direction.

I start by heading downhill using my best instincts and move south. As I walk along, feeling tired and light-headed, I enter Takeo's funeral again and the way I was shown a seat between two women. I imagine someone purchased a black dress for me. I kept touching the buttons lined up like the cuts I now have down my chest. We were a row of black cloth, like freshly tilled soil holding the seeds of loss. Dry tears washed my face. One of the women said something about grief. It seemed important at the time, though I couldn't grasp it.

I now realize that was my mother. The other woman nodded her head and whispered back. I saw Takeo's eyes in her eyes. They were supposed to repeat in my daughter's eyes. Those are the only things I recall. My mothers were there to hold me. The rest of the day was like nitrate film catching fire. Until we arrived at the cemetery.

Gradually, wending my way back with his compass, crashing and burning through the foliage, circling in a downhill effort, the campground comes into view. It's good to see I'm closer to Hidden Lake than I had imagined.

Deciding to take the fastest route, I go down the steep hill that takes me around the cabins. I am filled with a wild hunger and skittishness, and I'm eager to rest. Gazing over to take a fresh look at Paul's work, I see people in the cabin marked *Violet*, where Walter's name appeared. This is where Paul has been staying.

Whenever Salish slips into the lake, she goes quickly from bathrobe to water in a one-piece bathing suit. Even on the hottest days, she sticks to old cotton blouses with cuffs that are often buttoned at the wrist. She likes the extra covering of an apron. To see her naked is unnatural. Like her face, her body appears utilitarian. That sturdy body isn't with Gabe, however. Paul is the one to frame her. He has also stripped down to nothing. She comes up to him a little lower than I do. I hit the exact crook of his neck. All the wrong questions fill my mind: Why did they pick the cabins? When did this begin? Why would he want such a plain woman?

He picks her up almost like a child, one arm under her neck, one under her knees. I wonder what kind of thinking has him carrying her aloft. I don't recall my husband ever carrying me this way. Even after we married, he explained outside my front door that he didn't believe in things like thresholds. The real threshold, he said, is how well we get along, and we had already crossed that one. Paul was drunk from our celebration dinner, trying to sound poetic, and maybe he didn't want to pick me up only to drop me. I let it go and walked into my house as I had always done. After placing the bridal bouquet on the front table, I helped him to bed.

Paul cradles Salish until she's lying on a blanket on the floor of the cabin. He is different with her, moving as slow as the hours that fill a day at Hidden Lake. She seems swollen with emotion, actual tears down her cheeks. I'm finally able to turn away.

Looking at the water, I can't find a single turbulent spot. It's as if the lake came to a halt along with me. I turn back and take a one-minute film of their sex on my phone, to prove to myself later that this happened.

Seeing Leon where he sits on the dock, I go over and join him. I ask if I can record him with my phone.

He hands me the joint and says, "Sure."

I don't talk about my condition, just hand it back and say, "Maybe later."

"You've lost some blood." Looking at my T-shirt, he takes a drag. We watch the air go through the trees, a red-tailed hawk in the distance. "I could get a bandage."

"I'll go up to the house in a minute."

"Okay, if you're sure."

"I should have brought my car," I say.

"I should have brought mine." His face shifts. I watch a different temperament move in. "I'm sorry you got stuck with him."

"Thanks," I say.

"He met my mom right after she lost her dad. She said, after you got together, that he only likes women in mourning. I thought she was just bitter. Later, she told me she was sorry she said it."

I start a second video when the first one times out. "What are you going to do after you leave?"

He takes another hit. "Band's waiting."

"Did you know about them? Your dad and Salish?"

"I told you a month ago."

"No, you didn't."

"I said you guys were fucked," Leon says.

"Ah. I didn't realize what that encompassed." I'm trying to

recall if he actually said anything like this. "Thanks for looking out for me."

"No worries. And watch out for my uncle. Seriously."

"Meaning?"

"Jones says Gabe's the dude who goes to the school concerts and builds forts in the backyard and shit, but like five percent of the time, he goes nuts and turns mean on her mom."

"Has he hurt her?"

"Mostly he intimidates her, puts her down, I guess."

I take this in and the word *mostly*, thinking about all of them differently. Even Leon. I don't know if he's started thinking about heredity, if he worries that something in the male line could be buried in him. But I know he doesn't deserve to take that on.

"There are women's shelters—" I say.

"That's what Jones keeps telling her."

I nod and sit back for a minute. "When we're in Berkeley again, I want to have your band over to the house so we can talk about a video. I have a producer friend I'd like you to meet. He does a lot of indie stuff."

"Nice."

"You're going to have a good life, you know that, right?"

He takes another hit, and we both look out at the lake and just sit there for a while.

———

In the kitchen, I find the locks are back in place. I go after the electric screwdriver. It's connected to a charger in the office. Using a chair, I remove the hinges that hold the locks. Then

I open the pantry. I've seen it when it had enough supplies to feed us for a week and when it thinned out just before the next delivery. I've seen it after things were thrown onto the floor in mystifying chaos. But I have never seen this. It is *bulging* with food. Canned goods are stacked in towers and pyramids. Extra sacks of flour, sugar, rice. Giant drums of cereal. The refrigerator is full to the brim, and the freezer is stocked so tight, it's hard to get the door to shut after I peer inside.

Clearly, Salish plans a long stay. She must have built this up little by little. Maybe stockpiled it somewhere else for a while, feeling safe enough now to put everything back in place. Maybe she assumed no one would think of entering the pantry ever again.

I put the hinges and locks in my backpack. Getting out a large pot, I fill it with water. Then I line it up on a burner and add a dozen eggs. My mother counts the time from the second she turns the flame on, and that's seventeen minutes. Satchiko likes the yellow when it's still capable of running. Her boiled eggs ooze over cooked vegetables and fish, and have yolks that are almost orange. Takeo and I talked about moving to Japan, but we had purchased the house by then and went back and forth in our thinking. For a while we undertook a campaign to get his mom to move in with us in California. That's why we built the loft over the garage. I knew my parents would do their best to make her feel at home We had hoped for everyone to be together. Takeo and I were always like that, very close to family. Embedded, really.

It seems the desire of the Hidden Lake family is just the opposite: to disperse, to dissolve, to shred under the guise of restoration.

When the eggs are done, I take the pot over to the sink. I run cool water until the heat drains off. Placing half the eggs in the refrigerator, I put the other half in a bowl and take this upstairs along with my backpack.

Sitting on Catherine's bed, I lean against the headrest. When I peel the first egg, I eat it slowly, thinking again on how I could get the kids out. I know it will be impossible to shut my eyes and rest until I come up with an answer.

There's a knock at the outer door. A second. I've gotten absentminded about securing it. I listen to it push open and the sound of boots across the floor. Gabe bends down and studies me as if he's come upon a rare flock of birds trapped in a ravine.

"You found it," he says.

"By accident. I'll come out."

"That's okay. You look comfortable."

"I don't mind." I get up.

"No, no. I'm already through," he says, crawling into the opening. I see years of practice in his approach.

"I wanted to give you an update on Mason." He comes over to the end of the bed and takes a seat.

"His fever has started to break. But he really went through it last night. By the way, I didn't see you at dinner."

He touches my left ankle only for a moment, and I notice something wrong about his scent.

"I'm glad he's improving. But don't you think he should see a doctor?"

"We've talked with Dr. Liebold by phone. If things get even a little worse, we'll head for the hospital."

Given the distance, they should already have him at the ER.

I don't know what to say, but it seems important to keep up the chatter. I tell him about getting lost. "I wasn't that far away, but it turned dark, and I thought it best to sleep out."

"I wish I had known."

Catching my own reflection in the wardrobe, I wonder if anyone would hear me if I scream inside Catherine's room. "Are there more rooms like this?" I ask.

"One off the Wedding Room. The first owners had a big family, plenty of people working for them. It was a summer place. No cottages then. I think they converted storage rooms to bedrooms as needed. But it's a goofy design."

I wonder if he and Salish hear ghosts in the room inside their room. Hoping to seem at ease around him, around the way we could be found here, I start to peel another egg.

Gabe runs a hand down my calf, and I withdraw, tucking my legs under my bottom. Putting the egg back, I retrieve Catherine's writing from my pack and hand this to him. His eyes stop on each blurred and washed-out fragment.

"Where did you get this?"

"Here. In her room."

He shakes his head. "Someone wanted you to find it."

"I don't know why. I don't read Danish."

"I got the mail every day when I was a boy. It was one of my jobs. It looks like the letter Catherine wrote to Elizabeth after Walt died."

"Did your mother read Danish?"

"She took an interest. I think it was a way to have a code Emmett couldn't understand."

He gets up and goes over to the wardrobe. His shoulders

hunch in the mottled reflection. It would be easy for him to seal me in. To strangle me. Maybe he's gauging how much I know. Opening the side with the hangers, he just stands there for a while. Then he comes over and sits in the same spot on the bed again, but he doesn't touch me this time.

"Everything was different than the brochures, the cheery welcome signs and campfire songs. It wasn't just the way my father treated us. He shorted employees on their pay and was always trying to corner the women who worked here. He saw those things as his right."

"Did he hurt Catherine?"

"Hard to say. But when he learned she was seeing Walt, that's when he went crazy."

"So you saw the fight?"

"We all did."

I get up so he won't reach out again. I don't know what to say about a story that shifts and shifts again. You see that in films when people begin to face trauma in a way they couldn't before. But you also see it when people lie and lie deeper.

Going over to the window has me closer to the trap door. I see Jones is up. This is early for her.

"It's been hell being here. Everything flooding back," he says.

"What happened when they fought?"

"Elizabeth got a rifle out of the case. Later, at the hearing, Emmett claimed he was the one with the rifle and there had been an accident."

"You're saying *Elizabeth* killed Walter?"

"Yes."

I begin to wonder, with his mother's belief in retribution,

maybe the letter was Catherine's way of terrifying her—like leveling a curse. But I'm not sure it adds up.

I leave Catherine's room first, and he follows but doesn't try to linger. After he's gone, I get the last essential material to my father to back up. I think of Takeo's sweet face as if I'm going home to see him again.

I know from the conversations I've had with my mother, when I did the film on the abused wife, that until I get the children out, it's essential to normalize. That funny word, as if there's some standard of normal. With everyone except Jones and now Leon, I must act as if nothing has changed, that the events in the forest never occurred and the display in the cabin was a flicker of bad light.

———

I watch Paul fasten his tool belt, midmorning, and head back to the cabins with a thermos of coffee. Leon lags behind, as if tugged by a rope that's fraying through. Normally, Salish is down in the kitchen, ready to cook for the children while she cleans up from the early meal and starts bread making or looks at recipes. But I spot her out in the lake, breaking into a long stroke. She typically swims up and back in the shallow water that holds to the shore. Now she moves toward the center. Maybe this is where she will sink her guilt.

There isn't much wind, but a low breeze comes through occasionally. The house settles, and something rushes into the pipes. I imagine Elizabeth standing by the dining hall door, trying to steady one of her husband's rifles as the men fought.

But it's hard to know if she shot Walter to protect Emmett or if she aimed for Emmett and killed Walter by mistake.

There's a clicking and chattering, the sound of birds, a great flock of birds that flies into a tree near the house. I'm sure they're starlings, sweeping in, taking over, scattering my logic with their luminous green wings. I don't know how long I stand by the Quarter Room window, pinned in thought. After a while, I turn on the hot plate I brought up from the office and set a pan of water on top. Getting my tea bags out, I unfold one from its paper wrapper.

Placing a hand on my stomach, I close my eyes and drift again. I see Takeo's face precisely, and then he's gone. Maybe that's all I'll ever have, split seconds. I recall the long flights to Kyoto, how Takeo and I curled into one another, unable to tip our chairs back very far, surgical masks covering our mouths. We would sometimes wake at the same time, lower our masks, and kiss, soon dropping off again—though I know he watched over me for a while.

Thinking about the temples I visited with Takeo and his mother, I say the prayer she taught me in Japanese, hoping she will be around long enough so I can leave my shoes by her door again and enter her home. The birds move off suddenly.

Salish returns in her swimsuit and robe.

I feel a rash of sorrow and the physical pain from the last cut. Taking off my top, I'm like a die-cut perforation, ready to rip down the middle. I put a fresh T-shirt on. That's when I hear footsteps on the stairs. With her dripping hair and sturdy expression, she's coming for me. Let her come. She throws the door open. "Someone's taken the goddamn locks off and cooked a dozen eggs—don't think I didn't count—and your room *stinks* of eggs." Salish looks over at the bowl on my desk filled with broken bits of shell.

"Did you ever think," I say, backing away from the window, my words as measured as a cup of flour leveled with a knife. "Did you ever think we'd get so badly used?"

"I don't know what you're babbling about, but I want my locks."

I realize I've left my backpack in Catherine's room and the opening is sealed. I tell her to look around.

Another search begins as if we are forever digging for something that's already surfaced. She pulls open my dresser drawers, rifles through my desk, picks through the closet. "I won't cook unless I have my locks."

"That's okay by me."

"Right," she says, even more flustered. "You're making dinners for the whole house? And four kinds of breakfasts and..."

"I think we'll manage," I say. "I'll go down and get some eggs started."

"Everything's a joke to you. My life is a joke because I've done the hard work of raising a family while you've indulged yourself in making stupid little films no one will ever see."

"It isn't a joke to me that you're overworked and scared to death. That you're involved in things you don't understand. I know you think you're in love."

"Ten years. I've been married ten years," she says, her voice losing its spit.

"I'm not referring to Gabe."

She sits down in my desk chair, looks at the screen filled with files—the work I'm engaged in—picks up my sunglass case, and lifts the pages of a notebook and then another. She says in a voice so soft, I can barely make it out, "Please give me back my knives."

"There's not a thing in the world I can do to help you," I say. "Unless you're ready to get the kids out of here. Then I will be your best ally."

Salish stands, straightens her back, and walks away.

———

I head down for something to eat an hour past the time when she normally has her spread put away. I make sure my phone is in one pocket, my Swiss Army knife in the other. As I enter the kitchen, I find her sitting in front of the pantry door, arms folded and eyes weary. Leaning against a far counter, I consider my next move when Gabe appears in the passage filled with cabinets.

To his wife he says, "Mason needs you."

"Can you take my seat while I'm gone?" she asks.

"What? Mason *needs* you." His tone isn't patient.

"And I'm trying to protect our food supply."

He lifts his brow. "From Nora?"

She takes her chair and hooks the back under the handle the way I do upstairs. Except on this side, it makes no sense.

"I'll know if you move it," she tells me.

"While you're gone, I *am* going to move it. I'm going to fix a sandwich and cut up some fruit. I'll clean up after myself, and when you come back, you will have the whole afternoon to sit in this very spot and guard your suffocating little world."

———

Lily, Mason, and I play three long board games at a picnic table in the shade while I try again to formulate a plan. When their father calls them in for nap time, I return to the water. I tend to stay on the surface and see how far I can go without turning back. Today I swim into the center of the lake, where I'm compelled to dive. Taking a long, deep breath, I submerge, only returning when I'm desperate for air. I try seven times to reach silt, hoping to find an answer or two. I seem to go a little farther with each try but finally realize the center is deeper than I will ever reach.

CHAPTER FIFTEEN
Gathering Evidence

L ily comes into my room around 2:00 a.m., in a pink nightgown with small rosettes, one of her sister's old pajama tops
that stretches to her knees. Eyes open but sleeping, the little girl
I love comes up to the edge of the bed in the full-moon light.
I pull back the sheet the way I always do. Together we tuck in.

It's 4:00 a.m. when I wake up to the sound of scraping or
clawing. Takeo and I had raccoons in our attic once, and they
made this kind of noise. I reach for the light, my hand shaking.

The noise stops, the room still now. Lily sleeps soundly. My
computers are off, phone charging, spare camera in the same
place where I set it on the desk. I listen to the sound of my girl's
breathing, the puffs of sleep as if she's snared in a dream where
she starts to run then slows.

When I wake again, I find Lily gone. Bits of paper are
scattered on the floor. I get out of bed to pick one up. In each
repeating diamond shape, the flowers have been cut out of their
baskets. Turning round, I see where the wallpaper above the
headboard has been torn. The flowers remain in place on the
three other walls, but this one has gone through a deliberate
pruning. Poppies are scattered everywhere along the floor, like
a field of wildflowers.

Lily isn't hiding in my room. I tear down the stairs, through the house, and up to her bedroom. Turning on the light, I find her fast asleep, sheet kicked off. I check her breathing and look for even a drop of blood. Pulling the sheet up, I kiss her forehead. As I turn out the light and shut her door, I back into Salish, who's holding a bowl of water in a state of turbulence. Some of it slops over the side, a washcloth swimming about, and suddenly she drops the bowl. Water leaps.

She rushes into the room to check on Lily.

Once she's back in the hall, she shuts the door behind her and says, "I told him from the start. I told your husband, *you're the one*. If you get anywhere near my children again—"

"Did you tell him when you were fucking him in the Wedding Room or in the bedroom behind the Wedding Room? What do they call that, the Cheating Room? Let's go see what that's like," I say, moving down the hall.

She doesn't call for her own husband. She calls for Paul.

I grab the door handle and enter her room. Light pours in, and I can almost see myself in the window across the way, impatient for answers. I find a door covered in wallpaper, the seams almost hidden. I pry it open. Like Catherine's room, there's a bed and a side table but two dressers instead of a wardrobe. A window looks out toward our parked vehicles. I am in a space above the staircase.

There are vials of small teeth sitting on one of the dressers. Some sharp as fishhooks, some with saw-blade edges. The black pits of decay in the molars make me think these are the baby teeth of neglected children, given soda instead of milk in their bottles. I don't understand why Salish traveled hundreds of miles with these rotten teeth—why she keeps them on this dresser.

She has a half dozen old books on knives wedged between two bookends carved with a cowboy design. There are titles that say something about trailing points and drop blades, grips and handle materials. In addition, I find an assortment of dead insects, pieces of bark, rattles cut from rattlesnakes, a bottle marked *Nux Vomica* with white pellets inside. Several jars and bottles of herbs, in powdered and liquid form, most of them labeled, along with standard pharmaceuticals. I recognize Ambien as one my mother used in order to sleep at night when she went through menopause—until she discovered its side effects.

"This is where you make your concoctions," I say.

"Remedies."

"What have you remedied here?" I ask. "You need to take your kids and go. I'll help you. There are shelters. I'll make sure you're safe. I've still got some money."

"You'd like that, if we abandoned the property to you. You'd have enough food to live for months and—"

The eggs, days of shiny hard-boiled eggs, rise in my stomach and make their way toward my throat. I run to the bathroom.

———

Paul finds me sitting alone on the Wedding Room bed. The inner room door is closed. "You okay?" he asks, as if I've come down with something and Salish suggested he take my temperature.

"Can you bear a question?"

"Sure," he says, though he doesn't look very sure.

"Did Elizabeth kill Walter accidentally? I mean, do you think she meant to hit Emmett?"

He looks as if he's taking in too much oxygen. "That idea has gone through my mind. But not then, not in that moment."

"You must have fled to keep from harming your mother as much as your father."

This isn't a question. We're just getting things straight between us, like reading out a sentence we both expected at a hearing.

"Something like that."

"She must have gone into a long state of grief."

He almost says something when he changes course. "I'm sorry, about a lot of things. This place—"

"I'll miss the lake when I go."

He looks down at the rug. "So you're thinking—"

"Yes."

"Maybe when I finish—" he begins.

I hope to put him at ease, to secure the game, to leave without hindrance. "It would be hard for any of us not to feel undone right now," I say. "But when you come back..."

"We have so much invested," he says.

I note the double meaning and smile. "That's what I was thinking." I go over to him and touch his face, hoping this is the last time I'll ever have to see it again.

———

It's first light when I wake. Curled on my side, I look out the window. They have a lamp on across the way. In the stillness, I try to distinguish a bird's song, until I realize I'm listening to a mockingbird. One of its trills reminds me of the sound of Salish chopping vegetables. When I was a child, there was a mocking-bird that perched outside my father's office and mimicked the sound of his typing.

Usually, Salish turns off the lamp before going down to the kitchen in the early mornings. But there isn't any noise coming from downstairs. After too many sleepless days, I feel groggy and consider returning to sleep, even for a little while. I must have dropped off around six without supper. As I open and close my eyes, trying to find any will to get up, I'm aware of something close, and roll onto my back.

The glint of metal. Knives hang over my torso, tips down.

I become frozen the way a nightmare can paralyze, but I'm fully awake, looking at eight of Salish's blades suspended above me. As I take slim puffs of air, they seem to drop an inch. Or my thoughts drop an inch. Each knife sharp enough to kill.

Taking a breath, I realize my legs are tangled in the sheets. I try to kick them away, which only tightens them. Lying there like a specimen, I understand I need to wriggle my upper body while I work my feet around. But the more I try, the tighter the sheets become.

Takeo appears. Not in a clear or vivid way but as a shadow or a subliminal message in a film. He reaches down and unbinds me. I quickly shift off the bed as he dissolves.

"Wake up, Leon!" I shout at the top of my lungs. "Now!"

I run to the other side of the house and check on the three youngest. They sleep soundly. I head into Jones's room and shake her. She begins to cuss when my throat weeps. "Hurry."

We find Leon in the Quarter Room, studying the knives, ceiling light on. "Monofilament," he says.

"What?" I say.

"They're strung up on monofilament." He hits the handles, and the blades knock together like a toneless wind chime.

"Monofilament," I repeat. "I thought…"

"We have to get the fuck out of here," Jones says.

Leon says, "I don't want my dad making any of this okay. He can leave by himself when he's ready."

"Lily, Mason, and Timothy. That's it," Jones says.

"I've tried to talk with your mother—" I start.

"It's useless," Jones says.

"And Gabe?" I say.

Jones tightens her jaw. "No."

"Can you find the keys to the van?" I ask.

"Gabe leaves them under the mat on the driver's side," Jones says.

"Get your sister and brothers ready, tell them…tell them we're going to a movie theater in a big mall, and we're staying overnight in a motel. With a pool. Pack as little as you can, one backpack apiece. Each with a change of clothes, one stuffed animal, pj's, medications. Oh, and swimsuits. No more. Do you know where your mom is?" I ask Jones.

"You know," Leon says.

"Where?" Jones says.

"Later," Leon says.

"Maybe I don't want to know," she says.

While Jones goes back to the other side of the house, I get dressed; take a photo of the hanging knives; grab my backpack with my laptop inside, the small suitcase, and my best camera. Leon has his guitar, laptop, and backpack. We head down the stairs, and when we get to the bottom, I hear a sound like Timothy's arrows hitting wood.

The bright sun cracks the day open as we look out the dining room windows. Timothy faces a shed where he's made the design of a man with a black marker. In the brittle wood, there's a head, torso, arms, and legs. A man who splits into pieces with each hit. Looking at the bright fletching, I think of bird names Gabe has taught us, their calls. When the next arrow drives in, it goes straight for the man's heart.

I go outside and say, "Have you seen your dad?"

An arrow goes into the man's head.

That's when I see someone in the middle of the lake in one of the boats. I have to shade my eyes to make him out. I think it's Paul, but it might be Gabe. He sits very straight, an oar braced against his shoulder. The other end appears to be propped in the bottom of the boat.

Leon and I go over to Timothy, who's run out of arrows. The three of us watch the boat. The light leaps about, and the way his hair lights up, this is Gabe.

But it isn't an oar. When the rifle goes off, it sends him backward into the boat, the sound reporting against us.

Movement slows until there's almost no light at all. The water's direction shifts. A single wave touches the dock. Timothy's look is fixed like a doll's with painted eyes. I cover them and turn him away. Leon moves his body around both of us so Timothy can't look again.

"Take him inside and find Jones and tell her to get everyone in the van," I say.

The boat is moving now, as if time has finally been released.

Leon takes Timothy into the house, not once allowing him to turn and look, though he tries. I run to the cabins. A rushing noise takes over my eardrums. Out in the lake, the boat has started to drift toward the far shore. The door to Violet is open.

Her body is part on and part off a mattress resting on the floor. She's naked and covered in blood. Paul is collapsed near her. Three of the remaining knives have been driven into them. One in Salish, two in Paul. I see them there. I see them again. They appear like this as if I am watching individual frames. Blood, flesh, family. I walk into the cabin and take their pulses through a loss so full, it lights them up. I check to make sure and make sure again.

I get out my phone and record them to make a report. As I back out the door, unable to turn away from them, I see Paul's keys and clutch them in my bloody hands. I lock the door behind me so animals won't get in and eat them. This is what I think about. Every animal for miles, coming into the cabin and taking pieces of them away.

I walk a few steps and look back. My shoes have left bloody marks. I run.

Jones and Leon go through the game room with the kids. Their hands aren't in the air, but I am reminded of children being led out of a school after a mass shooting. I want to scoop up Lily, but I realize I have to get the letter in Danish. I run up the hill and through the kitchen and take the stairs two at a time. I wash my hands quickly and throw water on my face.

As soon I have the letter in hand, the bookshelf pops open, and a few of the paperbacks hit the floor.

"Hello?" I call.

When there's no answer, I push the bookcase shut again, hearing the mechanism click into place, sealing the room up with the cleaver and other items that might explain what's occurred. I nest one of my boots in front of it, tucking the toe under the lowest shelf, wedging it tight.

As I turn back, it happens again, sending my boot halfway across the room like a ball in a pinball game. I back out the door and hurry downstairs. Getting my things into the wayback, I find Timothy in the passenger seat, slumped against the door. I worry he will jump out to look for more death, to see what it's like when it stacks up. But I don't know what he saw before he got his quiver out. It's impossible to understand what he heard that pulled him from his bed—if he was only faking sleep when I checked on him.

Leon gets the seat belt on him, and I climb into the driver's seat.

Jones is in the middle row with Lily nestled against her. Mason looks peaked, bundled in a blanket in the last bench seat. He coughs a little but tells me he's okay, that the air-conditioning in the movie theater will be good for him. Leon gets in next to him and puts an arm around his shoulders. I have no idea how I will tell them what has occurred, but now all I can do is drive.

"We're going to a jumbo theater today." I don't say that the closest movie theater is three and a half hours away.

Leon wipes his eyes with his T-shirt, determined to hold it together.

As I turn to look at everyone, I think of a Virgin Mary I saw in Prague, her heart pierced through with swords. I'm not sure how I'll be able to help anyone. There is nothing pure about me, nothing bountiful or right in this moment. The sequence of decisions I've made to escape Takeo's death. My inability to act sooner. My need to record the hardest things.

We pull up to Brenners, and I tell the kids, "If anyone wants a treat or magazine or puzzle book for the road, grab it, but hurry."

Lily perks up. She asks Jones if we can see a kids' movie that was out months ago, as if she's waking up from the coma of Hidden Lake. Mason stirs a little and pulls his blanket in close. After Timothy descends from the van, Leon gets out and hands me a sealed envelope with my name written across the front. "It was sitting on one of the dining hall tables," he says.

"Are you okay?" I say.

"Did you see my dad?"

"No," I say.

He turns away and calls to Timothy, who is heading into Brenners. "Wait up, man."

Jones slides the side door open and walks Mason and Lily into the store.

"Buy some cheese and crackers. Nuts and juice boxes. And plenty of water." I step into waves of heat.

The letter is written on Hidden Lake Camp stationery. The logo is a simple drawing of the sun rising over cabins.

Dear Nora,

Recently, I discovered Salish was having an affair with Paul. I doubt she understood all he wanted was Hidden Lake. She would be the cook he needed to start up the camp. He must have made her feel like his life depended on her affection. It's

*hard to know exactly. Emmett used to say this place would be
Paul's one day, and I began to understand that's exactly what
Paul wanted, at any cost.*

*After he moved down to the cabins, Salish started getting
up at four or five in the morning to see him before she went
to work in the kitchen. Last week, everything came out. I
learned he would try and trap the kids here—another way to
use Salish. I'm sure he planned to have them working the way
Paul and I used to, once he got this place running again.*

*The worst part for me is knowing I too am our parents'
son and Paul's brother.*

*I realize none of this is fair or right but please look out
for the kids. I know Jones and Lily, in particular, adore you.*

Gabe dated and signed this letter with his whole name as
if he wanted someone to recognize this as a legal document, a
confession. I get out the letter I have of Catherine's in Danish.
The handwriting is almost identical.

I can't imagine how anyone tied those knives to the ceiling
without waking me, how the wallpaper was shredded while I
slept. Until I think about the Ambien. Maybe Paul and Salish
stirred some in my tea at night when I went off to shower.
Maybe they did everything they could to frighten me so I'd
leave. All of it churns inside. The secrets with answers and the
ones without.

I throw up against the hillside. With a bottle of water from
the back, I rinse and spit. Going around the van, I get the cap
off the gas tank. Once it's filled, I walk into the store and see
Jones helping the little ones to their selections. Leon is trying to

get Timothy to look at the car magazines. Mrs. Brenner is at the counter, her husband stepping out from the back.

"We're going to a big movie theater," I say.

"How fun," Mrs. Brenner calls out.

"You planning on coming back?" Mr. Brenner says.

I've never quite figured out why he is so sour on me. Maybe it's the idea that I'm a foreigner—a Californian. Maybe he thought we should have moved here a long time ago to take care of Emmett and Elizabeth.

"Of course she is," Mrs. Brenner says.

I pay for our purchases, trying to keep my hands from shaking. Just as I step outside, I see Timothy pick up the wooden lost-and-found box and launch it. It breaks the giant window in the store across the way. Glass drops like a wall of water, sheeting down to the bottom of the frame, raining over the tattered dresses and forms. Leon calls out to him as Timothy goes through the opening into the shop. Jones watches nearby, holding Mason's and Lily's hands in the slice of shade by the store. Mr. and Mrs. Brenner step outside and stand near the front bench. She describes everything to her husband in real time.

Following Timothy into the shop, Leon and I step through the broken glass. We go down the aisles and find Timothy sitting, knees to his chest, head resting there.

I bend down and say, "It's okay. It's going to be okay."

Leon squats beside him. "You know how you said you wanted to learn how to play guitar? We're going to do that. I'll show you on mine. We could start in the van with some chords."

While Leon talks to him in a voice that's almost a song, I straighten and look around. Dresses still on their racks, scarves folded on trays, tired lingerie with the elasticity gone. There are cargo shorts, flannel shirts, a small supply of hiking boots. It isn't lost on me that we are in the same kind of frozen time as Hidden Lake.

"We'll find a motel with a pool and spend the night," I say again, knowing there's nothing I can offer that will get him on his feet. I ask Leon to pick him up, and I'm surprised when Timothy doesn't resist, allowing Leon to carry him like a speaker set or drum kit, hoisting him into the van. Jones moves up front, Leon staying with Timothy. Mason begins a puzzle book with Lily. And we break away.

CHAPTER SIXTEEN

Pointing Out
the Bodies

S itting in the back seat of the county sheriff's car, I see that
Dave has gray and black hairs that need to be trimmed
along his neckline. His deputy, Ruth, sits in the front passenger's
seat. Her hair is buzzed close to one side of her head. On the
other side it whips about in the air from the open window.
These are things I notice many times over as we drive. We go at
a pace that eats into my stomach. Sometimes we lift into the air
and come down hard. The AC is barely working. When I turn
all the way around, I see the two ambulances that follow.

Dave says, "I want to get things wrapped up quickly, without
fuss."

Ruth isn't talkative, but she did find the child social worker
and a grief counselor two towns over. We expect them tomorrow, 11:00 a.m. at the motel. She got the doctor to see to
Mason, and he now has the kind of medication he should have
gotten from the start. Once the adults meet, we will tell the
children that three of their parents are gone.

I rush up streams of thought wondering how we explain the
reasons. None of them need to hear how the stolen knives were
driven in, yet I know the news cycle is coming like the blades
of a helicopter cutting through the hours. I don't know where
we start with Timothy because I don't know where he starts. He

shouldn't be gaslighted if he knows what happened before his father shot himself. And whatever we tell Jones, she will figure out the whole story soon enough because: Jones. Maybe she and Leon will comfort each other. I'll certainly be there for them all.

For the little ones, I made up excuses as to why we're watching movies on TV while lolling on big motel beds, eating burgers and fries, and slurping ice cream sodas, instead of going to the movie theater. "We're all good," Mason said. Lily repeated this. They kept their eyes on the screen as they assured me.

Timothy said he was looking at arrow and quiver sets on my laptop, complaining, "They need a better router in this motel." When I looked over his shoulder, I saw military gear. AK-47s. I gave it a couple of minutes, so I wouldn't upset him more, and told him I needed my laptop for some work I had to do.

All day we found something animated on the kids' stations. The café sent over many trays of food. I told the little kids the sheriff is a cousin and Ruth is his sister.

Dave has not asked me to step away from the kids. For this I am more than grateful. He has the two letters and understands what I meant about the same cursive in each. He also says he knows something about handwriting analysis. I kind of doubt it but go along.

Though they already drove out yesterday and took photos and dusted for fingerprints, they say they couldn't get enough ambulances to come out until today. I am to show them the grave sites and the marker up the hill with Walter's name. I think I've covered everything that occurred, leaving out ghost recordings and anything else of a spectacular nature. I have gone over the way knives kept disappearing, the sequence of deaths, and even the chickens again. That was the only time Dave looked at me with suspicion. "Who'd kill twenty good laying hens?" he asked. He doesn't strike me as a cynical man. Perhaps *disbelieving* is a better word.

When we pull into the drive, the dogs begin to bark, and Dave tells the EMTs to sit tight. We start toward the house, and I ask to use the bathroom. Ruth accompanies me up the back stairs and waits. Running the water full blast in the sink, I throw up in peace. When I raise my head, I am struck by a pain that pierces my right eye. I close it until the pain stops, rinse out my mouth, and put some toothpaste on my tongue.

Stopping for a moment in the hall, I look at the knives no one has cut down, the desk where I worked, the bed where this child was conceived. The bookcase is open, but as I inch into the room, Ruth says, "Sheriff is waiting." I watch her roll up her sleeves to get through the heat. I would say she can wait on the landing to cool down, but there isn't any cool today.

"You have dog food?" she asks.

I go down to the kitchen and open the cabinet where it's stored. Filling the three bowls, we put them outside along with extra dishes of water. The dogs eat and eat.

The boat has drifted all the way to the far shore. It's covered with a tarp, but vultures circle overhead. I point this out and stop a few feet from the cabin. They watch my reactions. I had no idea they would make me go through this again. The smell fills the air, even before he opens the door. Dave puts on a pair of latex gloves and retrieves the keys from an ID bag Ruth holds open for him.

"Coyotes?" she says, looking at the deep scratches in the door.

"Mountain lion," Dave says. "Surprised it didn't break the windows. You locked them in just like this, right?" he says.

"I felt for pulses, grabbed the keys, and locked up. Got everyone in the van, filled the tank, drove the kids to the motel, and called you."

"You said. Deputy, why don't you stay here with Nora for a minute?"

This is Dave's show, and we are here to help. I don't talk to him about what it is to be retraumatized. He opens the door and stands back. He gets out a handkerchief and covers his mouth before he goes inside, leaving his footprints in congealed blood. I don't understand his investigative technique.

Paul's arm is draped over Salish as if he's trying to keep her from taking off. This isn't the way I left them. The entire angle of his body has shifted along with his arm. But there are no drag marks in the blood. Their faces are covered in insects. Everything turns blue again.

As I stand there watching and unable to watch, I hear a voice I can't fully make out, like lyrics playing softly on a neighbor's radio.

"I have to sit," I say.

"Take her down to the water," Dave says.

I drop down on a log bench and look out at the boat while Ruth waits there, just over my right shoulder. "I forgot my sunglasses in the house, up in the bathroom," I say when I realize they aren't on my face.

The boat begins to unmoor in the overly bright sunlight. Slowly at first, as if the air is strong enough to give it momentum, or someone is hiding behind the stern kicking their legs to propel it forward. I ask Ruth if she sees what I see. When she doesn't answer, I turn around, but she isn't there. Neither is Dave. The door to the cabin is shut.

I hear the boat's sounds amplify in the water. Looking back, I see it's free of its tarp and it sweeps toward me with great speed, past the center where Gabe roped the rifle to the oar guides to allow for the correct angle. The boat hurries as if it's eager for me. It comes all the way up to the shore. I hear the hull scrape against the small rocks fixed in the mud. I go over to the boat and look inside.

The center thwart has been removed, the oars pulled from the rowlocks. There are repeating stabs of pain in my sight. I remember. The day Takeo died, when his skin was turning blue, he reached into the air as if someone had cut a hole in the hospice ceiling to pull him upward. I had forgotten just how peaceful he looked.

"When you're ready," Ruth says, touching my shoulder. I feel numb to time, so I'm not sure how long I've been in this state. But I know I'm still sitting on the log, and the boat bobs at the other end of the shore while the birds celebrate. The small black dog is by my side. Ruth hands me my sunglasses and a bottle of water. The cabin is secured again, and I don't go over to look inside.

Dave explains the next steps and asks if I can continue. As we head out on the trail, I see the EMT guys walking down to the lake with their stretchers. They are joined by a team that drove out in a truck with a winch.

Dave, Ruth, and I take the gradual, sloping path up to the meadow, and the black dog tags along for a while finally returning to the house to wait. The first thing I notice is the nest box knocked off its pole. I wonder if any of them are still in place. I imagine the swallows making new homes in the eaves of the cabins—moving in and encroaching along with the rest of the wildlife.

"Why don't you lead the way," Dave says, trying to catch his breath. He adjusts his holster, and I want to tell him there's no one left to shoot, but I take a measure of water and keep walking. I explain that it's next to the large boulder.

Crouching down, I look at the stone with Walter's name and dates. Seeds from an orange are scattered across its face, some resting in the impressions of the letters. I've been on hikes and seen scat with seeds and even tiny bones. An owl's pellet can be particularly compelling.

But in my mind, Catherine sat and talked with Walter, eating an orange, offering him half.

"Do you have any idea what they mean?" Dave asks me, rolling a seed between his fingers.

"None."

———

I'm light-headed when we get to the motel. The kids are all in the pool, except for Mason, who's stretched out on a lounge chair wrapped in a big towel, watching. I remind him that he needs to come in for his medicine in a little while. The air is hot, and I'm aware of the sound of crickets. Ruth takes me straight to the room I'm sharing with Jones and Lily, and waits while I get into bed. She opens the connecting door to the boys' room so I won't have to get up for anything. Stuffed animals, juice boxes, cereal bowls, sets of pj's, and makeup are scattered across the dressers. My backpack is there and my camera. I'm pretty dehydrated, and Ruth makes sure to leave me with plenty of bottled water and a fresh turkey sandwich. She props the outer door open so I can see the kids as they bob about.

A short while later, Jones and Lily appear, waiting just outside the open door in dripping bathing suits. Towels drooping, hair wet, eyes red from chlorine.

"I'm going to take a very short nap," I say. "Can you take Mason his medicine and help measure it out?"

"Sure. Then we'll get in the pool again for a little while," Jones says. She gets the bottle with the teaspoon and takes Lily's hand.

Lily says, "I'm going to dive to the bottom."

"I expect a full report," I call.

I'm aware of the children coming in and out. Wet towels heap up, the shower goes on and off. And I'm up. We pore through the menu again. The café sends over dinner with little umbrellas in the Cokes. Animation dances across the screen late into the evening, and I hold all of them close.

CHAPTER SEVENTEEN

The Way They
Talk to Us

In Berkeley, I wait for Takeo. I hear the sounds the house makes anew. I expect him to come around a corner or slip through a door. I imagine we'll talk about each day the way we used to, in bed at night.

When this doesn't happen, I make a point of reading aloud from books he loved, hoping my voice will carry and reach him.

Moonlight slides across the ceiling. The coyotes stir. The house is lashed in rain. Around 2:00 a.m. I wake up. Unable to return to sleep, I take a bath. When we remodeled the house, we put a three-foot-deep soaking tub, with two built-in seats, into the bathroom. Nightly Takeo and I would shower off and then soak together. I continue this ritual. There's a set of French doors I open so I can be inside but feel outside as the last of the rain settles. This, more than any other place, is where I hope Takeo will find me.

I think this time is about returning to the person I was when I was with him. And now we will have a child to look after. Each day, I make my bed with a set of old, soft sheets that were Takeo's and mine that I couldn't throw away. I have one of my favorite pictures of him on the mantel and another by my bed. I light the incense I brought from Sanjusangen-do when I went to see Satchiko last month. This is the temple where I first prayed for a child to the 1,001 statues of Kannon, when Takeo and I had our hopes. On this last visit, I prayed this child will be healthy in mind, body, and spirit.

Leon plans to come over one night before practice and look through things shipped to us from the camp by a church group willing to help. All the kids and I have slowly received items left behind, though some things are still missing or got switched up.

In the evenings, I begin the work on his band's video.

I go to a Buddhist temple at least once a week to hear prayer over the sounds of the children being separated from me and each other that run too often through my mind. Lily in the back seat of a Toyota Corolla with her sister, windows up, the way she cried for me to make it stop. Jones doing everything she could to comfort her. I convinced the sheriff to let them take the black dog. She sat by the window next to them and looked as bewildered as the rest of us.

The girls went to Salish's sister who lives in Seattle, all according to the will, though I made it clear I wanted to adopt them—and the girls said they wanted to be with me. I am, after all, family. I get texts and photos from Jones, in spurts, and I have asked Salish's sister repeatedly if I may see them if I drive up. I did this first on my own, and then I thought of asking my attorney who's handling my portion of the Hidden Lake sale. But when I sent Jones photos of the studio and loft, she said she was promised a car when she graduates. She plans to bring Lily on a little trip to the Bay Area to look at schools, now that she's decided on a gap year, and then we will see what happens.

I sent her the picture I took when I slept out in the woods that night, and Jones said the narrow band of light like a vertical ruler or ladder is definitely a spirit. She was sure, since nothing really bad happened to me in the forest, that Catherine liked me. I didn't know what to say but wrote back to thank her for this thought.

The boys were escorted by a guardian ad litem to an older aunt and uncle's ranch in Virginia. Timothy has his own ATV now and was taken to a gun show recently where they purchased his first rifle for him. Mason developed a rare form of asthma and hasn't adjusted well to the horse dander, the hay, and the bus rides to and from the public school an hour from their new home. When I heard this, I said I would surely take him. There's a good elementary school close to my house and any number of pediatric pulmonologists in the area. But his aunt told me he clams up when I call, and that hearing my voice wouldn't improve on anything. At least he talks with Jones and Lily. I keep my offer open.

When I try to take in the things that occurred at the lake, I'm aware the dead hold on to some of their answers, and you can't talk with the dead unless they're ready to talk with you.

Mom wishes she had been brave enough to ask her mother certain things before she died. Sometimes she talks with her mother's cousin in Cincinnati, but Mom doesn't fully trust the cousin's accounts of family, knowing how stories can slip out of register, even when they're firsthand and well intended.

The investigation wrapped expeditiously. The findings were straightforward: Gabe learned of the affair between his wife and brother, killed them, and committed suicide. Motive, victims, weapons, evidence. No one is sure about the things Dave referred to as mischief, like the orange seeds. That was the word he used for anything he couldn't explain, that he decided to leave out of his report. I think of the mischief he will never know about.

———

Looking at the kitchen clock, I realize I have to hurry and get the salmon out of the refrigerator and onto the grill, then pour butter and garlic in a slice down the top of the sourdough, since Dad loves it that way. While this heats in the oven, I open the bag of prewashed lettuce and cut up a couple of tomatoes for the salad. Checking emails in between, I find one from an old friend, Mia, someone I lost track of after I accepted Paul's proposal. She and her husband are willing to knock down their crib, haul it over to my house, and reassemble it. This is the third time one of these old friends has gotten in touch to say they want to give me baby clothes or loan me equipment. I'm not sure I can set everyone's wrongs to right, even my own. My closest friend, Lauren, gets back from India next week. I'll wait and look at new cribs with her.

"You still have much to unpack?" Dad asks, walking out of the spare bedroom and resettling at the dinner table.

"I go through stuff when it arrives from the camp, in case something belongs to the kids. But I decided to leave the rest boxed up until I miss something."

"That's what we should do," Mom says. "I'm thinking of moving my office to the house again."

They loaned me the money to keep my home, and I'm troubled that this is how they'll economize. Eventually, something will come from the sale of Hidden Lake, and I'm taking work all the time, but Dad might postpone his retirement a couple of years in the interim. They worry too much when I feel low now, so I brighten and say, "I remember when you had an office in our house. I loved that."

"One time, you started banging at the door when I had a patient. You were two, and the babysitter wasn't keeping up. Of all things, the patient was trying to decide if she wanted to have another child."

"Is that what they call immersion therapy?" Dad asks.

"Ha ha," Mom says.

"Did she?" I ask. "Have another child?"

"Maybe. I'm not sure, it was so long ago, and she only came for a few sessions. All I recall is my sweet little girl demanding to come in."

Placing my hands on my belly, I say, "I think mine might be demanding to get out."

My mother comes over and feels her kick.

After dinner, my parents and I work at the raspberry tart from our favorite bakery. I top off their coffees and ask them to get comfortable on the sectional. I'm aware that Mom has become too slender, her dresses loose and airy. The past few months have made her waver around me. Dad gets her wool sweater from the hallway closet and wraps this around her shoulders.

When I returned from the lake, I stayed with them the first two weeks, until I was ready to go home by myself. They sat with me while I stared out at the koi pond. They tried to distract me with silly British shows and costume dramas, and games of gin rummy and Scrabble. It was Mom who suggested I spend time in Kyoto. She hoped this might restore something in me. It did help, in certain ways. All the temples, many I hadn't seen before. I will go back once a year from now on.

I thought I would sit down and explain everything to my parents, but so far, all I'm able to tell them is the official version. I have kept my chest covered so they can't see the cuts. I apply vitamin E to them morning and night in the hope they'll disappear over time but I've also booked an appointment with my dermatologist. I don't think I should live with permanent scars.

Tonight I load one of the rough videos to show them pictures of the children again. The three younger ones float in black rubber inner tubes like bobbing seals. Salish holds on to the tubes of the two youngest and keeps an eye on Timothy. There's a rowboat out on the lake, and Paul puts up his oars. He signals for them to swim out. I'm aware as I look at this clip that if the youngest kids had gone for his challenge, they would have drowned before they started. None of them were good swimmers, except for Jones.

I look at Lily's face. She's happy as she asks me to watch her spin. It was one of the hotter days in that string of abnormally hot days. Timothy starts splashing water in his brother's face with ferocity before Mason leans back in his tube and kicks a fountain of water his way.

Salish waves at Paul as if she's in a swimsuit competition. I don't know if she had started sleeping with him by then, but I look for signs. "Watch the kids," she yells to me, and swims out to Paul. It isn't a request. I almost shout for her to come back, but I want to get along in that nowhere land for as long as I can.

Just as I'm about to turn my camera off and join them, Jones calls, "I've got them," and moves through the water grabbing Lily's inner tube as she simultaneously reaches for Mason's. Timothy stays put, but I can see the way Jones keeps track. I don't know where Gabe was that afternoon. Probably out in the field, understanding the bird population instead of his own.

The lens rests on Salish. She slows as she approaches the boat. Paul looks pleased. He helps her to climb inside. I pull back to the kids again and see that Jones, who continues to keep watch, turns for a moment to look at her mother and that boat in an unbroken way as if she can see everything to come.

I forgot I had footage of the house on this clip. A shot that starts at floor level in the Quarter Room ends up in the room within a room, catching the flight of dust, the old bed, the open wardrobe with the sad blue uniforms, the dresses, and the coat left behind. I half expect Catherine to appear sitting on the bed like a woman in an Edward Hopper painting, but maybe a Vermeer would make more sense now.

There's some dummy footage before Salish crystallizes again, wedged between the kitchen cabinets. Unbuttoning her blouse, she pulls it open. On her chest there's a gauze bandage with a spot of blood. I fumble to turn the camera off, aware of my parents' expressions as she pulls the gauze away and the blood runs.

I will tell them, in time, about the documentary I'm making. But this one will be a slow process. There are scenes I turn away from and scenes that have me pacing through every second to understand. In this work of splitting things apart, like apricot or peach pits, I look for the seeds inside the hard stones.

Hitting the rheostat to pull the lights up, I stand by Takeo's photo and think of unbuttoning enough to show them the way the knives talked to me at Hidden Lake. But when I look at their beautiful, fragile faces, I say, "We used makeup and fake blood. Sorry if I scared you. I was just playing with the idea of making a ghost story."

Reading Group Guide

1. How is Nora and Paul's relationship shaped by her recent loss of Takeo? Does that loss change as they commit to each other further?

2. When the bowie knife cuts Nora's leg on the drive to Hidden Lake, she worries that the trip will be about wounds. What themes do you think that incident actually set for the trip? How is it borne out in the other events of the book?

3. What was your first impression of Salish? Why do you think Nora struggles so much to connect with her?

4. When did you notice Paul's attentiveness and care falling away? How does his increasing self-isolation affect him? How does it affect Nora?

5. Compare Paul and Gabe. How do they each cope with the memories that surface at Hidden Lake? How do they reflect their parents?

6. Catherine is the big spiritual presence at Hidden Lake. How does her relationship with Walter parallel Nora and Takeo's?

7.   What did you think of Nora's protective impulses towards Lily? Do you think she considers Salish an unfit mother?

8.   When Nora finds Salish's paring knife and cleaver, why does she hide them instead of returning them? Do you have a final thought on who was stealing the knives?

9.   What draws Paul to Hidden Lake? Why is he interested in staying long-term and running it as a camp again?

10.   What is the role of grief in *Book of Knives*? What convinces Nora that "we leave our bodies as the dead leave theirs"?

A Conversation with the Author

What was your inspiration for *Book of Knives*? How do you begin writing a new book?

I was eager to write a ghost story. Each novel begins with an image, a line of dialogue, or a phrase. I don't plot out a book in advance. Sometimes this means I need to move things around later in the process, but it keeps me as excited to learn what will happen as I hope my readers will be.

The abandoned camp is unnervingly isolated and traps the characters with their grievances against one another. How long do you think you could keep it together in an environment like that?

I've lived alone during the pandemic, and so far, I've managed to keep it together despite needing a good cry now and then. Like Nora, I'm sure I would place the children first. And I'm sure I would love the quiet beauty and a chance to swim each day. Relationships can make us feel trapped whether we're in a city or isolated in nature. I'll get back to you if Salish or Paul knock at my door.

Nora describes filmmaking as medicine when things get especially tense. Do you feel the same way about the writing process?

I feel so many things about writing since I've been at it my entire life. No matter how challenging a novel or story can be, I live for the process. The closest analogy is "runner's high" or "swimmer's high." It's about getting into a rhythm and dropping into another state. Another way to put it is conscious and fluid daydreaming.

How would you describe the purpose of ghost stories? Do you think of *Book of Knives* as a ghost story?

I absolutely think of it as a ghost story, and I hope it conveys a good deal more in its reflections. I will leave the question about the purpose to the scholars who read widely in the gothic world. But I do see the relationship between some ghost stories and coming to terms with grief, unless one is writing to terrify as a primary objective, which I was not. I do know, however, that it's a scary read.

What are your writing routines? Do you have time set aside to write each day or squeeze in work wherever you can?

I write whenever I'm able. When my daughter was growing up, I learned to start and stop on a dime so that I could focus on her needs and be a good provider. Somehow, the balancing act has worked out, though I wouldn't have turned down a trust fund.

What are you reading now?

Mostly student work as I head into the last quarter of my teaching year. There are so many books on my must-read list, including the work of many friends. At the top of my stack is Colson Whitehead's *Harlem Shuffle*. I also teach from *The Best American Short Stories* and *Best Debut Short Stories*, which are marvelous collections.

Acknowledgments

Big thanks to: my agent and friend, Esmond Harmsworth of Aevitas; Anna Michels of Sourcebooks, who champions my ghosts; Kerry Tomlinson, for her heart and keen eye; John Solt, who sent Kenneth Rexroth's map to Marichiten; my daughter, Sienna, who found a spirit for me underneath the streets of Prague; my sister, Suzanne, who made sure I wandered in Japan in this lifetime; translation help from Susan Cokal, Gunver Hasselbalch, Carole Steinberg, and Hanne Rousing; the Emerson College community; the Boston writing community; my family and friends who are there for me while I walk in the land of a book.

About the Author

© Sharona Jacobs

Lise Haines is a past finalist for the PEN Nelson Algren Fiction Award, she is Senior Writer in Residence at Emerson College, and a former Briggs-Copeland Lecturer at Harvard University. Her stories and essays have appeared in *AGNI*, *Ploughshares*, *Post Road*, *Crosscurrents*, *Barcelona Review*, and elsewhere. Haines received her undergraduate degree from the creative writing program at Syracuse University and her MFA from the Bennington Writing Seminars. Santa Barbara, California, was her home for many years, and she currently lives in Boston near her daughter, a video game producer. Lise Haines's parents were journalists in Chicago where she grew up. She recalls writing her first novel about a cat when she was nine on her mother's Olivetti typewriter on green newsroom paper. Today, on a free afternoon, you will find her writing, curled up with a novel, lost in a museum, at the movies, out in nature, or exploring the city. Her favorite travels have taken her to Kyoto, Paris, and Venice.